Sugar Mill Stories

For Rolf

I hope you'll see and enjoy more of the Caribbean

Joe Hastings

Sugar Mill Stories

Lies & Truth in the Caribbean

Sue Hastings

Copyright © 2016 by Sue Hastings.

Library of Congress Control Number:		2016908596
ISBN:	Hardcover	978-1-5245-0455-7
	Softcover	978-1-5245-0454-0
	eBook	978-1-5245-0453-3

All rights reserved. No part of this book may be reproduced or transmitted in any form or by any means, electronic or mechanical, including photocopying, recording, or by any information storage and retrieval system, without permission in writing from the copyright owner.

This is a work of fiction. Names, characters, places and incidents either are the product of the author's imagination or are used fictitiously, and any resemblance to any actual persons, living or dead, events, or locales is entirely coincidental.

Any people depicted in stock imagery provided by Thinkstock are models, and such images are being used for illustrative purposes only.
Certain stock imagery © Thinkstock.

Print information available on the last page.

Rev. date: 06/30/2016

To order additional copies of this book, contact:
Xlibris
1-888-795-4274
www.Xlibris.com
Orders@Xlibris.com

HATUEY'S PROLOGUE

*Changes in latitude, changes in attitude,
nothing remains quite the same.
With all of our running, and all of our cunning,
if we couldn't laugh we would all go insane.*

—Jimmy Buffett

Sugar mills. What they mean to you, and what they mean to me, are two different things. I imagine you sitting in a comfortable chair, in some air conditioned room, as you read these words. If that is true, then likely you see sugar mills as romantic relics of a bygone era.

But if your grandfathers had toiled in those mills—maybe lost an arm there, or lost a soul—you would see the mills differently.

My people have always lived on Caribbean islands. Perhaps because of that, we have always understood that there are many ways of seeing, and many ways of telling what one has seen. Any person or object, or any occurrence, seen through your eyes, and described by your tongue, will naturally be seen through my eyes, and described by my tongue, in a distinctly different way. This was true in the past, when the islands belonged to my people alone. It is true today, when you consider our islands merely your playground. Right there, in my example, you may note a difference in the seeings and the tellings.

In the pages that follow, you will read a modern tale, a situation seen through four sets of eyes, including my own. But no one set of eyes can see everything. And no one tongue is willing to tell all.

Undoubtedly, you will apply your own seeing to this tale. Then tell me, where does Truth lie? Does Truth lie?

WILL'S STORY

Plantation life is usually thought of in the rosy, romanticized terms of the rich sugar planter lolling at his ease in a luxurious mansion, while myriads of Negroes toiled his fields and ground his cane in contented bondage. This picture is almost a myth as history proves—but not quite—for in the heyday of sugar and rum, it did look like this from the surface.

—Florence Lewisohn

November 28

Dammit!

Will Mattison did not shout the word—it was only a mutter—and he barely bumped his fist against the glass sliding door. But even that minor display of emotion irritated Mattison. He reminded himself that he was successfully controlling every aspect of this unfortunate event—just as his impeccable attention to detail managed every other aspect of life on Dos Marias Island.

Still, an unbidden torrent of angry words continued in his head: *Charles' death is a blot on my family's image. Dammit! Damn. It. All.*

The outburst—mild as it might have seemed to an observer—was simply not like Mattison. He'd spent the last fifty-two hours developing, and completing, the steps necessary to expunge any imagined 'blot.' Few islanders would hear anything about Charles' death, other than the version that he, Will Mattison, wanted them to hear.

So Mattison focused his gaze through the glass doors of his main living room; he concentrated on the panorama of success that lay below him.

A line of royal palms flanked his lane and halted, like obedient troops, at the electronic gate that he'd installed just last year. The modern marvel hung between his estate's 250-year-old Danish pillars, and beyond the gate, Will's road snaked down to the old harbor. Past the harbor lay the historic town where eight generations of Mattisons had created an empire. That empire now spread across most of Dos Marias and parts of the other, larger, U.S. Virgin Islands. And now, of course, the Mattison hegemony also held significant investments on the mainland.

On this morning, Will Mattison stood sentinel, watching for Ava Collier's arrival. His phone conversation with her—two days ago now—had gone well enough, he believed. He had told the woman only what she needed to know, and not a whit more. He then arranged Charles' funeral to fit Ms. Collier's ETA. He did not want her on his island any longer than was necessary.

But of course she had to come—no way to get around that. The dead boy, Will's son-in-law, was Ava Collier's son.

The mess had begun late on Thanksgiving night. Will and his wife Clio were already in bed when the telephone rang; it startled them from sleep.

"Oh, Daddy, come quick," Will heard. "Oh, Daddy, something horrible has happened." He thought that Maura sounded like a frail and frightened child.

Will stabbed his legs into chinos, pulled a polo shirt over his head, grabbed his car keys. He floor-boarded the Land Rover down the hill and then along the beach road, bouncing across ruts and potholes. Will slowed only to maneuver a tricky turn toward his daughter's waterfront property.

The gate was open. How many times had he warned Maura . . . He saw her then, standing almost in front of him. As he braked to a stop, Will frowned. Maura was almost naked in a sheer nightgown.

She stood with her arms spread and her palms turned up in helpless supplication. Her mouth, open, emitted no sound.

Will hurried to Maura. He huddled over his daughter, swaddling her with his arms, protecting her from whatever unseen evil had invaded her life.

Maura fluttered one hand over her shoulder. "Charles is there," she said, keeping her eyes shut tight.

Will ushered Maura into the house. When he had seated her, caressed her, and wrapped a shawl around her shoulders, Will listened to her story. Then he called his wife Clio, and his attorney Lloyd Lundell. While he waited for their arrival, Will Mattison contemplated Charles Collier's bloody body.

The rest of the night became a kaleidoscope of tears, solace, coffee, police, questions, mortician, pills. Will called Biohazard cleanup first thing the next morning. He did that right before he called Ava Collier, Charles' mother. Will told her the same brief story that he had told the others—the truth, the whole truth, and nothing but the truth.

He was beginning to believe it himself.

Ava Collier had been stunned, of course, to learn that her son had committed suicide. Will imagined the woman wringing her hands as she stammered, "I can't believe . . ."

Will had interrupted, urging Ava to make plans soon. She wept again. "I'm so far away, in the States. I can't see how . . ."

He didn't press the grieving mother too much. Will needed all the time he could get before Ava Collier arrived. He wanted everything settled by then. He wanted all the stories straight.

Will Mattison was a precise man with the soul of an accountant. He liked numbers in neat rows, numbers that he could manipulate to achieve desired effect. He had razed an historic manor to create its reinterpretation as his home. And in the last two days he had plotted out every moment of the funeral event—from Ava Collier's arrival, through the funeral service, and to the interment of Charles Collier's ashes.

Retaining the ashes on Dos Marias had not been Will's choice, nor that of his wife Clio. They had assumed that the ashes would go back to Texas, with Charles' mother. But Maura had wept, had said that she wanted Charles with her always.

By custom and law, the decision lay with her. And since Will's one weakness was that he could not deny his daughter anything, he devised a way to turn that one small concession to Maura into a singular point of pride for himself. He would put Charles Collier's ashes in the old sugar mill on his property.

Mattison's mill was in no way unique; some fifty Danish sugar mills dotted the island of Dos Marias. The conical stone towers—even the ones that had gone to rubble—stood taller than most island trees, drawing one's eye.

Mattison had always taken considerable care to patch and polish his mill. He wanted people to do more than notice it; they should have reason to admire it. He had not been content merely to maintain the mill's shape and stability, as some did. When an inspection of the relic disclosed areas of weakness, Will had undertaken a complete and authentic reconstruction. And now, in this crisis, he felt a fresh wave of self-congratulation that he had gone to so much trouble.

Yesterday, he had directed his men to clear out the mill's cobwebs and the wasp nests and the dry leaves that had settled at the joinings of circular walls, rock-paved floors, and wooden cap works. The workmen checked the integrity of the oak structure holding the wind blades at the top of the tower. They affixed Plexiglas over each long slit window, and a grating of iron bars over that. They constructed a gate of iron bars as well, and attached hinges and a hasp to hang the gate at the mill's gaping entry. After the interment, that gate would forestall any entry into the Mattison mill.

As a final touch, under Will's direction, his men created a low cairn in the very center of the circular mill room, using small stones left over from the reconstruction of the Mattison mansion. They had leveled the top of the cairn with the greatest of care, just as Will had instructed.

The sugar mill stood ready and waiting now, just as Will was waiting. He glanced at the gate again, saw a puff of dust on the road below, recognized the taxi that was arriving at his gate. He buzzed the driver through.

"Clio!" he called. "She's here!"

His wife, as usual, impeccably performed the role of a gracious hostess. She greeted Ava warmly, then prattled about some nonsense—the sort of thing that Ava might find interesting, Will supposed. The housekeeper offered breakfast-like snacks.

Maura came downstairs. His daughter soon demonstrated that she was, as usual, a dependable student. She recited for Ava Collier the story that Will had coached her to tell. And she did an almost impeccable job of it.

But as her story neared its conclusion, Maura said, "I could see Charles in the car. "I went out there, but the car door was locked. I pounded on the window, but Charley didn't move. And I thought . . . I . . . I thought . . ." Maura's voice had become shrill, almost frantic. "I went in to call Daddy and . . ."

Will Mattison cleared his throat to interrupt her.

Speaking to Ava, he said, "I can only add that I had been concerned about Charles for some time. He seemed occasionally distant, distracted, but I tried to let that go. Now, of course, I wish that I *had* taken action, to avert his decision to take his own life. I am sorry for your grief, Ava, which surely equals our own."

Ava just sat there, one hand covering her mouth, her eyes wide but unfocused. Clio went to sit beside her, patted the hand that lay in Ava's lap.

Mattison looked at his watch and cleared his throat again. "I told the mortuary that we didn't need a limousine, since there are only the four of us. Anisectus can drive the Mercedes, rather than one of the smaller cars. We need to leave soon, Ava. The powder room is that way."

When they arrived at the church, Will had some problem getting his women to take their seats properly. Once they were in the pew, he—always the family's guardian—sat at the aisle. Business associates and others passed by, leaning over the front rail of the pew to shake Will's hand, to exchange a word with Clio, to peer at Maura's ravaged face. A florist hurried to place a few late-arriving arrangements in front of the altar—birds of paradise, orchids, calla lilies. Will shook his head at the ever-frustrating island tardiness.

The excellent organ, a gift from the Mattison family some generations back, launched into an appropriate dirge. The priest delivered the agreed-upon eulogy. The women wept.

With restrained and impassive decorum, the funeral service plodded to its traditional end. Will had to nudge Ava when the time came to vacate the pew. He led her, along with Clio and Maura, to the Parish Hall. Mahogany antiques, most from the Maddison family collection, filled the large room.

Various associates besieged Will, but he kept an eye on Ava. He frowned as Charles' friends surrounded her. Where was his secretary, Simone? He saw her at last and gave a signal that sent her to Ava. Will could relax then: Simone knew what she was supposed to say.

Will Mattison watched Simone steer Ava away from the young men, into more neutral territory. He kept an eye on the innocuous nonverbals of their conversation. Then, when enough time had passed, he walked toward the two women. "Ava, I must introduce you to our Lieutenant Governor. Come with me now."

They walked only a few steps before Mattison stopped in front of a withered, infirm man. "John Lemtorp," Mattison said, "may I present Ava Collier."

Ava accepted the old man's handshake. He only mouthed a *Good Morning* as Mattison provided Ava with the relevant information. "John Lemtorp's family has maintained an unbroken residency on island for more than two hundred and fifty years. They were the first Danes here, and they built our first sugar plantations."

Lemtorp let his hand drop from Ava's. "My mother was a Kjaer," he said in a quavering tone. "They preceded the Lemtorps on island by a generation. But now, alas, there is no one left on island who carries the Kjaer name."

Will broke in on the old man's rambling. "It has been John's honor and obligation to represent both family trees," he said. "And of course Governor Lemtorp does that quite well." Mattison's tone was just a careful tinge short of patronizing. "Now, John," he continued, "I must escort Mrs. Collier to meet other notables."

He steered her toward Maura, who stood in a cluster of people her own age.

"Ava," Will said, "certainly you recognize these young men—Parker Flanagan and Byron Hendley—who, as you surely remember, attended Maura's and Charles's wedding. They represent the next generation of leadership for Dos Marias."

"Mrs. Collier, oh, I'm so sorry." Byron grasped her hand and began a long and rambling speech, teary and difficult to understand.

Will frowned when Ava used her left hand to loosen Byron's grip on her right. She pushed the boy's hand down, then turned to walk away.

But Will Mattison stopped her. "Maura is tired," he said. "I've told Anisectus to bring the Mercedes around. We can all get a little rest before the interment. It will be just us—and a very few others. At the sugar mill on the grounds of Estate Clary."

When they reached the mansion, Maura went directly upstairs. Will offered his women a diluted sherry, then suggested that they, too, retire to bedrooms for a brief rest. With Clio and

Ava out of the way, Will was able to take care of a few items of business.

After a while, he checked his watch: Time to rouse the women from their drowsy stupors. He prodded them back into the Mercedes, which Anisectus then drove to the proximity of the sugar mill. He urged the women from the car, greeted the churchmen and the few others he had invited, and launched all of them up the path toward the sugar mill.

As he led the mourners, Will enjoyed a great sense of satisfaction in what he had accomplished this day. The sun, though still relatively high in the sky, was on its way down; the glare tempered.

The mourners grouped themselves around the door of the sugar mill; the Bishop walked through it. Ava Collier made a move to follow him, but Will put out his arm as a barrier to stop her. The Bishop set the gold urn on the cairn in the center of the mill. He said what he had to say; the others listened. And then it was over.

"Now," Will said sharply. His laborers, who had waited off to the side, unseen, carried the steel grate and hung it on the steel pins they had embedded in the sides of the doorway. They bolted the gate shut, locking Charles Collier's remains away for all time.

Will Mattison led his family, and Ava Collier, back down the sugar mill hill. There, Anisectus waited with the car. Will ushered Ava into it, wishing her a good evening.

Anisectus knew to take her directly to her hotel. Another car was coming for Clio, Maura, and himself.

Will's women went directly to bed. He poured himself a brandy and once more, with the exactitude of an accountant, ran through his mental list of people to talk with about the current situation.

He believed everything to be in order. The banker, Arthur Hamilton, understood his role and would carry it out impeccably. As Simone understood and would perform hers.

Will wished that he might once more speak with Simone in person, but Duty demanded that he stay at home. On the other hand—he smiled as the thought came to him—that lovely woman probably did need a bit more massaging.

He pulled a cell phone from his pocket and pressed #5 on the speed dial. When Simone answered, he said simply, "I'm coming out there," and clicked off. He did not ask the woman if his visit would be convenient. She worked for him; she made herself available at his convenience.

Will did not bother to tell Clio, his wife, that he was leaving. She wouldn't like it, of course, and she would probably be tending to Maura, anyway. Or sleeping.

Simone had been a hotel housekeeper on Martinique when Will Mattison found her. He always stayed in the best hotel's best suite, and she took care of his room each time he came. They talked a little each day—about Martinique at first, and then on a more personal level. "You are too lovely for this hard work," Will told her.

Simone looked baffled. "Housekeeping is all I know," she stammered. "It's all that I have been trained for."

"Do you know *Pygmalion*?" Will asked.

"No sir, I don't remember anyone of that name staying in one of my rooms."

Will suppressed a smile and tried again, mentioning the musical, *My Fair Lady*.

Again, Simone shook her head. She had not seen that movie.

"It's about a girl like you, and a man like me," Will explained. "Because she met that man, she lived luxuriously. So you might live, Simone, if you will go with me to Dos Marias."

Simone's face turned from ingénue to suspicious shrew. "I'm not that kind of woman. My sexual favors are not for sale."

"Simone!" Will spoke sternly. "I can't imagine that you would think I see you merely as a toilet scrubber, bed-maker, and provider of carnal pleasure! You are a beautiful young woman, and I suspect that you are intelligent, as well. I will never lay an unwanted hand on you. I would like to educate you, train you, and make something significant of you."

She straightened up from the bed she was stripping; she held her chin high. "I am significant already. I always have been."

He laughed, a delighted laugh. "You see? That's just what I mean! You're not only a clever young woman, but also a spunky one."

In time, Will Mattison had convinced Simone to make the move to Dos Marias. She left her two babies with a sister on Martinique, and he set her up in a small apartment.

Six months later, Raoul followed her there. Will would have objected, of course, if he'd known in advance, but Simone—always attempting to be her own woman—had acted independently. That amused Will, and so he did not reprimand her right away. Instead, he investigated.

Most people called Raoul by a nickname, "Treacle." Will asked around, discreetly, and learned that Raoul had acquired the nickname—a British term for molasses—while he was overseas, serving in the U.S. Army. Raoul appeared to be proud of his nickname; it marked his special talent. Will assumed that talent had more to do with sneaky ooze than with sweet syrup, and he suspected that Raoul might have other talents worthy of cultivation.

Will believed that his apparent beneficence in allowing Simone to continue her liaison with Raoul would have its own benefits, as well. He cautioned her to keep the liaison secret, and to insist, at all times, that Raoul should use a prophylactic. Will Mattison regularly supplied Simone with the condoms.

And he made it clear to Simone that Raoul would be expected to vacate the apartment any time Simone was "on assignment." Will assured Simone that Raoul would be required to leave only for very occasional, very short periods.

Simone soon had some idea of what "on assignment" could mean. Will Mattison developed her skills to such a fine point that she could appear in public, greet people on his behalf, and make certain phone calls. And, of course, she catered to all his sexual whims.

By the time Charles Collier moved to Dos Marias, Simone's administrative abilities were on a par with the young man's needs. Mattison saw to it that Simone became Charles' assistant and office manager. She considered the opportunity a promotion, and she was proud to have earned it.

At that same time, Will Mattison moved Simone to a house in Cotton Valley. The irony of the name amused him. Cotton Valley was an area where once slaves had sweltered, stooped over endless rows of low cotton plants, picking out the fluffy balls. Within the last decade or so, as the population of Dos Marias had swelled with people from the United States and Northern Europe, Cotton Valley became a sort of subdivision. The new settlers, in their nice, but not palatial, homes, liked to believe that "Cotton Valley" denoted a place where only white people lived.

Simone had demurred, at first, when Will moved her there. She worried that neighbors would treat her rudely. She knew that she would never be accepted in the Cotton Valley community. But Will assured her that he would not let any real harm come to her. He believed that Simone would feel quite elegant in her fine house on a wide lot, with flowers and a bit of a view of the sea.

If she missed her children, if she felt sometimes a "house slave," that was her problem, not Will's. Simone understood that if she did not follow his orders in every detail, she would lose everything that she had gained. And she understood that being Will's mistress was an inescapable part of the bargain. Will believed that Simone would do anything—anything to give her children the advantages that she never had as a little girl.

This night, with Charles Collier's funeral behind him, Will Mattison drove toward Simone's Cotton Valley home, smiling. He congratulated himself again for having developed such an effective relationship. He made the last turn onto Simone's street.

Mattison saw her standing in her open front door, watching. He clicked his remote to open the garage door, and as soon as he was in, he clicked again, so that the door rattled down.

By then, Simone had shut her front door and opened the one leading from her kitchen into the garage. The routine was familiar, well-practiced by now.

Will stepped through the door and into her arms. His deep sigh seemed almost a groan.

"A hard day," she crooned.

"Not enjoyable," he answered, "but successful. That's the important thing."

Simone massaged his shoulders a while, then said, "I need your help now."

Will pulled away to look at her, questioning, with a hint of disapproval.

Simone winked. "This dress has a long zipper down the back."

Will turned around, putting himself behind her, and drew the zipper down the length of her cream-colored sheath. He pulled off his shorts and shirt and tossed them aside.

"Turn to face me now," he ordered, his voice husky with anticipation.

As Simone turned, her dress fell, revealing a matching cream-colored thong and a bra just barely sufficient to support her *café au lait* breasts. Now she removed those wisps of cloth.

He fondled the breasts and pinched the nipples. He ran his hands down to her lovely brown waist and pulled her against him, waiting to feel himself grow hard.

He fondled her buttocks; he pressed more firmly against her, but still his flaccid penis failed to respond.

"Lie down on the floor," Will directed. "On your back." The floor was stone, and Simone had put a petate there—a native woven mat. Will pushed it away; he wanted Simone on the rough stone. His erection rose at last.

AVA'S STORY

A wise woman puts a grain of sugar into everything she says to a man, and takes a grain of salt with everything he says to her.

— Helen Rowland

NOVEMBER 25

The telephone called her from sleep. The grief and horror would follow.

"Ava," a male voice crackled behind the bad phone connection. "Were you still sleeping? How many hours earlier is it there in Texas?"

"Oh, I'm okay," Ava said. She wasn't; she felt groggy. But it was the kind of white lie that a mom would always tell. Still, she could not imagine why some stranger was calling her at five a.m. on a holiday morning. From somewhere in another time zone, she thought. And he seemed bent on pestering her with a barrage of trivial questions.

"Are you awake enough to talk?" the voice persisted. "This is Will Mattison, in the Virgin Islands. I'm afraid—" the voice dropped, became somber—"that I must relay to you some very bad news."

Ava Collier came wide awake then. She knew the voice, and the significance of the name—her son's father-in-law. *Oh, my God!*

"Is Charley all right?" Ava took a shuddering breath. "Has something happened to my son?" She felt her hand trembling as she waited for Will Mattison to speak again.

She heard him clear his throat. "Ava." When he hesitated, she sensed how bad the news must be. And then he said it.

"I'm very sorry to have to tell you that Charles has died."

Ava's skin went cold. Her breath stopped. She willed her heart to beat and her ears to listen as Mattison talked on. She crumpled to the floor, curling herself against the wall. Cold support, but better than none.

"Maura called me late last night," Mattison said. I've been at her house ever since. Hers and Charles' house. Maura found his body. In their Escalade. Ava, your son committed suicide; he shot himself."

"No!" Ava cried. The word exploded from her throat, reverberated through the bedroom. She meant, *No, it could not have been suicide.*

Even so, instantly, an ugly thought wormed itself into her brain: *What if it was?*

She shook her head. *How* Charley had died hardly mattered. The only thing that mattered was the inescapable horror: She would never speak to her son again, never hold him, never . . . Ava pressed three fingertips to her forehead, as if that might arrest the reeling in her mind.

Mattison was again speaking into her ear. Ava wanted to pull the phone away, but she could not. The voice in her ear said, "I understand how hard this must be, but—."

Ava tried to steel herself for another blow as Mattison continued. "Charles will be cremated—before the funeral service, of course."

Cold enveloped Ava. *Her son, gone to ashes. Unbelievable.*

And, somehow, she was only a spectator, someone peripheral to the awful thing that had happened so far away. Ava was hearing her son's fate in past tense. Someone else had made the decisions that should have been hers to make.

Mattison's voice raced on, cold and factual now. Ava struggled to keep up with his words. "The funeral is scheduled for ten a.m. Monday, at St. Elmo Episcopal Church, on Dos Marias Island. You'll need to get here soon, if you want to see your son. Just let us know when you have booked a flight, and I will complete the arrangements."

Ava nodded, then realized that Will Mattison couldn't see that. She somehow managed to say something to him—some sort of assent—before she hung up the phone.

Today is Friday, Ava thought. *The day after Thanksgiving.* The irony of that word sent her to her knees. She grabbed at a chair, used it to pull herself up. When she had managed a few steps to her bedroom window, Ava stood there for a while, looking out at Aransas Bay.

She stared across the water to San José Island, imagined that her eyes carried her past that narrow strip of sand and brush, over the entire Gulf of Mexico, and into the Caribbean. She had often created that vision for Charley, when he was a little boy—her only child. "Look!" she had said to him, "if your eyes were strong enough, you could see all the way to Cuba."

Back then, she did not know of Dos Marias, smallest of the U.S. Virgin Islands. Now, Charley had lived there for the past five years. He had married a beautiful girl. A girl whose father now claimed that Charley was . . . *Dead?*

Everything in Ava's heart and mind rebelled against that. She wanted only to imagine Charley here, on her bay, Aransas. In memory, she saw him, eight years old, learning to sail a Sunfish. She imagined him playing high school football for the Rockport Pirates. She remembered. She envisioned.

The memories destroyed her for a while. She wept, imagining that her tears might overflow the bay. Later, when she could handle it, she called Ándrea, her dearest friend. That helped a little; talking provided her a degree of focus.

A mere six weeks ago, Charley had phoned her, jubilant. "Mom! I hope you're sitting down. Maura just passed the test. You're going to be a Grandma." She had stammered, overwhelmed, embracing all at once the myriad joys of the next twenty years. And then Charley had said, "Next Thanksgiving, we'll bring the baby to celebrate with you, Mom." The very thought had provided more joy than her heart could hold.

At the end of that conversation, after Ava hung up the phone, she had gone directly the box of stored Thanksgiving decorations that she hadn't intended to bother with this year. But with Charley's news, she wanted to celebrate! Her mind jumped a full year ahead, to the time when Charley and Maura and the baby would be with her. She would have to remember to find Charley's crib, carefully stored away, and . . . Ava's thoughts had run on, in joyful anticipation. Next Thanksgiving was going to be such a wonderful day, a magical, family day—the sort of day that she had not enjoyed for too long.

Now, following Will Mattison's awful phone message, Ava's mouth turned down in a bitter grimace. Without Charley, she would have no Thanksgivings. No Christmases. And likely no grandchild with whom she could spend a great deal of time.

Ava walked into her kitchen, opened the refrigerator, threw away the remains of roast turkey and cornbread dressing. She stuffed her Thanksgiving decorations into a black trash bag and shoved it into the back of a closet, hating the happy collection. She leaned against the closet's door, so that its contents could not assail her.

She could not get her mind around the enormity of her loss; she could not begin to imagine what her life would be next year, or even next week. She took a deep breath, remembered a phrase: *Stay in the now.* And then another: *Take small steps.* She had learned such phrases, leaned on them, when Charley's father died.

So Ava knew now, too well, that the next steps would be very hard. She steeled herself for them by setting an agenda. She called Joanne, her company's office manager, at home. Joanne, as expected, was consoling and efficient. She promised to see that everything was taken care of. She knew whom to contact.

Next, Ava dialed the number of an airline in Houston, wincing as she requested 'bereavement fare.' That earned her some consideration; it got her on a flight early Sunday morning. She remembered, from previous trips, that it would take her all day to get to Dos Marias.

She gathered some clothes together. *It will be warm in the islands, warmer than Texas has been for the past few weeks*, she thought. She watered plants, putting inordinate care into the small chore, willing the plants to stay alive. She checked her e-mail and responded, briefly, to a few messages, then deleted all the others. She packed a suitcase.

That was all. She could think of nothing more to do. Ava undressed and crawled into her bed. At last she wept. And, finally, she drifted into a sort of sleep.

November 26

Awake too early, Ava Collier sipped coffee and watched the sun rise. She ate a piece of toast with home-made dewberry jelly on it. She added a few last things to her suitcase, put it in the car, drove across the little bridge linking her tiny key to the mainland, and fueled up.

The journey began. At the intersection with State Highway 35, Ava headed northeast. She knew, from long experience, that the trip from Rockport to the airport in Houston would take three and one-half hours. During that time, Ava promised herself, she would focus only on the drive.

It was a trip that she'd made many more times than she could possibly count. First, she and Fred, Charley's father, had made the trip in reverse—from their Houston home to a summer beach getaway. They had repeated the journey, year after year. Until Fred's cancer. And the radiation, and the slow dwindling away. That was when Fred had told her a slogan remembered from his youthful days as a Navy SEAL: "The only easy day was yesterday."

Once more, the words seemed acutely, achingly true to Ava. There would be no easy days with Charley gone. Even while he was so far away, on the island of Dos Marias, she had always felt him with her. She still did.

After her husband died, Ava had decided to make Rockport her full-time home—hers and Charley's. She liked the idea of bringing up her boy in a small town. And Rockport appeared to be a prime place for her business skills.

Fred Collier had taught her all she'd need to know, during the years that they developed subdivisions in the greater Houston area. When Ava moved to Rockport, wealthy young retirees were streaming into the easy-going coastal town, and her soft assurance worked well with them. Later, when widows wanted to down-size, Ava developed Collier Cottages on Fulton Beach Road.

Now, Rockport had finally decided to develop its long-vacant downtown harbor front, and Ava held an enviable position as the builder-of-choice. She hardly went back to Houston at all anymore—and then only on business.

Ava filled her mind with such topics as she turned onto U.S. 59, drove through Victoria and Cuero. She stopped at Prasek's Barbecue for lunch. She chewed her Polish sausage slowly, trying to eat up more time. She dawdled in the souvenir area and then, with nothing left to do there, returned to her car and again headed it east.

She came to the sprawling Sugarland suburbs of southwest Houston, nodding toward the entries to subdivisions that she and her husband had helped to develop. Sheer determination kept Ava's focus on memories from that happy era. They carried her down the exit ramp that led to the Sam Houston Toll Way. Ava followed that road to the exit for the George Bush International Airport, then checked into a nearby motel.

She endured a long afternoon and a miserably sleepless night there. In memory, she kept hearing the startle of that telephone ring Friday morning—her "last easy day." In memory, she heard Will Mattison's voice when she answered the phone. Still, she would not allow herself to hear what came next. She blocked out all that Mattison had said; she filled the space with static. Or at least she tried.

NOVEMBER 27

When at last daylight came, Ava was already dressed and ready to check out of the motel. She stowed her car in a long-term lot and took the shuttle to the airport.

Not until after she had boarded the plane, not until it had lifted at last from the runway, headed for Miami, did Ava allow her mind to replay Will Mattison's entire message. It was excruciatingly painful, of course, but she had expected that. What she did not expect was that Will's words still made no sense to her at all.

Her son Charley was dead. That must be true, because Will Mattison would have had no reason to say so, otherwise. But Will also said that Charley had taken his own life, and Ava knew that was *not* true. She refused to believe that.

What's more, Will Mattison's way of giving her the awful news had been inexcusable, Ava thought now. He had been blunt, business-like, totally lacking in compassion or consideration. On top of that, the man seemed to be in an inexplicable rush to hold the funeral. He had given no thought at all to Ava's problems in arranging transportation from Texas to the Caribbean. No one could expect another to deal with that on such very short notice, at the close of a holiday weekend, and while enduring unimaginable sorrow and loss.

But Mattison had always been overbearing, Ava recalled. Charley had told her that his father-in-law interfered in his and Maura's marriage. He told her that Maura had no defenses against her father. Charley couldn't fathom why she wouldn't stand up to him, and her unwillingness to do so had created some tension for the young couple.

Ava's plane touched down in Miami, interrupting her reverie. She ate some lunch there, then transferred to a flight bound for Puerto Rico, largest of the Spanish Virgin Islands. Ava recalled her surprise, on an earlier trip, when she had discovered that Puerto Ricans spoke a version of Spanish very different from the Tex-Mex idiom that she sometimes used at home. She could hardly understand the Puerto Rican accent at all.

Ava waited miserably in an over-crowded room below the main concourse of the airport. Hours later, she at last crossed the tarmac to a Cessna 150. Only after that little plane was in the air, headed directly for Dos Marias, did Ava allow herself to recall the last *two* conversations she had with her son.

The first was his wonderful announcement that Maura was pregnant. But three weeks after that call, Charley had phoned again, pain evident in his voice. "I got ambushed, Mom, beaten up, by Maura's friend—*our* supposed friend—Byron. Maura took a tumble, too, but she's not really hurt, I think. She just stumbled, while trying to help. Because Byron was kicking me in the ribs. And he made a god-awful mess of my face. I'm e-mailing you some pictures. But don't worry. It's over, and we're both okay."

Charlie's photos were ghastly. Ava had quickly put them away, out of sight. And when she learned that her son had accepted Byron's apology—had even invited the young man to his home for dinner—Ava seethed. She tried to understand how Charley could just brush the brutish behavior away. Perhaps her son was a better person than she was, Ava thought, to be able to forgive a beating like that. Still, the fact that Charley and Maura had invited Byron to dinner reassured her that they suffered no serious or lasting physicals injuries.

Ava had expected to talk with Charley about the incident in more detail. But then Will Mattison had called with the news that Charley was dead.

So, in the past six weeks, Ava had received three emotion-charged phone calls from Dos Marias—about a baby, a brawl, and death. She had to wonder now: Were the three events connected? Were they a meaningful sequence? Ava shook her head, trying to dispel the repugnant thought.

Still, her sense of a connection persisted. Perhaps, if she had taken some action after Byron mauled Charley, Will Mattison's devastating telephone call might never have happened. It was what all moms believed: Be prepared; know everything; shield your child.

Ava stared out the plane's window, plaiting a damp handkerchief between her fingers. She watched lights twinkling on across the U.S. Virgin Islands. Bustling St. Thomas, the island that the other ones called "New York City." St. John, half incredibly wealthy, half quirkily lost in 1960's, and the most ecologically-aware of the U.S. Virgins. St. Croix, with its rum distillery, vast rain forest, and the hemisphere's largest oil refinery. And Dos Marias, the little-sister island.

The sky was fully dark when Ava's Cessna taxied to a stop at the small, sleek airport on Dos Marias. She walked across the tarmac and into the baggage claim area. Her wait there seemed interminable.

At last outside the airport, with her baggage in tow, Ava Collier hailed a taxi. "Take me to the Harry Sander Mortuary," she told the driver.

She saw him look at her; she saw herself in his rear-view mirror, then imagined how she must appear, through his eyes: *Another lady from the Continent. Not young, but not old, either. Just a little grey in her short, dark hair-do. Trim lady. She'd be pretty if she smiled, but this lady hasn't smiled once. Of course, going to a funeral parlor could do that to anybody.* It was, perhaps, a wishfully generous imagining.

The cabbie drove, and Ava watched the road carefully. She recognized, from her earlier visits, the divided four-lane highway serving the airport. But before, safe in a car with Charley, she had not noticed that the thoroughfare soon narrowed to two lanes. And now the cabbie drove her along an unlit road!

When he made a series of sharp S turns through steep hills, Ava sat straighter, looked sharper, wary of where the cabbie might be taking her. At last, with palpable relief, she saw a street of modest businesses. But the cabbie turned into a sort of alleyway between a fish market and a florist shop, and again Ava grew suspicious. The man might be lost—or, she thought, with a new pang of fear, he might be preparing to waylay her!

The taxi continued to creep forward. Behind the flower store, Ava saw the mortuary sign—blazoned in red on the side of a cement block building. *Harry Sanders* in large block letters, then below it, in small, flowing script: *Mortuary. Caskets. Funeral.* Bizarre, Ava thought.

Still, she sighed with relief when the cab stopped at the building's simple entry. Without waiting for the driver to open her door, Ava got out of the taxi.

"I'll wait for you," the cabbie said.

"No, no," Ava replied. "I have no idea how long I'll be. Go on, please." Then, seeing the expression on the taxi driver's face, she added. "But give me your number so that I can call you later."

"I don' min' waitin'." The man's voice sounded stubborn, almost surly.

Ava remembered that she hadn't paid him. "Tell me what I owe you so far, and I'll give that to you now."

With the transaction complete, Ava walked on to the mortuary and entered a reception area that seemed little more than a wide hall.

A dark woman sat at a battered desk, scowling imperiously at Ava. The woman's hair, a towering mass of intricate African braids laced with scarlet accents, looked like a macabre black halo. She tapped her desk as if to say, "Get on with it, Lady!"

Ava shifted her stare from the receptionist's braided hair to her mahogany fingers. Each ended in a long nail, curved like a talon and glistening steel blue. In the center of every rapier nail sparkled a carefully painted pearl-white cross.

Ava stared at the woman, at the unbelievable inappropriateness of this gaudy display at a funeral home. The receptionist's hair and nails seemed to Ava another example of how her entire world had gone insanely askew.

"Good night," the dark woman said.

There it was again, Ava thought. Bizarre. "Good night" sounded dismissive to Ava, very much like "good bye." And even if the words were meant as some strange sort of greeting, there was certainly nothing 'good' in this occasion or this place.

Ava mustered a calm, expectant tone as she said, "I have come to see Charley Collier."

The dark woman frowned. "We have no Cholly Callya heah." She shook her head with a quick, emphatic jerk.

"But Will Mattison called me," Ava told her. "He gave me this address." She hoped that her voice did not sound as lost as she felt.

"We have a *Charles* Collier," the receptionist acknowledged. "He be a *Mattison*."

Ava bristled. And she recalled that Charley's father-in-law had never used her son's informal name, a nickname that carried affection, and, for Ava, so many memories.

"Yes," she said. "Charles Collier. He is *my son*, and I call him Charley." Ava glared at the woman. "If you will direct me to—"

The receptionist interrupted her. "You cannot see Charles now." The woman sounded bored, as if repeating words that she had said a thousand times. "The family has been here and is gone."

"But I *told* you: I am Charley's mother." Ava had intended to speak in a tone that proclaimed complete control, but to her own ears, her voice sounded merely plaintive. And it broke, just a bit, on the final syllable.

Ava tried again, breathing the words from her diaphragm. "I am Charley's mother, and I want to see my son."

"His mother," the woman echoed. She swiveled her chair so that she could speak to someone in a room behind her. "This woman says she's the mother," the receptionist told her unseen listener, and Ava thought that the woman's inflection was odd.

Ava felt herself judged somehow. Her stomach turned. Bile rose in her throat. Ava touched the desk top with three fingers and fought for composure. She heard no voice from the inner office.

After a pause, the receptionist pulled a steno pad from her desk drawer. Poising a pen over it, she said, "Give me your name, please." Her tone suggested a mood of resignation.

Ava responded icily, "Ava Alden Collier."

The receptionist wrote, then pressed her hands to the arms of her chair, lifting her great bulk from its confines. Ava saw that the soft fabric of the woman's loose dress was printed all over with bright, super-sized hibiscus flowers—red, orange, and yellow. They swayed as the hefty woman shuffled into the back office.

Bizarre, Ava thought once more. *An appalling image for a funeral home.* She tried to listen to the back room conversation but heard only a muffled and unintelligible Caribbean patois.

The woman returned to Ava, still frowning. "You can go to the slumber room," she said with a sigh, "but we will close at 9:45, thirty-seven minutes from now. Then you will have to leave."

"I can see Charley again in the morning, though?" Ava had exhausted her self-assurance; she heard herself begging.

"You can come here if you want; the chapel will be open," the dark woman said. "But we must do the cremation overnight. Just go through that door there."

Ava did not move, could not move into the next phase of this nightmare. Watching her, the receptionist softened. She walked around her desk, took Ava gently by the arm, led her to a closed door, and opened it.

Ava took a shuddering breath as she stepped inside. She did not hear the door click shut behind her.

To her left lay Charley, her only son, her only family. Ava put her hand to the boy's cheek. "You're with your father now, I guess." She ran her fingers through Charley's soft, soft hair, so like his father's.

It seemed to her then that Charley's eyelids fluttered. She believed that she saw Charley blink several times during the thirty-seven minutes that she spent with him in that dim and muted room.

Charley lay beneath a pink knit thermal blanket that seemed slightly shabby, and certainly inappropriate for the sturdy masculine body of her adult son. The cover, pulled high up under Charley's chin, curved around both sides of his face and across the top of his head.

For one startling moment Ava saw Charley as a four-year old, wearing a bunny sleeper outfit that had swaddled his head that way. But this blanket—Ava reeled, imagining what its arrangement might hide.

With stern determination, she blocked from her mind an ugly vision of Charley's final moment. She focused instead on the thought that the pink cloth brought healthy color to her son's face, and she was glad for that. Leaning closer to him, Ava could see yellowish bruises—probably a result from Charley's fistfight with Byron three weeks earlier. A fresher split in her son's lip might have happened as recently as the night he died.

For the most part, though, Ava saw days long past. She patted her son and spoke to him of those memories, those good times. She tried to stay there, in the long ago, but the ghastly present kept imposing.

"Why, Charley? What has happened here?" Ava put her hands to her son's shoulders and imagined that his eyelids fluttered again. What was it that Charley wanted to say to her?

Ava stood, immobile. Without words, without thoughts, she contemplated her boy's dear face. For a while, she and Charley floated together in some vague, interim eternity. Then a soft tap on the door pulled Ava back into the awful room.

She started toward the door in slow motion, then changed direction, back again to her boy.

The taloned and haloed receptionist entered the room and spoke. "You must go now." Her tone expressed a gentleness not present before, something like an apology. "It is late. We have to take your son now."

She led Ava all the way to the mortuary's outer door. She ushered the grieving mother outside, to where the taxi idled, as its driver had promised.

The receptionist helped Ava into the cab and then asked, in a tone kinder that Ava had heard from the woman before, "Do you have someplace to go?"

"Yes. A reservation at The Tradewinds."

As the taxi took her there, Ava remembered that Charley had tried to describe island people to her. "They're bristly on the outside, Mom. You feel that they're stand-offish. That they don't want us around. But as I got to know them, I learned that they're the most caring people on earth. They're a nurturing people, and generous to a fault."

Now, Ava put her trust in Charley's words. They carried her to The Tradewinds, where the taxi stopped.

The upscale tourist hotel fronted on a boardwalk overlooking the boat-filled Dos Marias harbor. Beyond that, across a shallow reef, lay the broad Caribbean Sea.

Ava stopped at the hotel's bar for a glass of wine, carried it to her room, and collapsed on the bed.

NOVEMBER 28

Ava's first night on Dos Marias had not been a restful one, but she had expected that. She was up and dressed with too much time to spare. She took a tiny elevator down to the hotel lobby, crossed it, and headed toward the door.

Ava hoped that she might find a place on the boardwalk that was open for breakfast. Still, she knew she'd feel uncomfortable outdoors, too warmly dressed in a somber suit. Then she remembered that the Mattisons had invited her to breakfast. More accurately, she felt that Will Mattison had commanded her presence there.

I might as well get on with it. Ava pursed her lips like a disapproving old lady as she gestured to a taxi. The driver came to open her door, affording Ava a clear look at the huge stocking that bound the man's head. *It must hold dreadlocks long enough to reach his knees*, Ava thought.

"Do you know the way to the big house at Estate Clary?" she asked as she climbed in the taxi.

"Good mornin'," the driver said. "An' yas, Ah do know deh home ah Will Mattison. Oh, yas, Mom." The man kept up a constant stream of chatter as they made the drive, and Ava struggled to interpret his strong patois:

"Estate Clary," the taxi driver said, to begin his story. "Mistah Will's wife family have dat first. Dey be rich befo' he. But Ah reckon Estate Clary b'long entirely to Will Mattison now. Oh yas, surely."

Ava raised an eyebrow at the assertion. Odd, she thought, that the driver would speak of the Mattisons in such a manner.

His words seemed disrespectful, and potentially risky. Ava suspected that Will Mattison would not tolerate people of that class discussing his personal life so casually.

"Now deh first Mistah Mattison, he name Will too," the taxi driver rambled on. "He come to supervise a plantation fo' one o' dem Danish sugar cane men. Alla we slave worker call Mr. Mattison 'Iron Will,' because he dat hard on us."

The cabbie spoke as though the events had occurred within the past year, rather than two centuries earlier. Ava remembered Charley telling her that the Danes had freed their slaves on Dos Marias before the United States fought its Civil War. In any case, Ava silently agreed with this driver: "Iron Will" described the current Mattison as aptly as it might have described an earlier one.

The cabbie spoke slowly, and drove slowly as well. Ava suspected that the man regulated his taxi's speed so that he could finish his tale before reaching Estate Clary. He dawdled, as though they had all the time in the world.

On an ordinary day, Ava might have enjoyed the easy pace that characterized island culture. That was not so different from Rockport, Texas, after all. But she needed to get on with this day's sad business. Once it was behind her, Ava believed, she could begin to find the answers to all her questions.

The taxi arrived at a large gate; the driver pressed a button and spoke into an intercom. Then, almost before Ava was ready, she found herself in front of the Mattison mansion.

Twin curving stairways, thirty yards apart at ground level, met at a broad balcony—a gallery, the Mattisons would call it—some twenty feet up. Ava remembered that the main living area was there, high, to catch the breeze. Utilities—kitchen, laundry, and such—filled the ground floor. Above the public rooms, a top floor held bedroom suites.

Ava paid the cabbie, then stood for a full minute at the double mahogany entry doors, gearing herself for what was to come. Finally, she lifted her hand to ring the bell.

Almost at once, Clio Mattison opened the door. "Dear Ava," she murmured, her voice redolent with social warmth and suitable compassion, "Did you have a dreadful flight?"

Before Ava could formulate an answer, Will nudged Clio aside. His right hand grasped Ava's; his left hand held her elbow. He bowed, a bit. Mattison might have intended these gestures as appropriate masculine shows of sympathy, but Ava felt manhandled, controlled.

"Good morning, Ava," Mattison said. "I was having my coffee on the east gallery. Come enjoy the view with me." He turned to his wife. "Clio, you will bring fresh coffee?"

He walked Ava through a room rather like a hotel lobby, and wide open to the gallery beyond it. Will stopped as his toes touched a metal channel in the floor. "On the rare day when our weather is not perfect here in Paradise, I wheel out glass walls along this track. We can sit inside then, and still enjoy the view."

Today, however, seemed typical Caribbean, warm and soft. At that altitude, a light breeze freshened the gallery. The air smelled sweet, and Ava inhaled its comfort with a feeling akin to gratitude. She and Will stood without speaking, lost in private thoughts.

Clio came, carrying two mugs of coffee. "Would you like for me to add a splash of mango rum?" she asked Ava. "It's a delightful enhancement."

"No." Ava shook her head. "Thanks."

Clio smiled that odd smile that people often employ at funerals—somewhat sympathetic or maternal, but for the most part smug. Because this horror wasn't really happening to them at all.

"Will tells everyone that he likes this gallery for the sunrise," Clio said then, gesturing to the left. "I love it for the two Marys." She nodded toward the right, then responded to Ava's quizzical look with surprise in her voice.

"Those two mountains give our island its name! Didn't I tell you the story the last time you were here? *Dos Marias* means 'two Marys'."

Clio made a sort of disapproving pout. Then, without waiting for Ava to say that she, as a Texan, certainly knew the meaning of those words, Clio continued. "I don't know if it's true or not, but tradition holds that when Spaniards discovered this island, the officers aboard ship argued over naming it. The Castilians among them wanted to honor the Mother of God, but the Basques favored a particular manifestation of the Virgin, known as Aranzasu."

Ava fought to keep from pursing her own lips then. Clio certainly might have recalled that Ava had just arrived from a Texas county named for that same Virgin of Aranzasu. Clio might have recalled that Charlie had grown up there. Charlie had believed that the coincidence of names in Texas and in the Caribbean was something very special for him and Maura; he'd thought that it promised them good luck, and a blissful future.

In any case, Ava thought, Clio certainly might have refrained from rattling on about such inconsequential things now, with Charley dead. But the woman continued to talk. "That name, Aranzasu, has something to do with thorns, I think—Our Lady of the Stickers, maybe. That would be appropriate for the drier end of our island."

At last Clio lapsed into silence for a moment or two, perhaps lost in her own historical musings. When she roused again, she continued: "Well, as I was saying, tempers ran high among the sailors as they argued about a name for the island. In the end, the ship's captain came up with a compromise.

"One of the two prominent hills would honor Mary the Mother of Jesus, while the other paid tribute to the Virgin of Aranzasu. If one of our hills stands a little higher than the other, no one then or now has been inclined to squabble about which was which. Those first sailors simply agreed that the island itself would be called 'Two Marys'—*Dos Marias*."

Will Mattison reached out and put his hand on his wife's arm, startling her, and Ava as well. "As usual," Mattison said to Ava, "my Clio is living up to her name, the Muse of History." Apparently not wanting a guest to believe that he intended his words as harsh or patronizing, Will then raised his wife's hand to his lips and kissed it.

"Clio is right, of course," he continued. "The name *Dos Marias* survived sequential island occupations by the French, the English, and the Danes. It even survived transfer of ownership to the United States of America. "But—" Will waved a cautionary finger and assumed a pontifical tone. "The name may not survive our current onslaught of American sailing tourists. They insist upon calling our island 'Dos Mari**n**as,' adding a despicable *N*. I suppose they do it because they so enjoy the beautiful, welcoming harbors on both the north and south sides of our island. But I won't accept their pronunciation! Nor will I accept nautical charts that label my island that way!"

Ava had no inclination to respond to any of these trivialities. Instead, she intended to bring the conversation back to the business of this awful day. "How is Maura?" she asked.

"She should be down soon." Will looked at his watch and then, inquiringly, at his wife.

"Maura is doing as well as can be expected," Clio answered in a placid tone. "She slept some last night."

Ava nodded. "It's all the more difficult, I guess, since she can't take any medications now."

Ava had assumed that Will and Clio would both understand that she was referring to Maura's pregnancy, but neither of them responded. The awkward moment brushed away as Doulsie, the house servant, refilled Ava's coffee cup.

But the veneer of frippery had been broken, and Ava took advantage of that. "Please tell me what happened to my son."

"Maura will be down soon," Will Mattison said again.

"Well," Ava said with finality. She felt her lips pursing again, like an old woman's, and so she changed her tack once more: "I also want you to tell me about the fight that Charley and Byron had."

Clio put a delicate hand to her own lips. "That was horrid, wasn't it? I don't know what got into Byrie."

Ava suppressed a frown, irritated that she probably would not get any straight answer on this topic either. Clio's use of a childish nickname for Charley's assailant revealed the depth and warmth of her relationship with Byron Hendley. It seemed clear to Ava that Clio had never wished for such a close relationship with Ava's son, since she consistently referred to him as Charles.

Clio rattled on. "Why, that Byrie has sat at my dinner table since he was barely old enough to tuck a napkin under his chin. His mamma and I were Coterie Debutantes together, and of course she served as my maid of honor when Will and I married.

"Byrie and Maura have been playmates and best friends almost since the day she was born, just three months after him. I always thought they would marry.

"Oh, of course I don't mean that I'm sorry that Maura married Charles instead!" Clio reached out a hand as though to touch Ava's arm in reassurance. "Maura and Charles *had* a good marriage! I just meant that I've always felt close to Byron, because we've known him for such a very long time. And now . . ." Clio paused a bit, considering, before she continued.

"Now I will not break bread at this table with Byron Hendley ever again. Not ever!" She made a little fist, and tensed her arm muscles so hard that the fist shook.

Will frowned and made a slight movement of his head, shushing his wife: Soft as a whisper, Maura had come into the room.

Ava thought that she looked like a schoolgirl—or a lost Alice in Wonderland—with her long honey-colored hair falling straight down her back, almost to the waistband of a dark blue pleated skirt. She wore a demure white blouse, and over it had wrapped a gauzy alpaca shawl in pale gray-blue.

Maura's demeanor shocked Ava. This was not the girl she knew. This Maura seemed only a shadow—seemed a ghost of the bubbly, confident young woman that Ava had met three years earlier. Her affect seemed something more, something darker, than the deep sorrow of losing her husband.

"Good morning," Maura said now, in a vague voice. She leaned over Ava as a hint of embrace.

Well, it wasn't a good morning, of course, Ava thought, and it certainly couldn't be one for Maura. Then a flicker of memory came to her—Charley must have said it—that islanders said *Good morning,* or *Good afternoon,* or *Good night* at the onset of any encounter. So Ava echoed Maura's greeting now.

Charley's wife—Charley's *widow*—sat then, primly, on the edge of a chair. She appeared very pale, but no puffiness around her eyes gave any indication of tears. The thought came to Ava that Maura looked like a student, tense before an oral exam.

"Would you enjoy some herb tea, Darling?" Clio asked.

Maura just shook her head. "I have some water," she murmured, showing the trendy plastic bottle in her hand. She looked then at Ava. "Have you seen Charles?"

"I visited my son last night."

"I didn't. I didn't go. Does he look all right?"

Ava nodded, then spoke to Maura in a comforting tone. "I could imagine that Charley was just asleep. He appeared to be trying to wake, to tell me something."

Maura seemed to stifle a shudder. "I'm glad he looks well." She glanced over her shoulder. "Doulsie? I thought Doulsie was right behind me, with breakfast."

The dark servant *was* there, holding a silver tray of miniature sticky buns. "Good morning," she said, setting the tray on a glass-topped table, next to a stack of small crystal plates. "The eggs soon come," she said, as she left the room.

"Doulsie makes delicious breads of all kinds," Clio told Ava, "but we do not have them often. Will is diabetic, so we all curtail our sweets. It seems ironic, doesn't it? Our ancestors made their fortunes producing sugar, and now it is Will's undoing. However, at a time like this . . . Well, you know what they say: *A spoon full of sugar . . .*"

Doulsie returned, presenting eggs scrambled with sausage, stuffed into silver-dollar-sized biscuits. Ava shrank from the plethora of finger food; it made her nauseous.

As an accompaniment, Doulsie offered Virgin Bloody Marys or plain orange juice. Ava accepted the orange juice and sipped it as the Mattisons nibbled—four individuals awkwardly making small talk.

After a while, Maura set down her plate and made a little smile in Ava's direction. "You are wanting to know what happened, of course." And so she began her recital.

"It's always been our tradition," Maura told Ava. "On Thanksgiving night, all the kids go out. We've been with our families all day, and the night is *our* time to party. The girls always go one place, and the guys always go to another. Of course, now Charles is included. *Was* included." Maura shook her head, reprimanding herself; she pressed two fingers below her right eye.

"This is always just the old, established families," she continued, "so Charles went out with Byron, Parker, and Ronald. Maybe a few others?" Maura looked at her father for confirmation.

After Will's nod, she continued. "Charles was already home when I came in that night—about eleven o'clock, I think. We talked a little. I said that I was tired and ready for sleep. Charles said he'd be along in a few minutes.

"I brushed my teeth and cleaned my face and got into bed. I waited, but Charles didn't come. Then I heard a clattering noise in the study, so I got up.

"Charles was sitting at his desk there, and he had all his guns spread out—pistols, shotguns, shells and bullets, everything. I asked him why he was doing that, and I told him that I didn't want to see those things and that he should put them away.

"He was very understanding, very caring. He always is—always *was*. Charles put all the guns back in the cabinet. I asked him to come to bed. He looked very surprised all of a sudden and slapped his back pants pocket. He said that he must have left his wallet in the car, so he had to go get it.

"Charles is—Charles *was*—always doing that, forgetting his wallet someplace. I watched him walk out the door, and I went back to bed.

"I waited and waited, but he didn't come. I got up again and looked out the kitchen window. I could see him in the car. I thought that maybe he had gone to sleep. He does that—he *did* that—sometimes too." Maura grimaced at her error, then continued.

"So I went outside to wake him up. I could see him just sitting there. But I couldn't get the car door open, and Charles didn't move, even when I called to him. That frightened me. So I went back in the house and called Daddy."

Ava noticed that Maura glanced at her father then, as if for reassurance that her story was complete. She had not shed a tear; she had rarely stammered or hesitated. Will gave her a subtle nod, after which she just sat, staring at her hands.

Ava went to kneel in front of her, to hold those hands. They seemed chillier than Charley's had been, the night before. "I'm so sorry," Ava murmured. "So sorry. At least we'll have the baby."

Her own words surprised her. Nothing could take Charley's place. But a woman needs to know that something will live after her. Ava had to believe in a baby that would carry on for her and Charley both. And surely Maura must have shared that need.

But the girl said nothing at all.

Clio came to stand behind Ava, placing a hand on her shoulder as a gesture of compassion. "We think of you as family, Ava. We do not show grief publicly, and we may not always express our warmth for you, but we do care."

Will Mattison cleared his throat. "Well of course we do. I should say, though, that I had been concerned about Charles for some time. He seemed occasionally distant, distracted, but I tried to let that go. Now, of course, I wish that I *had* taken action, to avert this tragedy."

Mattison looked at his watch. "We must leave soon. Ava, the powder room is that way."

Ava stood, ready to follow the suggestion, and then pursed her lips yet again. Iron Will had tried to direct her just as he directed Maura—as though they were both just school girls, requiring his firm hand.

Over the double doors of the St. Elmo Episcopal Church, four large and gilded digits decorated the keystone: *1734*. Clio pointed to the numerals, to make certain that Ava saw them.

"Even before that, we had an Anglican chapel on island," Clio whispered, pride and ownership evident in her tone. Her phrase, *on island*, rather than *on* the *island*, was a British usage that most citizens of Dos Marias had fondly adopted.

Ava paid no attention. She was staring at the pews, crowded with more mourners than she could have imagined might live on the tiny island of Dos Marias. People of all colors and ages, and all with horror-struck eyes, watched the family's slow process down the length of the church's center aisle. Along that passage, and along the side aisles as well, engraved paving stones marked the resting places of St. Elmo's earliest parishioners.

Will Mattison escorted his daughter, and to Ava it seemed a painful mimicry of the way that he had walked beside Maura on her wedding day. Then, as now, Charley waited for them before the altar.

He waited today in a golden urn, placed with precision in the center of a white cloth that draped a small mahogany table. The table almost blocked the steps leading up to the altar, and the urn shimmered in a shaft of sunlight.

Ava stopped cold when she saw it. Mattison gestured to Clio, instructing her to urge Ava into the first pew. But neither Clio nor Ava would go.

Ava reached for the urn and picked it up. Maternal instinct cupped one of her hands beneath the widest part of the urn. She held its neck with her other hand, and sensed the weight of it. A chill ran through Ava as she realized that the urn's weight felt very little more than the weight she experienced when she first held her eight-pound, two-ounce baby Charley, thirty-two years before.

Ava was unaware of the passage of time; she did not know how long she stood, cradling Charley. When at last she became again aware of herself, she repositioned the urn on its table, her hands trembling. Ava fumbled in her purse for a handkerchief and stumbled into the pew. She wiped her nose, dabbed the handkerchief under her eyes, and knew it would never be absorbent enough to last out this day.

Clio, following Ava, seated herself and arranged her skirt. She patted Ava on the knee. Ava looked up and away from Clio, to the broad, dark beams of the nave. Those beams, replicating the framework of a ship's hull, gave Ava the odd sensation that she was swimming through a great overturned schooner. She imagined that it held her, and all the other mourners, trapped forever inside.

But she was not swimming, she thought then; she was drowning. Surely she drowned in salt tears.

Maura sat next to Clio. Will, always the family's guardian, sat between Maura and the church aisle. Ava had a vague awareness of people who passed by, leaning over the front rail of the pew to hug Maura, to shake Will's hand, to exchange a word with Clio. Ava recognized no one in that sad line; the strangers looked at her with mild curiosity and then moved on.

Soft tones sounded. An excellent organ, somewhere behind Ava, launched into the Albioni *Adagio,* startling a dove that rested in the rafters. The bird flew straight across the pews and out one of the tall windows on the far side. Ava's eyes followed the flight until the bird vanished. She imagined that it might be Charley's free spirit, sending her a sign of consolation.

The organist continued with something more ecclesiastical, and Clio stood to sing. Ava sensed that all behind her were standing, so she stood too, but she could not, would not, sing with them. Crucifer, priest, and bishop strode past her to the altar, their voices raised in song.

Ava knew little of the ritual of the Episcopal Church. As the service progressed, she followed Clio's cues. It all seemed meaningless—until Bishop Gardiner climbed a spiral stairway to the pulpit.

"Good morning," the tall, gaunt man said, and the congregation responded heartily: "Good morning."

"We are here on a sad day," the bishop continued. "It is always sad to say goodbye, but especially so when the Goodbye leaves us with so many unanswered questions. A fine man is gone, our Charles is gone, and we are puzzled. This friend, son, in-law, husband cannot answer the one question that every one of us yearns to have resolved: Charles Collier, why did you kill yourself?"

Clio reached for Ava's hand and held it tightly.

Bishop Gardiner raised his hands to the level of his head and repeated his question, thundering it now. "CHARLES COLLIER, WHY DID YOU KILL YOURSELF?"

Then the bishop slumped dramatically and lowered his voice to a rumble. "*What* was this young man's secret torment? *Why did he feel so alone? And at that fraught, awe-filled moment when he arrived at the throne of our Heavenly Father, what did Charles say?*"

The bishop paused, looking down. He seemed momentarily lost in contemplation, and he shook his head.

"Well, my dear friends," he sighed at last, "we will never know the answers to those questions." He looked out across the congregation again, and it seemed to Ava that Bishop Gardiner was making eye contact with various parishioners from time to time.

"The answers to those questions are none of our business, actually," the bishop continued. "They are the business of God and Charles alone. But we do have other answers." The bishop tucked his chin to look down upon Maura Mattison Collier.

"We do know that Charles is now with a loving and compassionate Father," he said. "We know that whatever pain and torment Charles was suffering have been relieved."

Maura sniffled; Clio slipped her a fresh hanky.

"We know that Charles is at peace," the bishop continued. "We know that he understands our love, and that he loves us more deeply than ever before. Knowing that, we know all. Knowing that, we too are at peace. Let us pray."

Ava heard a rustle around her; she felt Clio fumble for the kneeling rail. But Ava would not kneel. She just leaned over, her elbows on her knees, her head supported by clenched fists. She'd had a difficult time following the bishop's words, but a distinctive impression remained: Bishop Gardiner had been saying what Will Mattison wanted him to say.

The bishop's key phrase echoed in Ava's mind: *Charles Collier, why did you kill yourself?* And Ava responded with a silent rebuttal: *Bishop Gardiner, why did you ask that obscene question? It was absolutely the wrong thing to do.*

Ava believed—she felt certain beyond all doubt—that Will Mattison had persuaded the bishop to voice that query. It was entirely inappropriate, and the bishop should be ashamed of himself for following Will's orders.

Charley did not kill himself, could not have killed himself; he had too many reasons to live. Ava knew—unshakably knew with an even greater clarity than before—that her son, her dear Charley, did not commit suicide.

The emotion brought her some momentary relief. Then Ava's questions returned, like a tsunami wave hitting the shore. She wanted to cry out, to rouse everyone in the cathedral: *Tell me who has killed my son!*

With restrained and impassive decorum, the funeral service plodded to its traditional end, but Ava heard hardly a word of it. Clio had to nudge her when the time came to vacate the pew.

The congregation flowed from the Sanctuary to the Parish Hall, a large room filled with mahogany antiques. Tapestries brightened the stone walls; mahogany louvers shaded the broad windows and funneled a cooling breeze into the room.

Ava stood alone, studying the strangely mixed group. *Charley's killer is in this room,* she thought. *Any one of these people might have murdered my son.*

She saw the tanned faces and breezy style of America's leisure class, the eager intensity of ambitious entrepreneurs with offshore corporations, the husky build and blond hair of assorted Scandinavians. She noted a tall, dark man who stood a little apart from the others. He wore white linen trousers and a matching linen tunic that fell almost to his knees. It was decorated with a scroll pattern worked in golden cotton and gold metallic thread. A brimless hat, straight sided and flat topped, and of the same white linen as his suit, completed the ensemble. The distinguished gentleman looked like a prince of Nairobi, as perhaps indeed he was.

Ava blinked, feeling disoriented, trying to remember where she might be. She focused on East Indian women in saris, and West Indian men with dreadlocks. She compared Latinos in custom guayaberas to those in carefully laundered work shirts.

She listened to Spanish, to island patois, and to something that might have been Danish or German. The sounds, overlapping, created an unsettling Babel.

I will find my way here, Ava promised herself. *I will get to the bottom of all this. I will understand the truth of my son's death. And then, God willing, I may learn how to accept this unacceptable thing. I may learn some means of moving on.*

She turned, hearing American English spoken near her ear. "Good morning, Mrs. Collier. My name's Craig, Craig Fahrenthold. Charley was my best friend."

Ava looked up into the young man's grim face. Craig had called her son Charley, rather than Charles. Craig might actually *be* a friend. She took the hand that he held out to her, and managed a small smile.

Craig struggled to return the smile. "We went sailing together last weekend," he said. "Charley was in such high spirits!" He waved his hands to show how high, then he continued in a deep, quiet voice: "There's no way Charley could have been contemplating something like what this bunch is claiming."

Craig made a disparaging gesture that took in everyone on the far side of the room. He shook his head in disgust and kicked at an imaginary pebble. Or some other imagined thing or person.

Ava accepted his words as a welcome confirmation of her own conviction, but before she could respond to Craig, another young man joined them.

"I'm Rick Rowland," he said to Ava. "I saw Charley that night—earlier, I mean. I can't believe this happened, and I *won't* believe it happened the way Will Mattison says it did. Damn!

Mattison even got the Bishop to tell the story his way! How could he do that?"

Craig Fahrenthold nodded. Speaking to Rick in a half-muffled tone, he said, "We've got to get together and figure this out." Turning to Ava, he continued, "We'll be available, Mrs. Collier, any time you'd like to talk with us."

Ava choked back a sob. These young men had been so fond of her son that their love and support now surrounded her, too. "That's very kind," she managed to say at last.

"It's the least we can do," Craig responded. "All of this," he gestured again with repugnance, "is a Mattison thing. We loved Charley best."

Craig paused as Ava nodded her understanding. "Charley's real friends are getting together tomorrow night at Pirates' Den," he continued. "We need to say goodbye to Charley in our own way. We'll toss down a few drinks and share some memories. And we hope that you might join us."

"Yes," Ava said. "I think I'd like to do that—get together with you, I mean. It's what I need, too—to be with friends. Isn't Pirates' Den the bar in that old Danish hotel near the boardwalk?"

"You got it."

"I'm staying at the Tradewinds, just across the street. I'll meet you at Pirates' Den tomorrow evening. Just tell me the time."

With a plan agreed upon, the young men moved away. Clio, who had been watching the exchange, smiled. *I must remember to call . . .* she thought.

Ava put a hand to her chest. The discussion with Craig and Rick had been gratifying—more than gratifying!—but it was exhausting too. Ava felt that she could not take many more heartfelt conversations, no matter how well intentioned they might be. She stood on one foot and then the other, steeling herself as another sympathizer approached.

The woman—the color of richly creamed cocoa, neither dark nor light—appeared to be just entering her middle years. Slim and tall, she exhibited a graceful poise, and her exotic island hairstyle completed the look of subdued majesty. Tiny, tight braids radiated from the midpoint of the woman's brow line, tracing the contours of her head. At the nape of her neck, the miniature braids coiled—deliberately off-center—into an elegant bun.

Ava would have considered that woman the epitome of composed perfection, except for her face. Her eyes seemed puffy, and discolored blotches marred her skin. She transferred a damp handkerchief from her right hand to her left before offering the right hand to Ava. Her voice, when she spoke, rang with a cultured British tone.

"My dear Mrs. Collier. I am Simone Beranger." She took Ava's hands in her own. "It has been my privilege and pleasure to serve as your son's secretary for the past year. Charley was—." Simone dropped Ava's hands to raise the wet hankie to her face.

Ava waited as the woman recomposed herself. Simone, like Craig, had said the name *Charley*. She seemed to know Ava's boy truly, and she spoke of him with affection. Ava found that she could take some comfort in that idea.

Simone raised her head, and Ava saw with surprise that the dusky-skinned woman had amazing green eyes.

"I'm so sorry, ma'am," Simone said. "I didn't mean to break up like this. You have enough grief without my emotional behavior." She stopped, swallowed, and continued. "But Charley was more than an employer to me. He was, and I will always consider him, one of my dearest friends. It is not often that a woman like me has an employer like Charley."

Ava grasped Simone's hand it as though it were a lifeline. "Thank you, Simone. Please don't apologize for your grief. In an odd way, it gives me comfort. But I really need to sit down.

Could you help me find something light to drink, and a place where we might visit for a few minutes?"

Simone led Ava toward a damask-spread table where two impeccably-gowned dowagers waited behind elegant cut glass punch bowls. "With or without champagne?" one of the old ladies asked.

"Just a splash," Ava responded, surprising herself. She smiled a bit to think that she had said it. *Charley would have been glad for me,* she thought. *Charley* is *glad for me.*

While one of the little old ladies filled two cups with champagne punch, Simone's eyes scanned the room. She spotted a quiet corner with two empty rattan chairs and led Ava there.

"Mrs. Collier," Simone began, when they were seated, "I want to be whatever help to you that I can be. Ask me anything at all. Ask me to *do* anything at all."

"Begin by calling me Ava. I have very few acquaintances here, and I'd appreciate your friendship."

"Ava then." Simone smiled back, her emerald eyes shimmering with a last trace of tears. "Is there anything that you would like to take from Charley's office? I'm sure that the Mattisons will be down soon, to go through things, but I might put aside something for you, before they arrive. Pictures, personal items?"

Ava's face brightened a bit with a fresh idea. "Have you seen Charley's collection of antique fountain pens? I want those, since I gave him most of them. And does he have any recent snapshots of himself in the office? I'd appreciate something like that."

Simone emitted a soft, throaty chuckle. "You should see the sideboard in his office. I always fussed at him about what a job it was for me to keep his picture frames dusted. He had photos and more photos, each individually framed, and all crowded together. I recognized you from some of them. And yes, I do know where his treasured fountain pens are."

Simone nodded, as though thinking things over. "You really *should* come to Charley's office—if you would like to. If you think you can."

"I can, and I will," Ava responded. "Could I meet you there tomorrow?"

"Of course," Simone said, her voice warm and reassuring. "Maybe you would have lunch with me too, before you go through the things in Charley's office?"

"I would like that very much," Ava said, her voice little more than a whisper.

"I would, too," Simone echoed, dabbing the hankie at the corner of her eye once more.

Will Mattison interrupted their moment. "Ava, I must introduce you to our Lieutenant Governor. Come with me now."

He took her by the hand, led her half way across the room, then stopped abruptly. Ava saw a wrinkled and feeble old man, sitting in a huge leather easy chair that seemed about to swallow him.

"John Lemtorp," Mattison said, and then went into a biography of the man—the sort of detail that Clio would have found important. Ava was not interested. But she noted that Mattison's tone seemed just a careful tinge short of patronizing.

Simone had slipped away, leaving Ava to the repugnance of meaningless conversation with an old man. Leaving her aware that Simone, who seemed so genuine and helpful, had been a welcome respite from Mattison's conceit. Leading Ava to consider that Simone might be an ally in the imminent battle.

That was how she looked at everything now. She was identifying the enemy, and her allies. Ava was consciously girding herself for an all-out battle with the Mattisons.

When Lieutenant Governor Lemtorp had said all the platitudes that he could muster, Will Mattison steered Ava toward Maura, who stood in a cluster of people her own age.

"Ava," Will said, "certainly you recognize these young men—Parker Flanagan and Byron Hendley—whom you met at Maura's and Charles's wedding. They represent the next generation of Dos Marias leadership."

Ava could hardly forget that Byron was the young man who had given her son a beating, but might not have recognized him without the prompt from Will. She studied the small young man—sharp-featured, with a shock of untamed dark hair falling across his forehead and almost into his deep brown eyes. Ava thought at once of a Texas borderlands coyote, conniving and opportunistic.

She doubted that Byron possessed the leadership abilities that Mattison claimed for him. The boy had made a drunken fool of himself at Charley and Maura's wedding reception, and Ava noted that Byron seemed about to do the same thing now. She supposed that he had been drunk on the night that he attacked Charley, as well.

"Mrs. Collier, oh, I'm so sorry." Byron grasped her hand and began a long and rambling speech, teary and difficult to understand.

Ava used her left hand to loosen Byron's grip on her right. As she turned to walk away, Will Mattison stopped her. "Maura is tired," he said. "Anisectus is bringing the Mercedes around. We can all get a little rest before the interment. It will be just us, and a very few others. On the grounds of Estate Clary, of course."

Ava sighed. All these people. All these demands. She was just so weary.

Back at the Mattison mansion, Clio showed Ava into a small, quiet bedroom. Ava lay there, eyes closed. Perhaps she dozed, for she startled at the sound of someone rapping on her door. Clio.

"Look out your window, Ava," Clio, once Ava had let her into the room. "That rock tower on the next rise is our old sugar mill. Will has made it into a mausoleum for Charles. Don't you think it's a pretty site?"

Ava only nodded at the inanity.

"We need to go there now," Clio continued. "To the sugar mill. For Charles' interment. Freshen up a bit, and meet us at the front door." Clio backed out of the bedroom door and shut it quietly.

Ava checked her hair in the bathroom mirror, pressed a damp washcloth to her eyes, and decided that she had done all that was required. She found the front door, and the Mercedes waiting there. Maura, Clio, and Will were already inside.

Anisectus drove them to the base of the sugar mill's hill and parked on a small, level area where the bishop and his crucifer waited with a few others. Of course, Will Mattison organized their procession and led the mourners up the hill, toward the mill's wide door.

Immediately behind Will stumbled the crucifer, awkward on the uneven path. Behind the crucifer, Bishop Gardiner moved in haughty majesty, holding the funerary urn before him. Maura followed, supported by her mother. Then the others

Ava Collier brought up the rear, trailing the procession, feeling unnoticed and unremembered. For a moment, irritation edged out her grief. Ava resented Will's slights and Clio's acquiescence. They should recognize that only she, of all the group climbing that hill, had a blood relationship to Charley— only she and her grandbaby, traveling in Maura's belly. Ava alone, of all those gathered, had known and loved Charley for so many precious years.

Ava edged forward through the procession, keeping her eyes on the urn. She must be ready to rescue Charley should the bony bishop stumble. She would rescue her boy as surely as she had when he was a toddler, about to dart into a busy street. She was as ready to rescue him, as she wished she might have done, last Thanksgiving night.

A mongoose skittered across the path in front of the procession and disappeared into the bush. A round, yellow sugarbird startled on a branch and flew to a limb farther away. Ava did not see the creatures; her eyes did not stray from the stony path and the urn in the bishop's hands.

At last, the procession attained the hilltop. The bishop stepped with obvious relief onto a paved ramp that rose to the mill's entry, marched those last few yards, and posed benevolently. Will Mattison strode to his own place and indicated the spot where each of the other mourners should stand.

Ava ignored him; she chose the spot nearest Charley and would not budge.

Bishop Gardiner cleared his throat, then spoke in a lugubrious, oratorical tone that would have been better suited to a great hall than to such an intimate gathering. "Each of us comes to a threshold like this," the bishop said. "Most of us come, at least once, as mourners at such a portal. And every one of us comes, at last, as the mourned. So we have come today, and so Charles comes, to his final resting place. Let us pray."

The next words were ritual, out of the Episcopal Book of Common Prayer. Ava heard very little that the bishop read. After an interminable while, he turned and walked into the sugar mill.

Ava started to follow the bishop, but Will Mattison stopped her. She stood stock still, shocked and hurt. She peered into the sugar mill, a hefty cone of rough, gray stone. In its center stood a stolid cairn, less than four feet tall, less than three feet in diameter, constructed of the same weathered stone. Without doubt, that mill offered more than enough space for all of them to stand inside, circling the cairn.

Ava chafed at Will's dominance, but accepted it as fuel that would feed her simmering anger. She would need that anger, that fuel, to carry her through the days to come.

Bishop Gardiner set Charley's urn atop the cairn, said a few more words, made the sign of the cross over Charley again, and backed out of the mill now turned to crypt. A flash of sun found its way through one of the narrow windows and glinted on the gold of the urn.

Will Mattison's henchmen moved forward. Ava caught her breath as the men fastened a steel grate across the mill's door. Maura whimpered.

Jailed, Ava thought, clenching her fists. *And what did Charley do to deserve that?* The sugar mill tomb was not at all what her son would have wanted. Charley always sought open air, craved the wide sea, demanded freedom.

I'll get you out of that dungeon, my son, Ava promised, so that none but Charley could hear. *I'll give you the liberty of wind and wave.*

The procession retraced its precarious path, back down the sugar mill hill. Mattison ushered Ava into the waiting Mercedes, but neither Clio nor Maura joined her there. Will Mattison wished her a good evening, and as soon as he closed her door, Anisectus started the engine. "To the Tradewinds," Will told the driver.

Ava sank into the luxury car's deep maroon leather upholstery, grateful for its cool comfort. She released one quiet sigh of relief, feeling her exhaustion now.

When Anisectus had deposited her at The Tradewinds, Ava ordered a light rum drink at the bar and took it up to her room in a plastic cup. She stripped out of her suit in less than a minute, flinging it into a corner with considerable force. But she felt, as she did it, that she was shedding all the trappings and pretensions of the Mattison clan.

Ava stepped into the shower and stood in its spray, leaning her head against the far wall. She found herself sobbing, and she let the grief pour out.

One slow moment at a time, Ava's heaving abated. But her resolve remained undimmed. *Live to fight another day,* she thought as she toweled herself dry. When her head hit the pillow, the last words in Ava's consciousness were repetition: *Fight another day.*

NOVEMBER 29

Sun slipped between the shutters in bright bars of light, reflected off the dressing table mirror and into Ava's eyes. She opened the shutters and stared out at the harbor, seeing without seeking. Ava simply allowed her eyes to take in the panorama that lay before her. She did not emphasize or discount any aspect of the scene. She believed that answers were there, or somewhere on this island. She expected to glean some information from Simone this morning. And Ava felt confident that, in time, she would know much more.

She dressed, went to the hotel dining room for a light breakfast, and then wandered along the boardwalk. All of the streets of the historic town center ended there. The narrowest of the old lanes, now closed to vehicular traffic, offered strolling space for tourists. A few wider roads provided access for taxis and delivery vans.

Ava glanced at her watch—a habit, she thought, with little value on Dos Marias. She sat down on one of the benches that lined the boardwalk, pulled the smart phone from her pocket, and tapped in Charley's land line, intending to talk to Maura. A recording told her that Maura could be reached at her parents' home. The voice on the recorder was Will's.

Ava found the idea of calling Estate Clary distasteful, but she yearned for Maura to know that she intended for the two of them to be close. They would always need to be close. Ava wanted—she needed—to be an active part of her grandchild's life. And one day, Ava vowed, she would free the grandchild from Mattison's grasp as surely as she would rescue her son from the sugar mill prison.

She found the Mattison number in her phone's memory and clicked on it. Doulsie, the house servant, answered. When Ava asked for Maura, Doulsie informed her that the girl was having her massage and could not be disturbed. The old and faithful servant did not suggest that Ava might speak with Will or Clio Mattison.

So that's how it will be? Ava thought with wry acceptance. *They're done with me so soon? I'm yesterday's news, and they see no reason not to ignore me now?* Still, Ava hoped that if she could reach Maura directly, she might learn that the girl still cared. She wished that Maura might be the kind of woman who could stand up to her father, but Ava knew that she wished in vain.

She deliberately walked in a more brisk pace along the harbor, working off her agitation. She passed a dilapidated sugar mill, plastered with peeling posters—an awkward poor relation of Mattison's venerable structure. She surveyed the collection of tour boats, sports fishing boats, scuba diving boats, and sailors' live-aboard boats that bobbed at moorings in the harbor. A dinghy dock gave the sailboat people instant access to a variety of picturesque restaurants, bars, and shops, most still closed at this early hour. But a dive shop—*wUnderWorld*—teemed with activity; tourists milled in excited anticipation of their scuba adventure on the deep reefs of Dos Marias.

Someone hurried past Ava and jumped onto a small cat boat. It reminded her of the little sailboat she'd bought for Charley, when they moved to Rockport. Before long, Charley had become so proficient that they sailed that little boat all the way across Aransas Bay, to San Jose Island.

They had stumbled through soft white sand, watching for thorn bushes, watching for rattlesnake holes, until at last they came to the Gulf shore. It was a wild shore, a natural shore, with none of the trappings of modern tourists. Walking at the edge of the surf, they'd searched for sand dollars, picked up orange strands of whip coral, overturned the discarded shells of small crabs, stepped carefully around iridescent blue Portuguese-man-o-wars. Those jelly fish shriveled, shrinking in the hot Texas sun.

Always, returning home, Ava and Charley had promised each other that one day they'd have a bigger boat—a forty-foot ketch, maybe even a forty-two. "I'll buy it for you, Mama," her little boy had boasted. "I'll buy you a big boat and we'll sail around the world."

Now, on this alien shore, Ava heard Charley's voice clearly, making that promise anew. Her eyes filled with tears. *We should have had more time,* Ava thought. *I shouldn't have stayed so busy, or so often put things off.*

Shaky, she found a bench and sat. She shook her head to clear a touch of vertigo. And in that movement, she glimpsed someone.

A youngish man, twisted and disheveled, stepped from behind the dilapidated sugar mill and fully into Ava's field of vision. The man's huge head, disproportional to his body, sprouted an unkempt mass of dreadlocks that made the head appear even larger than it was. He wore a heavy army jacket, crisscrossed with empty ammunition belts. A military-issue canteen dangled at his waist, just above white cotton shorts that looked suspiciously like underwear. The man ambled along the boardwalk in battered leather sandals so loose that the soles flapped when he walked.

Ava pressed a hand to her chest, shrinking from the vagrant. She turned her face away, anticipating that he would beg for a handout.

"Good mornin' Mom!" The hobo contemplated Ava, shuffled a few steps nearer, and leaned sideways, peering into her face. "Ah say *good mornin'*. In dese islan', yo impolite when yo don' say 'good mornin''."

"I'm sorry," Ava answered in an even tone that was not really apologetic. "Good morning. And good bye." She turned up the corners of her lips to soften the words just a bit, but she turned her shoulders away from the man to indicate her rejection of such an unkempt—and almost threatening!—individual.

The drifter did not move away. He leaned toward her again and looked earnestly into her eyes. "Jah be watchin' yo, Mom. Jah know yo trouble. Jah watch, and Jah take care o' yo. Jah want dat yo have dis, Mom." The man scrabbled in one of his jacket's many pockets, found what he was looking for, and pressed a smooth, hard something into Ava's palm.

"Well," she sighed, reaching into her purse with that hand. Ava dropped the hard thing in the purse, pulled out a few coins, and offered them as a way to get rid of the vagrant.

"No *Mom*!" The vagrant shied away as though she had slapped him. "No, *Mom*! Ah don' take nothin' from yo. Ah jes' give yo what Jah say dat yo need. Jah watch. Jah take care o' yo."

The misshapen man pulled himself to a semblance of erectness and gave Ava a formal salute. Then he turned on a heel and a toe and strode away, mimicking—as nearly as his crooked body would allow—a militaristic style.

Jah, Ava recalled, was the Rastafarian name for God. And she supposed that "mom" was the islanders' pronunciation of "ma'am." She'd heard it before, from the taxi driver.

Ava groped in her purse, where she had dropped the thing that the hobo had given her. She pulled out the hard, smooth-edged lump; saw it to be wing-like, an inch and a half long, perhaps a quarter-inch thick. It was pale green in color, like an old Coca-Cola bottle. Ava realized then that she held a scrap of sea glass, sanded smooth in tumbling surf. She supposed that the vagrant had picked up this piece somewhere along a sandy shore.

Ava rubbed it, recalling that Charley had shown her a necklace of sea glass that he had bought for Maura, early in their relationship. Multi-hued specimens of the glass, artfully set, resembled rough-cut jewels.

But sea glass was not the focus of Ava's musing now. The point was, why this man had approached her. At the very least, Ava thought, she'd add the vagrant to her mental list of the strange individuals that she'd encountered on Dos Marias. Two taxi drivers, the receptionist at the mortuary, and now this misshapen man. Each seemed to communicate some essence of the cultural puzzle on this island. Somehow, Ava thought, these people represented a message for her—something that she should try to understand.

Or not. Probably she was imagining things, Ava thought. And most certainly, her overriding emotion was that she should not trust anyone on Dos Marias.

She willed herself to see, in memory, the people that she had talked with in the Parish Hall at St. Elmo's. She sorted them into three basic groups: Will Mattison's associates, Charley's friends, and "the next generation of leadership" that Mattison had introduced her to. Ava wanted to learn more about each individual in each group, and she reviewed them in her mind.

These thoughts occupied her morning, until at last Ava's watch indicated that the time had come when she would meet Simone at Charley's office.

Behind the narrow streets on which fronted the oldest buildings in town, somewhat newer buildings rose—the sturdy edifices built by successful Danish businessmen almost two centuries earlier. Now the reconstructed buildings attracted up-and-coming attorneys, would-be property developers, and many Economic Development Centers like the one where Charley had worked.

The stated objective of these centers was "to enhance the business climate and foster progressive economic development" throughout the U.S. Virgin Islands. Approved companies were expected to comply with the intent of the EDC program, encouraging investment and creating jobs in the U.S. Virgin Islands. Too often, however, EDC staffs remained small, and the majority of profits flowed back to the continental United States. As a result, Federal authorities had been pressuring these businesses to justify their operations. Some international banks had closed the hidden offshore accounts of their well-heeled American clients, and in so doing had thrown unwanted light on carefully guarded secrets.

Ava mulled on these facts as she walked toward Charley's office, her pace slower and slower as she neared her destination. Was the company for which Charley worked under suspicion for shady dealings? He would never have been guilty of that himself, Ava was sure. But what if he had been a whistle-blower? Charley's murder might have been revenge.

Ava stopped dead still. She tried to calm her emotions, tried to get her bearings. She saw that she was only steps away from Charley's office building.

Ava willed herself to mount the stairs briskly. At the second floor, she opened a glass door that led into the suite of offices that Charley had shared.

There, Simone Beranger rose from the receptionist's desk and came to meet Ava. She put her hands on Ava's arms in a sedate sort of hug, then stepped back, gesturing around the room. "Good morning, Ava. Welcome to our domain."

Ava remembered to echo, "Good morning."

"Charley's office is just beyond this one," Simone said. "Shall we go in? I'm eager to show you something special there."

Ava steeled herself. Entering her son's empty workspace would be a difficult hurdle.

But when Simone led her into that office, Ava saw that a huge basket of fresh flowers obscured Charley's desk.

"Someone has just sent these?" Ava asked.

"Yes," Simone replied, "the other tenants in this building. That was thoughtful of them, wasn't it?"

Ava only nodded, pretending to study the flowers as she batted away tears. She tried to focus on the floral arrangement's interesting blend of unusual tropicals and more ordinary blooms.

When Ava had control of her emotions again, she spoke to Simone, trying to make her voice light. "Where are we going for lunch?"

"There's a new place, back in one of the courtyards, a little more than a block from here," Simone suggested. "It's an easy walk. They do light lunches, for the most part, but you could order an excellent fish platter, if that appeals to you."

Simone's voice softened to a reassuring tone. "It's a nice place, quiet. A place where we can talk." She touched Ava's arm as she said it, as though they were intimate girlfriends, and steered her out of the office.

Simone led Ava along one of the old, closed streets to reach the restaurant. As they walked, Ava told Simone about the hobo who had approached her.

"I know the man you are describing," Simone said. "Most people call him 'Boardwalk Bum.' He has a name, of course, but few people bother to learn it. They call him '*Boardwalk* Bum' to distinguish him from "*Street-corner* Bum," another homeless man. That one stands motionless, every day, at an intersection of the highway leading to the airport."

Ava fished the sea glass from her purse and held it out to Simone. "The Boardwalk Bum gave me this. He said Jah wanted me to have it."

Simone turned the chip in her hand as though evaluating it; she kept her eyes on the glass as she spoke. "Rastafarians believe that the presence of Jah in His children and in the world is the triumph over the tribulations of everyday life." Then, looking into Ava's eyes, she added, "Maybe this symbol will help you to that triumph as well." Simone gave Ava a sweet smile as she handed the sea glass back to her.

They walked only another few steps before Simone turned into a narrow passage and pointed toward a wrought iron gate that hung open. "This is the place," she told Ava.

The restaurant owners had filled their courtyard with a wide variety of potted plants and a few small trees. Several interesting orchid specimens drew Ava like magnets. "What my customers in Texas would give for these!" she said.

"Yes, they're lovely," Simone agreed. She led Ava to a small table near the edge of the garden, and when they were seated, she asked: "Do you have a particular interest in plants?"

"Well, I suppose Charley may have told you that I'm a home builder," Ava said. "And I don't stop when the walls go up. I want a complete picture that includes a wealth of growing things. You might be surprised to know that orchids can do well in South Texas, with a little care.

"When Charley's father was alive," Ava continued, "I focused on that part of our business—the decorating and landscaping—almost exclusively. Then my husband died of cancer, and I thought my sorrow over his death would never end. But Charley saved me."

Ava stopped, choking back emotion. She cleared her throat before continuing, determined to overcome her grief and get her words out. "My boy became the repository for all my love and my reason to work. Everything I've done in my adult life has been for Charley's sake." Ava shook her head, unable to speak for a moment.

"After Charley married and moved here," she continued, "I began pulling out of the day-to-day operations of the organization that I'd built. I was planning an early semi-retirement so that I could spend more time enjoying the Caribbean with my son and his family."

Ava sighed deeply, looked down to her lap, then out across the room. Simone put a gentle hand on Ava's arm. She waited for the woman to speak again.

When Ava did, she changed the subject. "I've talked longer than you expected, I'm sure, Simone. That's enough about me. Tell me about you."

Simone shrugged. "I'm just a girl of the islands—the British ones, as you have no doubt guessed from my accent. My father was mostly African. His people, brought to these islands as slaves, intermarried with people who had always been here, and then a bit of French got thrown in—as you've discerned from my name. It seems a wonder to me that the name Beranger survived in my personal heritage, but it did, and here am I. My move from down island to Dos Marias occurred no more than a few years ago. And I believe that is all that can be said about me."

Ava shook her head. "I don't think so. I have a feeling that there's a great deal more to you than you've told me so far." She watched for a response from Simone and saw only a slight smile, before Simone looked away.

Ava continued. "Let me see if I've got the story straight so far. Your father was part French—from way back. And somewhere you got the blood of some native islanders—you mean like Caribs and Taínos?"

"Yes." Simone spoke just the one syllable. Then: "I'm surprised you know those names. Few of the Continentals do."

"I studied up, after Charley moved here," Ava said. "But you are mostly African?"

"Yes, of course," Simone nodded. "My father's French blood—not much more than a drop, in the grand scheme of such things—came from a slave master many, many generations back. That man had an on-going sexual relationship with a woman that he owned."

Simone felt an old and familiar twinge of resentment as she said it, but she did not allow Ava to see her emotion. "That slave master ended up truly fond of the baby that he and his slave had produced. The master liked that baby so much that he gave the boy his surname, Beranger, the story that went with it, and the sense of pride at being French—at least in part. But of course that boy could not marry into the White world. Eventually he met and married a dark woman who had Carib blood."

Ava nodded. "But he kept the French name. And I suppose that my Charley told you about a long-ago Beranger who explored the coast of Texas and Louisiana?"

Simone chuckled lightly. "Of course he did. He said that's what made us such good working partners." She put a hand to her mouth then, looked down at her lap, and shuddered.

Ava put a hand to Simone's arm, and the two women sat, silent, sharing their grief. When Simone spoke again, her aim was to change the subject abruptly. "Look over in that corner . . . the small tree? It's called Poor Man's Orchid, and it's a favorite of mine. In fact, I live on a street named Poor Man's Orchid, and I'm really surrounded by them there."

Ava blinked her eyes, trying to turn her attention to the sprawling tree that Simone had indicated. Its sturdy branches and bi-lobed leaves were not at all orchid-like. But each bloom displayed an arrangement of petals similar to those of an orchid, and the lowest-hanging lavender petal held in its hollow a smear of deep purple. "Do you suppose these trees might grow in Texas?" she asked.

Simone laughed softly. "I'm told that they revel in cool-weather climates. You could probably give it a try."

"And that one?" Ava asked, pointing to a taller tree with clusters of red-orange blooms standing straight up on the branches.

"African tulip tree," Simone said. "I know they do well in Florida, so they might work on the Texas coast, too. Here, we call the tree Sorcerer's Stick, because those stalks of blossoms look like a magician's wand that turns into a bouquet."

Ava studied the tree for a moment and smiled. "The blooms do resemble Dutch tulips," she agreed. "But I see the sorcerer's magic wand, as well."

Simone chattered on, identifying native plants around the atrium. Ava only half-listened. Instead, she mused that Simone had side-stepped the opportunity to tell much of her personal story. From the little that she did say, Ava gathered that Simone must be an intelligent and passionate woman. And a woman who might have complex feelings toward her employers.

Ava tucked the thought away for further consideration, then said, "Simone, I appreciate this diversion, I really do. It has been good for me, but now I must get down to business. I've been trying to recall the names of some of Charley's friends that I met at the funeral. Craig Fahrenthold is one, I know. Can you tell me something about him?"

"Craig is a broker," Simone said, shifting her attitude adroitly. "He's good at his business. In fact, I think he's one Continental who may actually stay in the Caribbean. He has been on island for about five years now."

"What do you mean, he's a 'Continental'?" Ava asked.

"That's how we islanders refer to people from the continent—from the U.S. in particular," Simone responded. "People like you. Dos Marias is made up of Islanders who have been here forever, Original Settlers like the Mattisons, and now the Continentals. In that category, I lump all the Johnny-come-latelies, the part-timers, the people who don't stay long, because their allegiance remains elsewhere."

"But you think that Craig may stay here permanently?" Ava asked.

Simone shrugged. "Who's to say, really? It seems to me Craig has the attitude, and the adaptability, that one needs, if he is to settle successfully into our way of life here. I sense that he is comfortable with all that we are—and are not." Simone made a rueful face, then continued, "I like him! Craig is a very nice man, and he was Charley's best friend and sailing buddy."

Ava turned her head away and blinked her eyes. Sometimes, it seemed, a simple phrase just wrecked her.

"There's someone named Dick, too, isn't there?" Ava said. "I met him at the funeral?"

"I think you must mean Rick," Simone answered. "Rick Rowland. He's with one of the U.S. alphabet agencies—ATF, DEA, FBI, CIA, something. Did you meet his girlfriend too? Brooke Randolph? She has been here for a number of years, so I suppose Rick finds her knowledge of the area helpful to him."

The waiter arrived with their meal before Ava could ask Simone more about Rick's intriguing work, or about his girlfriend. Simone resumed the conversation by bringing up other names.

"I think that you met Parker Flanagan and Byron Hendley, too. Yes?"

Ava nodded. "I remember Byron from Charley and Maura's wedding. And I think Maura mentioned someone named Ronald?"

"Yes," Simone said. "Byron, Parker and Ronald are all from families who rank among the most pedigreed on island. They are men whom Maura has known since they were all toddlers together."

Simone began telling little stories about those island families—what sorts of plantations their ancestors had, where their homes were on island, what they did now. The conversation did not provide any meaningful information, Ava thought, but it did carry them through lunch and their walk back to the suite of offices.

Once there, both Simone and Ava fell silent. Ava squared her shoulders, raised her chin, and re-entered her son's private domain.

Simone waited a few moments before following her. She stooped before a deep drawer in the bottom of a mahogany bookshelf cabinet as she said, "The fountain pen collection is here."

Simone pulled out a monogrammed wooden box and rose with it in a single fluid motion. She re-crossed the room to place the unopened box on a corner of Charley's desk, close to where Ava stood. Then Simone stepped back.

Ava took her time in opening the box, aware that she was about to unveil both treasure and pain. Her eyes fogged each time she lifted a pen. And for each pen, she had a short vignette to tell Simone. There were pens commemorating Charley's high school and college graduations, the one for his first important job, the one at his wedding. And a number of others.

"Well," Ava said when she had handled all of the pens and patted them back into place. She closed the box firmly. "That's that. I'll take this box with me." She placed it on an antique marble-topped mahogany table near the door. "And will you please make a list of names and phone numbers, and e-addresses of those I might want to contact. Craig and Rick. Charley's banker, certainly. Then, any of Charley's other friends that you think I might meet or want to talk with.

"And now—" Ava looked around the room—"to the photographs." She sighed, holding up her hands in a confused, overwhelmed sort of gesture. She saw a window box and a credenza crowded with frames large and small. Ava had never realized that her son was so sentimental.

A wavy pewter frame held a snapshot taken of Ava and Charley on a beach somewhere. Near it stood a miniature Texas flag. A carved wooden frame, painted with flowers and vines, displayed Maura on their wedding day. A bone-shaped frame held a photo of Charley's dog.

Ava took a deep breath and put a hand to her mouth and chin. "Is there any rhyme or reason to the arrangement here? I'd like to pick out some of the most recent pictures."

Simone chuckled in sympathy. "They'd be more or less at the front, I guess. Look here! Charley and Maura at Solitude Beach. And there—Charley with the new puppy."

"I hadn't even heard about that one," Ava said sadly.

"They hadn't had him for long," Simone answered. "Charley named him Sgt. Shore, because the puppy looked so self-important patrolling the beach—like a kid playing soldier."

Again they both fell silent. After a few moments Simone said, "I had a carton brought up earlier in the day, Ava. Pack in it as many of these pictures as you want—including the frames, if you like. I'll handle the Mattisons, and I'll have the photos shipped to you in Texas. They may even get there before you do."

Ava nodded. "I'll give you my business address then, and alert my secretary to be looking for the arrival of a large box."

A telephone rang. "I'll get that at my desk," Simone said, "and leave you to this."

So Ava worked alone. She went out once to ask for bubble wrap, which Simone produced, and again, much later, to ask for packaging tape. Simone's quiet way, Ava thought, was designed to give her comfort, to ease the pain of her task in Charley's office.

After a while, Simone came in again, opening a cabinet door that concealed a small refrigerator. Ava saw that the box held Cruzan mango rum, 151-proof rum, a top-quality Scotch whiskey, Cokes, orange juice, and the same trendy bottled water that Maura had carried the day before. Lead crystal double old-fashioned glasses gleamed on the shelf above.

"I thought you might be ready for something to drink, Ava." Simone said.

"Yes, some orange juice would be good," Ava answered. "I guess Charley kept all of this liquor for entertaining his clients?"

"For clients, of course," Simone agreed. "But also for himself, at one time or another. Depending on his mood or the time of day." Simone paused.

Then in a hesitant voice, she said, "Lately, I've thought that Charley seemed troubled."

Ava cocked her head suspiciously. "How do you mean?"

"Well, perhaps my feminine intuition was making a mountain out of a molehill," Simone said. She waved a hand, as though to dismiss her own words. "Still, Charley just seemed less full of life than he was a month or so ago. So he drank a little more. I didn't say anything; I felt certain that he would work out whatever was bothering him."

Simone broke off then, setting her lips in a firm line. "I've probably said more than I should have. Please forgive me if I'm overstepping."

"No," Ava answered. "I need to know what you think, what you have seen, what your opinion is in this situation."

"Well, I guess I've done that!" Simone said in a voice that sounded rueful, apologetic. "Now let me call someone to take your box to our shipping department."

Within minutes, a man came with a dolly, set Ava's box on it, and started for the door. Simone was busy on the telephone as Ava followed the porter into the hallway. She did nothing more than wave a short goodbye

Throughout the afternoon, Ava tried recall each thing that Simone had said, or even hinted at. What disturbed her most was Simone's description of Charley's mood during his final days—a choice of words that seemed eerily similar to what Will Mattison had said.

Ava took a shower, washed her hair, chose something casual to wear to meet Charley's friends at Pirates' Den. She felt quite certain that Byron, Parker, and Ronald would not be attending. Those were Maura's friends, and not men that her Charley has been close to.

She walked the short distance from her hotel to Pirates' Den, where weather-beaten bar tables spilled out of an old stone building and onto the boardwalk. A few tourists sat there, and from their conversations, Ava gathered that they were awaiting the evening's crab races.

As Ava tried to make sense of the race preparations, Craig Fahrenthold came to sit beside her. "I got here early. I'm glad to see that you did too."

Ava nodded. Then, unwilling to get down to serious business so soon, she pointed toward the busyness that she'd been watching: "I'm trying to figure out this crab race thing."

Craig grinned, nodded, launched into the story. "The bartender pays local youngsters to collect hermit crabs once a week and bring them to him for this event. Charley said that you have hermit crabs in Texas too, but that ours are much bigger."

Ava nodded. "Yes, these are indeed larger."

"Our hermit crabs occupy abandoned turban shells, whelks, or small conchs," Craig continued. "The bartender paints a number on each shell for identification. Since the crabs will never move in a straight line, he starts them at the center of a large circle that he has painted on the deck." Craig pointed to it.

"The first crab to reach the outer perimeter is declared the race winner. Bettors on the victorious crab—if there are any—win themselves a free drink, the house specialty, Frozen Pirate's Grog."

Craig laughed and shrugged. "It's just tourist stuff," he said. He and Ava watched for a few more minutes before he suggested, "Let's go on inside."

He stood up and led Ava into a semi-enclosed area with stools arranged along an antique mahogany bar. At its far end, an inconspicuous door led into a private room.

As he opened that door, Craig said, in a mock-serious raspy whisper, "A dark den for skullduggery indeed."

Ava smiled a bit, appreciating his attempt to put her at ease with the little joke.

Mottled maroon walls barely reflected the red light of simulated candles in black wrought iron holders. Booth benches, upholstered in burgundy faux leather, seemed to slide into the shadows.

Craig offered Ava a captain's chair facing the entry and sat down next to her. "So we can see who's coming," he said. They had just settled in when a couple stood silhouetted in the light of the door.

"Brooke and Rick," Craig told Ava.

She rose to greet them, and Brooke slid her arms around Ava's waist. She leaned her head against Ava's breast. "We miss him, Ava," she said. "Oh, we miss Charley!"

A waitress approached. "Gloria, halleluiah!" Rick said, as he pinched the girl's rear. Then he looked around at Ava, sheepish as a little boy caught in some indiscretion. "Her name is Gloria," he explained.

Ava decided that Rick must be the class clown, and she was glad of it. His adroit nonsense had saved her from the maudlin moment with Brooke.

Ava had imagined that the waitresses at Pirates' Den might dress like pirates' wenches, but apparently Dos Marias was too casual for that. The girl wore only a very snug spaghetti strap tee, and quite evidently nothing beneath it. Her very short shorts suggested no possible underpinnings there, either—at least nothing more cumbersome than a very slim thong. A butterfly tattoo peeked over the top band of the girl's shorts, low in the small of her back. She wore a half-dozen faddish island bangle bracelets, gold and silver, and large gold hoop earrings. One of her sandaled feet displayed a toe ring as well.

Ava could understand why Rick saw Gloria as a pinchable type. She was indeed a pirate's wench, even without the traditional costume.

The waitress looked at Ava, tapping her pencil against an order pad.

"I don't know . . ." Ava said.

"Bring the lady a rum cooler," Craig suggested. "Or would you rather have a beer, Ava?"

She looked at a list of ales, all unfamiliar to her. "The rum will be fine," she said to the waitress, "but make it light."

Before the drinks arrived, another guest sat down with them. "I'm Mark Dotson," the young man said. "I tried to get close enough to talk to you at the funeral, but never could. I work in the same office as Charley. I mean, where Charley worked."

Ava nodded to show that she understood. "I was at the office today. Simone helped me get some of Charley's things together so that I can take them home."

"Yep," Mark nodded. "That's where Charley's things should go. And I'm not surprised that Simone was there to help you. Whenever Charlie and I handled projects together, we always depended upon Simone's expert assistance."

He winked, but Ava wasn't sure she got the joke, if there was one. Mark sobered as he continued, "Two of Charley's clients flew in for the funeral yesterday. I thought you'd want to know. Not many brokers would get that type of appreciation from their clients. A lot of people in that crowded church yesterday were there simply to see and be seen, but not these guys. They came because they wanted to honor Charley and their relationship with him."

Ava nodded, grateful for Mark's words, but unable to come up with a syllable of her own.

Craig put his hand on Ava's arm, interrupting them. "Ken and Sandi Leland are just coming in the door," he said. "Ken is the top salesman at Auto Antillean. It's the major vehicle dealership on island, carrying most brands you might think of—American and foreign makes. Sandi is a charming asset, very much the 'corporate wife' type."

Just as the introductions were completed, the waitress, Gloria, returned to set frosty concoctions before everyone. "This is a rum cooler?" Ava asked, incredulous.

"Hell no," Rick laughed. "It's a Pain Killer. That's what we *all* need *this* night!"

Rick's girlfriend, Brooke, looked at Ava and smiled. "It's really yummy. But you'd better drink it slow. The bartender takes two Cruzan rums—mango and dark—and whirls them in a blender with coconut cream, orange and pineapple juices, and ice. He pours it into these special glasses, sorta like hurricane glasses, and then adds a splash of 151-proof rum—that's the real potent stuff. On top of the foam, he sprinkles fresh-grated nutmeg. Yummy!"

Ava thought the cocktail looked more like a dessert than a libation. She sipped at her Painkiller with cautious doubt, knowing it couldn't live up to its name. Instead, in liquor's way, the strong drink might add to her misery.

Various people appeared in the room from time to time. Some said a few words to Ava; others bought rounds of drinks and toasted Charley. Neither Byron nor any of his buddies arrived—nor any friends of Maura's, so far as Ava could tell.

The people she met all claimed affection for Charley, but a nagging question stayed in Ava's mind: *Are any of these people pirates, rather than Charley's true friends, and if so, how can I tell which ones?*

Ava rapped on her glass to get the group's attention. "I am so glad to have this evening with you. Thank you all for being here, and for inviting me to be here. Would it be all right if I asked a few questions? I don't intend to make the evening a downer, but there are some things that I do need to understand."

"You were on the agenda all along," Craig said. "We *know* Charley wouldn't off himself. That's just not who he was. We want to set the record straight."

Ava nodded her gratitude, trying to ignore the awful "off himself" phrase. When she could speak, she said: "Yesterday, before the funeral, Maura told me her story of what happened that night. She said that Charley was out with some friends—but she mentioned Byron and Parker, I think. Not any of you, I think—except . . . Rick, did you tell me you were there?"

Rick shook his head. "Not really. Early in the evening, I saw them, so I stopped by to say hello. I didn't stay long, but long enough to know that Charley was *fine*. He was the same Charley we've all known and loved. I left pretty soon, because I don't like those guys he was with—and I know that he didn't enjoy being with them either. Charley only went out with that bunch when he felt he had to, to keep Missy Maura happy."

Someone interrupted him. "But that wouldn't be so miserable for him that he'd do something desperate."

"Okay," Ava interrupted. "So none of you would have any sense of how Charley was feeling that particular night. And of course you couldn't know what happened when he got home."

She summarized the tale that Maura had told her about finding Charley with his guns, and Charley then going out to his car. Ava concluded her story by saying, "Maura said that she waited, and when Charley didn't come back, she went out and found him in the car. It was locked and he wasn't moving. Maura went back in the house and called her father."

"The Hell you say!" Ken uttered the words like an explosion. "Charley is in a locked car, not moving, and his loving wife just goes back inside to call *Daddy*? She doesn't try to get into the car? She just waits until *Daddy* gets there? Damn!"

Ken's wife, Sandi, patted his arm, then looked at the group. "I would break the windshield. I would scream bloody murder.

I would do *something, anything*. I certainly wouldn't just wait until help arrived."

"Yeah," Mark agreed. "Charley might have been alive then. Maybe Maura could have saved him, if she'd done something on her own."

"But we're missing the point," Craig argued. "That line of thinking assumes that Charley went out to the car intending to kill himself. And we all know that's just not the case!"

"Well . . ." Sandy pondered. "But why would Maura lie about a thing like that?"

She was not rebutting, just clearly puzzled.

"Yeah," Rick agreed, but his voice reeked anger and suspicion. "Why would she lie about it?"

Ava could not follow every conversation in the confusion of voices that arose. She tapped a spoon against her glass once more. "How can we get to the bottom of this?"

"What we know," Craig said, "is that someone shot Charley. What we *don't* know is who did it. Was it an accident, or was it a planned hit? And if someone set out on purpose to kill Charley—who was it? And what was his—or *her*—motivation?"

"And where do we go from here?" Ava's tone defined her pain and indecision.

"I brought you a business card," Mark said. "It's the name of a guy in the District Attorney's office—Miguel Losoya. He's supposed to be working on Charley's case."

Ava hesitated in taking the card. Calling the DA's office would be almost too difficult to bear.

Craig, watching her, said, "I know Miguel. I'll talk to him, Ava, and get back to you, if you want."

Ava shook her head. "I appreciate your help, and I'd like it if you would call him first. But just tell him that he'll be hearing from me. I feel that talking with this . . . Losoya? . . . is something that I must do myself."

"Excellent!" Craig grinned.

"Gloria!" Rick yelled. "Another round. We got some serious pain-killin' to do!"

As cocktail glasses slowly drained, conversation in the room became even more animated. Stories of happy times with Charley elicited waves of laughter that washed across the room, blurring the sharpest edges of sorrow.

"Remember when Charley was new on island, and we took him out to eat? The waitress served that titty bread that they stuff with knockwurst and top with chili. Charley kept looking at it and saying, *Titty bread? Titty bread?* He decided those knobs must be the nipples, so he gnawed on them."

"The waitress put Charley in his place, though. 'Yo bout to lose it mentally,' she told him, and she hit him on the head with a spoon. 'Git back inside yo skin,' she said."

The young men, remembering, pantomimed the action and roared with laughter.

"Charley always had fun talking to the locals. We sailed over to Tortola one weekend, and for some reason we were at a dock, instead of anchored out. Late in the evening, Charley saw a light moving around in the cockpit of the boat next to us. He worried that a robbery was underway. So he went over to check it out. A Rasta guy came up from the cabin and told Charley he was *baumin deh bote*. Charley just about freaked, thinking that the guy said he was bombing the boat. But what the Rasta meant was that he was the bug exterminator."

"That exterminator was Boots—the Rasta-looking guy who keeps a pencil in his beard? His wiry hair keeps the pencil convenient for him.

"Charley made friends with Boots and always invited him to have a drink with us when we were on Tortola. One night, Boots got to talking about going 'into the bush' to get a goat, and what good eating it was. Charley got all excited and he told Boots about Tex-Mex *cabrito*, barbecued baby goat. That made Boots' eyes sparkle, like Charley was his long lost kin.

"Boots told Charley that he'd been raised very poor. His father, a charcoal maker and seller, went into the bush to collect wood and burn it. He carried home big burlap bags full of the charcoal, balancing them on his head. Sometimes his hair would be smoking when he got home, Boots said."

"Huh! No local ever talked to me about things like that. But they'd always tell Charley. He just had a way of bringing them out.

"Do you remember the other story that Boots told Charley about his father? About how to tame a pig? Well, according to Boots, you tie one leg of a young piglet to the leg of a donkey, so that they sleep together for one night. After that, the piglet will never leave the donkey's side. Even when it grows to be a big hog, it will follow the donkey around."

"It wasn't just locals who caught Charley's interest. Remember that time we went over to Leverick Bay for a weekend, and met that woman on a bareboat charter? Her husband loved sailing, but she didn't even like to swim, because she was afraid of sea creatures. She was afraid of lizards too, but when a baby gecko got on to the boat, that tourist thought it was so cute that she adopted it. The gecko seemed to be starving, though, since bugs are scarce to non-existent on boats. When Charley heard that, he jumped up, got in our dingy, and went ashore. He stirred up the garbage bags so that he could collect flies for that woman's gecko. He caught them live, and popped them into a beer can that he retrieved from the trash."

"Yeah, Charley could do fool things like that, but he seriously helped people too. We were anchored over at Red Hook one time and saw a catamaran adrift—*Peregrine*, out of a charter fleet, according to her markings. There wasn't anybody on board, and Charley worried that the boat was heading for the rocks. But we had no idea how to locate the people who had chartered her.

"We went on up to Molly Malone's Bar, where we were headed anyway, and Charley spotted a touristy guy checking his e-mail. Charley went right over and asked the guy if he was on *Peregrine*. When the guy said yes, Charley told him the boat was in danger, and promised we'd all help him. The tourist rushed to close up his computer and just about ran to his dinghy.

"When we motored back out to the mooring area, *Peregrine* really was close to the rocks—but still bobbing on the water, not aground. The tourist got aboard and started the engines, while Charley circled around in our dingy, watching for any sign of trouble."

"Red Hook is a helluva place. Great bars, great partying. But sometimes you can't get an anchor to hold, and other times you get snagged—seriously snagged. Once we'd been there for a weekend, and when we got ready to leave, Charley went to lift the anchor. As soon as it came above the waterline, he saw that it had hooked a load of shit—parts of an old anchor, a snarl of rope, and heavy chain leading down deeper than he could see. Charley got the boat hook and tried to flip it loose, but no luck.

"I left the engine in idle and went to help him. We worked until we got all the mess off the anchor, but then some of the trash ropes snarled in the boat hook. Charley held onto that hook while I got another one, but I still couldn't free the one Charley was hanging on to. The boat was drifting, and after a while, Charley couldn't hold it against the current. The hook slipped from his hands and floated free.

"I went back to the helm and circled around so that Charley could grab that hook with the other one. No problem! So I thought we were finally on our way, but when Charley tried to raise the anchor, it had snagged itself again, rock solid. I couldn't believe it!

"I lowered the dinghy while Charley dug everything out of the storage compartment to get to a spare anchor. We put it in the dinghy and motored forward to drop it, so it could hold us when the other anchor came free. Then, back aboard the boat, Charley got into his dive gear.

"He swam down to the original anchor. It had somehow got itself totally hooked in a grid of shiny new chain—I guess it was part of a hurricane grid, where boats can be secured for a storm. Anyway, Charley released the anchor without a lot of trouble, but as he pulled on it, he saw that it wanted to bury itself in the sand. He came back to the surface and told me to start the electric winch, but raise the anchor just a little at a time. He was going to flip it over and hold it in a position where it couldn't plow in as I brought it up.

"Finally done, right? Wrong! We raised and secured that anchor, and then Charley went forward to raise the second anchor by hand while I was at the helm. We still had a strong current, and the boat drifted over a private mooring buoy. That damn dangling second anchor had snagged the line of that buoy about ten feet below the surface.

"Charley got back into his dive gear and swam down. That anchor was harder to free than the one on the bottom had been, but Charley did it! We got the hell out of Red Hook, and as soon as we were in the deep Drake channel, believe me, we downed a beer! It was the only one left on board, so we went straight on over to St. John's and sat at Skinny Legs for about two hours to drink our fill."

"No question that Charley was the kind of man you want aboard your boat. He knew how to do what needed to be done. But sometimes it's the simple little things about him that I miss the most. Like when we were in that latte bar—the one with the sign saying that unattended children will be given an espresso and a free puppy? Well, Charley goes over to the attendant and stands there pigeon-toed, like a little kid. He says his Mommie is away off in Texas, so he's very unattended. He wants them to give him his puppy. And his espresso, of course."

For Ava, the tales were the best imaginable homage to her son. Each story ended in a gale of laughter, followed by a drink to drown the threat of tears. The sentiment convinced Ava that these people were genuinely Charlie's friends. She felt comfortable with every one of them, and willing to trust them all. At least for the time being.

But the room had become stuffy, over warm; Ava craved fresh air. She was thirsty, but she didn't want another Pain-killer. "It's time for me to go," she said, standing.

They all stood, to let her out. And each had to say another word of condolence, another little story of why Charley was so special. When Ava finally made it through the door, she sighed. Her hotel entry, so near, was surely the maximum distance that she could manage.

November 30

Morning. Ava followed instructions on the hotel room's antiquated coffee maker and flipped its switch. When her coffee was ready, she carried a cup to the table on her balcony—a *gallery*, the Mattisons would call it. Charley probably used the term as well. Ava smiled, thinking that.

She watched the dive of a pelican, the arrival of a small dinghy, and the departure of a seaplane. She began to think about her day, eager to get out of the murk in her mind, to achieve some clarity of understanding. She wanted to talk to Charley's banker, and she should call the man in the DA's office that Mark had mentioned.

Although making any call would be difficult, Ava knew that she could handle it. At the same time, she recognized the risk: Making a call might tip off someone to her suspicions, might lead her into treacherous waters.

Ava went inside to get her purse and returned with it to the gallery. When she reached into the purse for her smart phone, her fingers touched the piece of sea glass that the boardwalk bum had given her.

She pulled it out and examined it closely, turning it in her hand. Now, it seemed to her that the green-blue glass represented a sea wave, rather than a bird wing. *What was it Simone said?* Ava mused. *Something about triumph over the tribulations of everyday life.* She rubbed her thumb across the glass; she imagined that it was a warm Caribbean wave, capable of buoying her up in any storm.

Ava floated on that wave for a while, then set her shard of sea glass on the table. But she did not pick up her smart phone; she was just not ready to get on with the day's tasks.

Instead, she went into the bathroom to shower and wash her hair. Then she dressed in cotton slacks and a palm frond printed shirt—appropriate garb for almost anything in the islands, she imagined. Anything, of course, except a funeral.

She found the card that Mark had given her, called the office of Assistant District Attorney Miguel Losoya, and made an appointment to see him that afternoon.

One down, Ava thought. Right away, she punched in another number—the one that Simone had provided for Charley's banker. She supposed that she had met him at the funeral, though she couldn't recall his face.

"Mr. Hamilton!" she said, when the banker's receptionist had put her through, "This is Ava Collier, Charley's mother. I'd like to see you this morning." She made her voice perky, confident.

"That would be doable, Mrs. Collier." Hamilton sounded like an older man, and a cautious one. "Whatever time you get here will be fine. I have few appointments today, and schedules are always flexible here on island."

That 'on island' thing again, Ava thought, *instead of 'on the island.' I should remember to use that, to appear to fit in here.* Aloud, she said, more energetically than she felt, "Thank you, Mr. Hamilton. I'm on my way."

Ava hung up the phone, slipped a notepad and the hotel key into her purse, and strode purposefully through the hotel and down the street, in the direction of the bank. It felt good to be moving; the activity buoyed her up.

Arthur Hamilton was indeed older, probably past a reasonable retirement age, Ava guessed. He had tired eyes and a weary, guarded demeanor. And he was dressed in a suit and tie, unlike the younger businessmen that Ava had seen in Charley's office building. Ava assumed that Arthur Hamilton and Will Mattison were friends, and if not that, then certainly business associates of long standing. She decided that trusting Hamilton would be a doubtful proposition.

"You reared a fine son," the banker said, when he and Ava had completed their opening formalities. "Charles had unlimited energy and enthusiasm for his clients and work, which he mixed with a deft sense of humor. It's my perception that Charles had not yet capitalized on the large number of friends and business associations that he had made, but the number of them was impressive, without a doubt."

Ava studied the parquet floor beneath her feet.

"As I assume you know," Hamilton continued, "Charles served on the Hospital Board here, a prestigious and time consuming volunteer position. He took that on willingly, and it reaped significant rewards in terms of additional contacts." Hamilton took off his glasses, polished them with a cloth that he took from a desk drawer, and carefully readjusted them on his nose.

Still Ava said nothing.

"So we are left to wonder why this tragedy occurred," Hamilton said then. "I can assure you that there was nothing, absolutely nothing, in Charles' personal or business *portfolios* that could have led him to despair . . ."

Ava noticed Hamilton's stress of the word *portfolio.*

"He could not have been stressed about *funds*," Hamilton continued. "He had no reason for concern in that area. Charles was in very good shape financially and I should think he understood that quite well."

Ava interrupted the banker's monologue. "I have read some things about the government cracking down on offshore accounts. Had that affected Charley's business? Had it cut into his income?"

Hamilton straightened his tie—rather primly, Ava thought. "Charles' firm doesn't do that sort of thing."

Hamilton paused, then added: "Mrs. Collier, put your mind at ease. Charles' *financial dealings* were sound. He *had* recently made a very large *withdrawal* that I did not understand, but I was confident that he could handle it."

Hamilton paused, as though considering how to proceed. Then: "I do believe that *something* was bothering your boy. I am sorry to tell you, but Charles had seemed unhappy in his last days, withdrawn. I suspect that he was quite depressed." The banker looked away as he spoke; he would not meet Ava's eyes.

She cocked her head. "Is that so?" she asked, in a tone that did not hide her suspicion. "Charley's friends all say just the opposite—that he was happy and looking forward to the future."

Hamilton raised his hands, as though to say, "What else can I tell you?"

"All right," Ava said, resigned. "How are Charley's accounts being handled now? Is there anything that I need to do in that regard?"

Hamilton drew back, a surprised look on his face. "Will Mattison has ascertained that the accounts are in order. He asked me to open a new one—with only Maura's name on it—and move all of Charles' funds there. Of course, Maura signed all the papers. She was on every one of those accounts from the beginning. She did not come into the office, however. Will conducted the business with me here—to spare Maura that stress, you understand."

Hamilton nodded, as though encouraging Ava to do the same.

But she was having none of it. Ava saw no reason for her conversation with Arthur Hamilton to continue. She concluded it adroitly, hiding the suspicions that were boiling in her gut, and sending sneaky tendrils through her heart. Although Hamilton had appeared hesitant to tell her that Charley had seemed disturbed, Ava suspected that it was a feigned hesitancy. After all, Will Mattison and Simone Beranger had both used almost exactly the same words to describe Charley's frame of mind.

As Ava left Hamilton's bank building, her churning stomach reminded her that she'd had no breakfast. She looked at her watch and decided that a good brunch might help her discomfort. It wouldn't ease the queasiness of suspicion, but something hearty to eat should distract her, at least, and get her through the afternoon meeting with Miguel Losoya.

Ava found the brunch, as she had expected she might, on the boardwalk—Lobster Benedict, with a generous assortment of fresh tropical fruits on the side. A young couple—obviously honeymooners—sipped Mimosas at a nearby table. The cocktails had been made with a careful last-step addition of grenadine. That sweet red syrup sank to the bottom of the glass, and then inched upward through the champagne and orange juice, creating the delicate color blend of a mimosa bloom.

Ava had often enjoyed a Mimosa cocktail as the supreme accompaniment for Eggs Benedict, but she did not order one now. She'd need all her wits for the conversation with Losoya.

Dawdling over her meal, Ava watched the ebb and flow of wavelets around the rocks that lay below her boardwalk vantage point. Brown amphibious crabs, some as large as tennis balls, scurried there. She saw a couple of large hermit crabs in black and white turban shells, too, and supposed they'd likely be conscripted for the next week's race at Pirates' Den.

Conversations from her evening there echoed in Ava's mind. With an impatient gesture, she looked at her watch again and nodded. She paid her bill and headed toward the District Attorney's office.

On Water Street, just two blocks south of the tourist boardwalk area, an old residence housed the District Attorney's workplace.

Beautifully restored with bright yellow paint and gleaming red shutters, the building presented a curiously ostentatious display of luxury for a governmental agency.

Miguel Losoya, junior in the DA's entourage, had an office at the back of the building. If he had any time for gazing out the window—which he did not—Miguel would see only Danish ruins and slum housing. His battered desk always held a pile of folders that he hoped to find time to go through someday. Dented and rusting file cabinets bulged with less recent data. On the wall opposite his desk, Miguel had hung the room's only decoration, a framed quotation from Henry David Thoreau:

In southern latitudes, man degenerates at length.

Losoya considered it an astute observation, but believed that he was an exception to it. Or perhaps Thoreau had written of Anglos, men from northern latitudes, who arrived late to the warmer climes that somehow defiled them. Miguel's own heritage was Puerto Rican; his people had lived on various Caribbean islands for as long as anyone could remember. Miguel considered himself immune to the sins of the northern newcomers, who often treated him as though they were better than he was.

Miguel had gone through the public school system—though there was no system to it, and very little real schooling. Each afternoon, as soon as school let out, and every day of every summer, he had reported to a menial job. In the course of that employment, he had managed to impress a few people, so that he was able to rise up. He had attended the University of the Virgin Islands and earned a scholarship to a law school on the continent. There he met and married Yoli.

Once he had passed his bar exam, Miguel Losoya returned to the islands, bringing Yoli and a new baby with him. He was determined to make a difference. Now he had two daughters—one in school, the other almost ready—and his wife ran the library where Miguel had devoured books as a child.

Today, Ava Collier wanted to talk with him. Miguel understood why, and he understood that she could cause problems for him.

In anticipation of Mrs. Collier's visit, Miguel had cleared from his desk as much clutter as possible. He set the folder covering Charley's death on top of everything else, opened it, and skimmed again its meager contents. He was just getting to the part that puzzled him most when he glanced up to see a woman—undoubtedly Charley's mother—at the door.

Miguel stood, stuck out a hand. "Good afternoon, Mrs. Collier. I'm Miguel Losoya."

Ava studied the athletic young man with close-cropped hair and clothing that carried a vague Ivy League flair. "Good afternoon," she said. "And please call me 'Ava.' Texans don't generally stand on formality. If you had known my son, I think you would have known that."

Miguel smiled. "No doubt I would, Ava Collier. And my past doesn't incline me to formality either. But please!—take a seat."

When Ava was settled, Miguel spoke solemnly: "You should know that District Attorney Naigle doesn't have much enthusiasm for this investigation."

"And that means . . .?" Ava asked, her voice carrying notes of suspicion and distress.

Miguel answered her question with one of his own. "Have you met Naigle?"

When Ava shook her head, Miguel continued. "He's a very determined individual, and quite secure in his job. He hasn't said that I can't look into your concerns—not yet, anyway—but he'll do his best to keep me busy on other things."

Seeing the look on Ava's face, Miguel hastened to add, "That said, I must admit that I believe there's something here worthy of investigation. My reading so far raises issues that I find difficult to ignore." He leaned forward, to emphasize his next words:

"But I remind you that this incident is not yet officially a *case*. Our final report will not be completed in less than three months."

"Three *months*?" The tenor of Ava's words measured the depth of her despair. "But that's ridiculous. And certainly I can't be here that long. I have to get back to my business in Texas."

Ava paused, shaken, needing reassurance. "It *is* ridiculous, isn't it?" she asked, looking Losoya in the eye. "There can't be any excuse for things moving so slowly?"

He answered in a guarded tone. "In contrast to your experience in the States, I suppose that it does seem that we proceed at a leisurely pace. But there's a saying here in the Virgin Islands: *Soon come.* It connotes about the same thing that *mañana* does in Spanish."

Miguel smiled at last. "Most people know that *mañana* translates as 'tomorrow,' but the joke is that it actually means nothing more than 'not today.' So if I had just one piece of advice for you, it would be this: Settle into our island ways, my friend; take life a bit easier. What you seek will soon come—tomorrow, or pretty soon. Answers always come in their own time."

Ava pressed her lips together and looked at her hands, baffled by Miguel's words, "my friend." She could not think of Miguel as a friend, any more than he could consider her to be his friend. She had no reason to trust Miguel to begin with, and even less now, than before he made such a silly presumption.

"Well, let's get busy on what we can do," she said. She almost pursed her lips again, but stopped, pretending a wry smile instead.

"Mrs. Collier—Ava—when was the last time that you spoke with your son?"

Who's interviewing whom? Ava wanted to say. The question raised her suspicions again, somehow. *Patience,* she reminded herself. She'd get her answers.

Ava managed to keep her tone even as she responded to Miguel's question. "I talked with Charley a little over three weeks ago. He called to tell me that he and Maura had been to a restaurant with some of their friends. Byron Hendley, who had been drinking heavily, became belligerent and attacked Charley. My son e-mailed me some pictures, showing that Byron had mauled him in the worst possible way. I can e-mail the photos to you if you think they might be helpful."

Miguel looked up, eyes wide with surprise. "Indeed I would appreciate having those photos, Ava! Thank you. But tell me, why do you think Charley wanted you to see such pictures?"

"I wondered that too, at first," Ava answered. "I thought it would have been more like my son to try to shield me from something so awful. I can assure you that it would not be at all like him to seek sympathy in that way. Now, I think I should have realized that the photos were my son's cry for help. I believe that Charley was trying to send a message that he was in danger. I think he sent me the pictures as evidence of that—evidence that I could preserve for him."

"Did Charley tell you what the fight was about?" Miguel asked.

"It had to do with Maura."

Again, Losoya looked up in surprise. "With Maura Mattison, Charley's wife? What exactly did Hendley say to Charley? Or was it something he said to Maura?"

Ava rubbed the back of her neck. "Charley told me that Byron made a toast to 'Maura's baby'—the baby that Maura is expecting. That irritated Charley, because, after all, it was his baby, too.

"I know that Maura and Byron are life-long friends, and I know that my son wasn't threatened by their relationship. But if

Byron was insinuating that he continued to have an unusually close relationship with Maura, then my son could have had reason to be irritated. I didn't ask Charley for details, since he didn't offer any. I didn't think it was necessary, or appropriate, to do so. Now, of course, I wish that I had pressed him to say more."

As Ava fell silent, Miguel wrote quickly, then tapped his tablet. "You say Charley claimed that Byron was drunk the night he attacked him. Was Charley drinking too?"

"I suppose so," Ava said. "It appears that most of his friends drink rather heavily. I saw that for myself last night, when I met with some of them at Pirates' Den."

"Did Charley have a problem with alcohol?" Miguel pressed.

Ava hesitated, choosing her words with care. "Some of the people I've talked with here are suggesting that my son drank more heavily than I had realized," she said at last. "So I've had some concern. Not just about his drinking on the night of the fight, but in general. But as I think deeply about that possibility, I am convinced that my concerns are just mother-worry."

Ava paused again, thinking. Then she looked Miguel square in the eye. "Even if Charley was a heavy drinker, there's no reason to imagine that his drinking would lead him to suicide. I'll argue toe-to-toe with anyone who believes that my son chose to kill himself."

Miguel made a note as Ava continued. "Let me give you another example of who my son really was. It's an example that seems just like Charley, but would be very difficult for me."

Losoya looked up, trying to assess Ava's intent, and her tone.

"On the weekend following Byron's fight with my son," Ava continued, "Byron was at Charley's and Maura's home for dinner. They invited him! That's hard for me to imagine. I would not have been so generous with someone who had mauled *me!* It's hard for me to imagine that Charley and Byron hade settled their differences so promptly. And I certainly do not believe that the fight was so insignificant that Charley just shrugged it off. If that were the case, he'd have had no reason to send me those photos of what Byron did to him.

"But my Charley was a generous man. And thoughtful of his wife. So he simply set the differences aside. And in the end, I believe that was his undoing."

Miguel wrote lines of words on his pad. "Did Charley ever suffer from depression; was he on medication? Did he take antidepressants, mood elevators, anything along that line?"

Ava blinked and pulled back in surprise. "I don't think so! No. I've just told you that my son was so stable, so generous, that he could even welcome Byron into his home after a fight." The look on Ava's face told Losoya that his question had insulted her—and her son.

He glanced down at his notes, leaving Ava in no doubt, now, that he was following a checklist. "Was Charley—or were he and Maura—planning a trip somewhere?" Miguel asked. "Might he have been taking Lariam?"

"Charley hadn't mentioned a trip to me," Ava said. "You might ask Maura, though—or Simone Beranger, Charley's office assistant. And what is Lariam anyway? I'm not familiar with that."

"Lariam is an anti-malarial pill, useful in some parts of the world. But it is known to cause suicidal tendencies."

Ava's mouth drew into a tight line, and when she spoke, anger was clear in her voice. "Before you ask, Mr. Losoya, I'll assure you that Charley wasn't taking any of those stop-smoking pills that make some people suicidal, either. Charley has never smoked. I want you to know that it's very clear to me from your line of questioning that you agree with the Mattisons—and Bishop Gardiner. You *do* think my son's death was a suicide, and you're trying to build a case to prove it."

"Not at all!" Miguel raised his hands in a placating gesture. "You know I have to ask *all* the questions, even the hardest ones. That's the only way we'll discover the truth."

Truth? Ava wondered. She felt she'd been a witness on the stand, under cross-examination. She sensed that somehow she was giving Losoya much more than the Assistant District Attorney was giving her, and she suspected that, somehow, the information she had shared would be used against her.

Ava closed her eyes. Even her own mind was going against her, half-quoting trite lines from TV cop shows: *Anything that you say here can and will be used against you.*

Ava took a deep breath and set her face with a calm, determined look. Then she spoke just five words. "All right, then, let's continue."

Losoya folded his hands together and leaned toward Ava, looking professorial. "When we ask how any sudden death happened, we consider the three obvious possibilities: suicide, accident, and murder. Now, of course none of us wants to believe that Charley took his own life, but we must give that possibility fair consideration. We must ask if some medication had warped his thinking. If the answer to that question is *No*, then we ask if there was some situation in his life that could have created such despair. It could be—for instance—in the area of finances, illness, or trouble in the marriage."

"I understand," Ava said, almost as an apology. Antagonism wasn't going to get her anywhere. She would give Losoya something he wanted: "I talked to Charley's banker this morning—Mr. Arthur Hamilton." She waited for a sign of recognition from Losoya, then continued. "Mr. Hamilton assures me that Charley was on solid ground, as far as his finances were concerned. But Will Mattison has moved Charley's accounts around now, and put them all in Maura's name. I have to wonder why he was in such a hurry to do that."

Ava paused, to be sure that Miguel understood her and was taking notes. "Also, last night, when I met with some of Charley's friends, their conversation did not suggest that Charley had any marital problems. Or worry. Or illness. In fact, everything his friends said supported the opposite—that Charley was a happily married man who loved his job and his life on island."

"Good," Miguel said. "Then let's look at the possibility of an accidental death. Since Charley died by gunshot, we must consider who might have been involved."

"According to Will Mattison," Ava said, "no one was at Charley's home except his wife Maura. I can't imagine that girl handling a gun, much less shooting the husband she loved. So someone else must have been with them—Byron Hendley, for example. I can't stop thinking about the earlier fight he instigated with my son."

"Yes," Losoya said, as careful as though he were picking his way across a mine field. "It is conceivable that a gun might have gone off in some sort of a tussle."

"But what if my son's death was *not* an accident?" Ava persisted. "What if Byron, or someone else, went to Charley's home with the clear intent to murder him? Would you be willing to consider that Byron had a reason to do that?"

"Let's apply Occam's razor," Miguel said in a coaxing tone. "Examine the most obvious possibilities first—the accident scenarios—and come up with the simplest solutions. When—*and if*—we must eliminate those scenarios, we'll address the thornier ones. We'll take a hard look at premeditated murder and, of course, at suicide."

Ava sighed, and the sound seemed to come from her toes. "I think we're done here, Mr. Losoya. You don't intend to do a thing about any of this, do you?"

"We are investigating–"

"What about an autopsy?" Ava interrupted. "Did you even do one? Or, considering the 'leisurely pace' of this office, did you just unfortunately run out of time?"

Losoya ignored Ava's sarcasm. "I'm sorry to say, Mrs. Collier, that you are correct. Mr. Mattison's request for a cremation did deny us the opportunity to examine your son's body with the care that we would have preferred."

Here it is again, Ava thought grimly. *Iron Will. That man always manages to be one step ahead; he thinks of everything, it seems. But why? Why has he been in such a hurry?*

"Mrs. Collier . . ." Losoya said, recalling her attention. "Ava Collier, I am willing, right this moment, to give you all the notes that I have regarding this investigation."

"I would appreciate that." Ava snapped her words. "And then you can continue with whatever *important* things you have to do." She wanted him to hear the icicles on every word that she spoke.

With Losoya's slim investigation folder in her hand, Ava walked to the door. Miguel Losoya followed her and said, almost in a whisper, "There is a great deal of corruption on this island, Mrs. Collier. I hope that you can appreciate my position."

When Ava returned to her hotel room, her first reaction was fear: The door was open. She imagined a break-in, an element of some strange plot against her. Then she saw a utility cart with mops, rags, aerosol cans, and fresh linens. A cleaning woman, who had knelt at the toilet, scrubbing, stood when she saw Ava.

"Good—" she began. Then, abruptly, she put both hands out straight in front of her, as though to push Ava away.

"St. George! St. George!" the dark woman screamed.

"What in the world . . ." Ava began.

"Look deh!" the housekeeper said, pointing a bossy finger. "Don' yo move. See dat centipede? Yo just about to step on he. Ah shout to stop he from stingin' yo."

Ava drew back, avoiding the insect, but studying it. The thing looked like consummate evil. About four inches long and less than an inch wide, the ugly creature had multiple pairs of legs along its flattened, segmented body. Jaw-like mandibles, a pair of antennae, and a set of small claws completed the creeper's satanic aspect.

Ava leaned closer to take a better look.

"Don' *do* dat!" the housekeeper hissed. "Our centipedes has a painful poison in dey little claws, and dey fast-movin' too. Dey comes aftah yo."

Ava looked skeptical. "A worm wouldn't prey on humans."

"Centipede do." The cleaning woman raised her chin with a touch of arrogance, and spoke again in a knowing, stubborn tone. "Centipede mos' certainly do attack humans, when yo gets in he way." She shuddered to make her point, then smacked the centipede with her dustpan and carried it to the trash bin.

Even after the housekeeper had completed her work and left Ava's room, the centipede's impression lingered. Ava saw it as an embodiment of all the foreboding and evil that she sensed on the island of Dos Marias. She called Room Service to bring her a glass of chardonnay and sat down in the room's most comfortable chair. She picked up the report that Miguel Losoya had given her and began to read.

FRIDAY, NOVEMBER 25, 1:45 AM

*W*e arrived at the Collier residence at 14 East Shore Drive. Mr. Will Mattison met us in the driveway and identified himself as the father-in-law of the homeowner Charles Collier and the father of the homeowner's wife, Maura Mattison Collier. Mr. Mattison told us that Mrs. Collier was in her residence, indisposed. He denied us access to her for questioning.

Mr. Mattison showed us a white Escalade, 2016 model, which he said was Charles Collier's personal car. We looked through the window of the vehicle, where we could see a white male slumped over the steering wheel.

When we attempted to open the door of the vehicle, we found it locked. Mr. Mattison denied having a key or remote opener and said that Mrs. Collier didn't have them either.

Ava could read no further. *My God!* she thought. *Mattison suggested to me that he had opened the car door. I believed that he must have tried to save my son. Why didn't he and Maura try? How could they just stand there, waiting for the police?*

Ava pushed her chair back and walked to the gallery. She watched the waves. There could be only one explanation for Will and Maura's behavior: They did not try to open the car, because they already knew that Charley was past helping.

She gasped, leaning against the gallery rail for support. If Maura and her father knew that Charley was dead, then Ava could think of just one explanation for that, too: They had seen it happen—or they had participated in Charley's death themselves.

Alert and icy calm, Ava returned to her reading of the report.

We broke the car window to gain access. When we opened the door, we leaned the male occupant backward, and confirmed that he was dead of a gunshot wound.

Ava took that to mean that Charley was slumped *forward*. But wouldn't the impact of a self-inflicted gunshot propel a person backward, not onto the steering wheel? Ava forced an ugly image out of her mind, determined to read on.

There was no exit wound. Mr. Mattison made a positive ID of Charles Collier. We removed the deceased and put him in a body bag for transport to the morgue. We noted that there was a cargo liner on the front floor of the Escalade. There was not much blood in it.

I picked up my radio to call for a hearse and a tow truck, but Mr. Mattison stopped me. He said that he would take care of the body and the vehicle. I tried to insist upon our protocol, but he was very determined, and since it was Mr. Mattison, I consented to leave the body and the vehicle in his care.

I did take the gun to Forensics, and it came back clean.

Bert Joseph had signed his name at the bottom of the page.

"What were you thinking, Bert?" Ava spoke aloud. Determined to learn more, she flipped to the next page of the report, hoping to find clarification of the assertion that the gun was clean. But she found none.

Ava remembered Losoya's words then: "A lot of corruption on this island." "Sure looks like it," she whispered to herself.

Behind the police officer's report, she found a sheet of notes that Miguel must have scrawled.

Bert confirms that the Escalade's door was locked. He told me that Mr. Mattison said that Miss Maura was 'so rattled' that she couldn't find a key to the vehicle. I asked Bert if he'd ever before seen a suicide lock a door. Bert said that was possible, but that he had never mentioned suicide in this case. He said he only reported on a dead man, in a locked car, shot in the chest with a twenty-two caliber.

Ava dropped her wine glass.

She stared at its shards for a while.

Then she stood up, stooped over, and picked up the shattered pieces of glass.

She got a towel to sop up the mess on the floor.

She rinsed the towel and hung it to dry.

And in all that controlled time, Ava's mind was running wild.

She drew three deep, calming breaths and forced herself to think rationally.

Ava knew beyond doubt that if Charley had wanted to kill himself, he wouldn't have chosen a small bore firearm, like a twenty-two. Charley was a Texas boy, raised with guns. He understood them well, and he acted prudently with them.

Furthermore, by no stretch of the imagination would Charley have shot himself in the chest. Even she, Ava, if pushed to the point of despair and wanting to end her life, would not aim a gun at her chest. She would put its muzzle in her mouth. She would want to make sure that she wouldn't wake up in a hospital and have to explain it all.

But Ava knew that she would never reach such a point. Even this awful experience had not brought her to that point of despair. And she knew beyond doubt that her son had not felt that way, either.

Ava supposed that it would have been like Charley to keep a small pistol in his car for protection. Maura probably would have known that. Mattison might have known that. So they had concocted a story implying that Charley had gone outside, intending to use the gun in his Escalade—that puny twenty-two—to kill himself.

But evidence that Charley had a gun in the car did not in any way confirm the theory that he had committed suicide. Ava felt convinced that these simple facts added up to proof positive that her Charley had been murdered. She picked up Miguel's notes again to read the final paragraphs:

The Escalade seems to be gone from this island; I can find no trace of it. I asked Bert why there was nothing in his report about a twenty-two, or about the victim being shot in the chest. Bert said only that he had reported that the body was slumped forward, with no exit wound. He repeated that a twenty-two was what he had picked up in the car.

Ava mulled on that again. Was Bert suggesting that he had omitted the pistol caliber from his official report because he had been told to do so? If that were the case, he could have hoped that his "no exit wound" phrase would suggest a small caliber weapon.

She read on.

I asked Bert to confirm that the gun had been cleaned. He said he had come to no such conclusion. He said that he considered the weapon "clean" because Forensics found just one single partial print. And it was Charley's.

Ava laid the document on the table and tapped it with one fingernail. *That's it!* she thought. Of course Charley's fingerprint would be on his own gun. But just one print? She'd expect many of them. So the gun had been wiped clean. But how? No one could commit suicide and then erase his own fingerprints from the weapon.

No one could commit suicide and then erase his own fingerprints from the weapon!

The report that Losoya had given Ava left her with no doubt that Mattison controlled everything, everywhere on Dos Marias Island.

Ava's heart was racing—a sensation akin to joy. Her mind raced, too, as she reviewed her meetings with Simone and the banker, Arthur Hamilton. Ava would not trust either of them. But Losoya? Well, maybe. Because he gave her the report, with his personal notes attached. He didn't have to do that, so he must have wanted her to know.

In any case, Ava now saw her job as abundantly clear: She must be the one to identify Charley's murderer.

Ava thought again of the centipede in her room, and of the housekeeper's fear of the thing. Ava had said that a worm wouldn't prey on humans. And the maid had answered stubbornly: *Centipede do, when yo gets in he way."*

Will Mattison, too, was apparently capable of attacking a human, if that person got in his way.

DECEMBER 1

Exactly one week after Charley's death, the first thing in the morning, Ava dialed the number of the beachfront home that her son and Maura had shared. As before, Will Mattison's recorded voice let her know that Maura was still with her parents at Estate Clary. The recording did not provide the phone number there. Ava found it in her smart phone, and pressed the button.

Clio answered and when she heard Ava's voice, she immediately said, "I'm surprised that you are still on island, Ava dear. How are you occupying your time?"

Ava thought that Clio sounded distant, cool. "Actually," she said, avoiding a direct answer, "I called to talk with Maura."

"You just missed her, I'm afraid," Clio answered. "Anisectus has driven her to see the therapist."

Ava bit back a question: *Which therapist might that be? The massage therapist again, or a real shrink this time?* Instead, adopting a tone as much like Clio's as she could muster, Ava asked, "How is Maura doing? How is the baby?"

"Oh, Ava! I am so *sorry!*" Clio paused before going on. "Ava, I wish I didn't have to tell you this way, over the telephone, but Maura lost the baby. I thought you *knew.*"

Ava slumped into a chair, too shocked to ask when, or how. She was too hurt and angry to ask why she had not been called, why she had not been involved. She did not remember, later, what she *did* say to Clio. She had simply ended the conversation and clicked phone off.

Ava sat, frozen, trying to get her mind around the awful news. From the moment that Will Mattison had locked Charley away in that sugar mill, Ava had fought to hold at bay the black waters of despair. Now her last defenses were gone; her last trust in the future was gone. A relentless flood of sorrow washed over her.

And the irony of it was that gentle Clio had been the one to utter the incredibly casual words brutally drowning Ava's remaining shreds of hope: "Maura lost the baby. I thought you knew."

I will never have family again, Ava mourned. *No one, no one at all, will carry any part of who I am, or what I might envision, or what I might have said that could provide a sense of meaning in a time of need. No one will even remember me.*

Ava made a grim face, chastising herself for fruitless self-pity. She had no time for that now, and self-pity did no good, anyway.

But she might find some benefit in learning exactly when and how Maura had lost the baby. Did Maura's grief over Charley's death cause her to miscarry? Did she have an abortion? If so, was that before or after Charley's death? Maybe Charley *did* kill himself—out of despair, because she had aborted the baby? But why would Maura have done that?

I need to phone home, Ava thought, *because I'm staying here so long.* She looked at her watch and frowned. Rockport, Texas, lagged two hours behind Dos Marias' Atlantic Standard Time, so it was just 7:00 a.m. there. Ava's office would not open until 9:00, and that would be 11:00, on Dos Marias. She frowned at her watch again, willing its dial to move ahead.

After a long and impatient wait for time to pass, Ava clicked her smart phone to contact Joanne, her assistant. She had not spoken to Joanne since that first call, right after she learned of Charley's death. Now Joanne's South Texas accent soothed her with a breath of mesquite and salt cedars.

"How are you doing, Ava?" Joanne asked. "Have you learned what happened?"

"The situation seems to be very complicated," Ava told her. "That's hard for me to handle, on top of so much sadness. There's no use going into the details with you now, Joanne, because the details keep changing—shards of glass in a kaleidoscope. I'll tell you the whole story when I have enough answers to make any sense."

Ava paused, to stop the tremble in her voice; she pushed the grief down. When she spoke again, her voice carried a more businesslike tone. "I will get those answers. And that means I'll have to stay here a little longer than I had expected." Ava meant to stop there, but heard herself saying, "And Joanne, Maura lost the baby!"

She was sorry that she had said it, even to a friend. Her relationship with Joanne was much more than that of boss and employee; from their first meeting, their bond had quickly grown to that of two trusting friends. Still, there were times when no words seemed right. The thing that Ava had blurted out now, led both of them into more platitudes, and then to a dreary awkwardness.

Ava changed the subject. "How are things there?"

"Do you have your laptop?" Joanne asked, sounding a bit miffed. "Have you checked your e-mails?"

"I do have the laptop," Ava said. "I have not looked at my e-mail. It's hard to make connections here sometimes." Her excuse was only half-true, and she'd only been gone a week, anyway. "You know my smart phone number," Ava continued, "and I'm up to handling any emergency that you can't wiggle us out of. Just please manage the complaining cottage dowagers for me. I don't need any of that. I promise you that I will stay in touch, and I promise not to be gone any longer than necessary."

Joanne persisted with a few business issues that she thought required Ava's judgment. "No, I won't respond to that," Ava told her, again and again, on each topic. "You know who can handle which things up there. Anyone who doesn't feel up to the job can call me himself. I'll free him of any future responsibility, and set you to finding a replacement."

Joanne was silent for a moment. Then: "We're all concerned about you Ava. If there's anything—"

"I know, Joanne," Ava interrupted. "We'll all get through this. I'm signing off now."

She needed to be outside. Ava looked for her purse, found it, checked to see that her room key and her sunglasses were there. In the process, she found the sea glass that the Boardwalk Bum had given her. She decided to slip it into the pocket of her jeans as a charm. She needed to hold on to anything that might conjure up a good result. And on this island, who knew what that might be?

Ava scanned her floor for centipedes, stepped into the hall, and locked the door of her room. She took the stairs to the hotel lobby and crossed it quickly to step outside.

But Ava soon discovered that out-of-the-building was not "out" enough to suit her. She wanted to get out of the downtown area, away from centipedes and the boardwalk bum and the sphere of Iron Will's influence. Out to a wild and deserted beach, maybe. A place that she could drive to on her own.

She remembered Ken, Charley's friend who worked at an auto dealership. She remembered the company name.

Ava hailed a taxi. "Take me to Auto Antillean," she said.

Once there, Ava asked for Ken Leland, who came out right away.

"Good morning, Ava. Great to see you again! To what do I owe the pleasure?"

"Two things. I need wheels. And I want to talk with you about my son, when you have time."

"Even if I didn't have time, I'd make room for Charley. Let's take care of your transportation issues first, and then talk. I guess that getting wheels means you're planning to stay with us for a while?"

Ava shook her head. "Not very long, I think. But I want the freedom to move around, not depending on taxis, for the few more days that I may have to stay here. I thought you might tell me where I could rent something reliable, something that would serve me for a week or so."

"We handle rentals right here at Antillean," Ken said. "I could put you in a Tahoe—four wheel drive, good for island roads, low mileage. How about we give her a run, and have our personal talk at the same time? I'll drive, to acquaint you with The Rules of the Road, island style. And that will allow you to focus on our talk, as well."

They walked onto the lot to look at the vehicle, but Ava only made a cursory inspection before saying, "This looks fine to me."

"Always remember," Ken told her, "We keep to the *left* side of the road, and we give horses the right of way."

"Why do you drive on the left?" Ava asked. "This island is part of the U.S.!"

"It is," Ken confirmed, "but we bought it from the Danes, and it was English for some time before that. The islanders' drive-on-the-left mentality preceded automobiles. When the U.S. took over, someone made a decision that it might be possible to train *people* to keep to the right, and probably the horses, but we'd never train the mules."

Ken chuckled as he opened the passenger door for Ava. When he had walked around to slide into the driver's seat, he said, "You'll notice that this car is American style, with the steering wheel on the left side. Just like you've always driven—not on the right, as the Brits have their steering."

"That's good," Ava sighed.

"Well, yes and no," Ken said. "At first it bugged me a lot to see an approaching car on my *right*, with the driver so far away from me that I couldn't look him the eye. You *know* there's a benefit in meeting on-coming drivers eye-to-eye! But you can't fully appreciate that until you've experienced it—your face and the other driver's face two car widths apart, looking into opposite ditches. But insurance companies insist on American-style cars—uniformity of the law, or something."

Ava sighed. "This *will* be a challenge for me to get used to. And you said something about giving *horses* the right of way?"

"Correct," Ken answered. "It's in the driving test that you'd have to take if you stayed here long. There are still many people on this island who don't have cars or trucks, and those people depend on horses for transportation. We try to give them all the consideration we can."

Ava kept her attention on Ken's driving, imagining her own hands on the wheel as she drove on the wrong side of the road. And at the same time, she was trying to make mental notes of the route that Ken took.

Sights along the road distracted her: She saw a pedestrian carrying a large iguana. Another man, trudging along in a dirty, faded orange tee shirt, had wrapped his head in a purple satin turban. She read a huge billboard: *AIDS Prevention is as easy as ABC—Abstinence. Be Faithful. Condomize.*

She thought that Charley must have hooted at that—not at the sentiment, of course, but at the structure of the statement. Charley had always been a stickler for good English, for consistency and balance in the correct usage of verbs and nouns and adjectives, as well as an intelligent balance of ideas.

Ken slowed for a traffic back-up, suspecting a wreck. After a moment, he said, "It's horses. Look."

Ava saw two unsaddled horses milling in the middle of the main road, trailing the tethers that they had somehow detached. Half a block behind them, a rather large woman in a colorful muumuu waved her hands over her head in circling motions. She emitted high, shrill shrieks, trying to call the horses back. The animals ignored her. After a wait that Ava had feared might be interminable, the horses ambled to the shoulder of the road, and Ken eased by.

Ava shook her head at this new addition to her series of encounters with bizarre island life. She considered the occurrences as mirrors of the altered geography of her internal world, a life turned suddenly unfamiliar, unsettled, barren of any landmarks or guideposts. Well, Ava thought, she had wanted "out" this morning, and this surely must be it.

Aloud, she said to Ken, "A strange world you live in."

"I don't even notice the strangeness anymore," Ken chuckled. "That's the weirdest part—that we begin to think of odd-ball things as normal. This island takes you in, if you let it." He drove only a short distance, then eased off the road, at a sort of parking spot overlooking the sea.

They sat silently for a moment, as Ava took in the view.

When she spoke, she said, "I wouldn't want to stay on this island, now that Charley's gone. I plan to stay just long enough to get all my questions answered. I don't trust Will Mattison, I don't trust Banker Arthur Hamilton, and I'm beginning to think I shouldn't even trust Charley's assistant, Simone Beranger."

"Right on every count," Ken concurred. "I glad to hear that you're onto them already. Of course it's reasonable for you to assume—for *all* of us to assume—that Will Mattison knows more about Charley's death than he has let on. The key question is *Why?*" What could have happened that anyone thinks should be hidden?"

Ava nodded, but furrowed her brow. "Yes, I agree that something's hidden. And, like you, I can think of no reason why anyone would want to keep a secret like that. I'd think that Will Mattison would want to get to the bottom of things, and would want to share that information—at least with me."

Ken made a noise more like a sneer than a chuckle. "With Mattison, it's all about image and control. Don't waste energy trying to figure out what his motivation is; that's just the man's personality. And he does control almost every person and every event on this island."

"Oh dear!" Ava sighed. "And yet, I suppose I shouldn't be surprised. Yesterday, I went to see Miguel Losoya, in the DA's office, but I came away with the clear impression that I'll get little help there. Can you believe—they didn't even do an autopsy!

"Losoya blamed that on Mattison, and I don't doubt that he's telling the truth. But you'd think that a District Attorney—even an assistant one—could insist on an autopsy. You'd think that he *would* insist on that." Ava heard herself getting shrill, out of control.

She took a deep breath to calm down, then explained. "It just seems a very strange thing to me, that the Law isn't willing to investigate a crime. I'm feeling now that it's all up to me."

"It's up to all of us who love Charley," Ken answered, his voice somber.

"Yes, I appreciate that," Ava answered. "And—thank you. Truly." After a pause, she said, "Now: One item on my agenda is to find Charley's Escalade. Can you help with that?"

"The vehicle isn't at his house?" Ken asked, clearly shocked by the idea.

"No." Ava shook her head. "Miguel Losoya said that he doesn't know where the car is."

"Well," Ken said, "I can look up the VIN—the vehicle identification number—and we can use that to locate the Escalade. But what do you want to do with the car then?"

"I think we should do what the DA didn't do—have that vehicle examined," Ava told him. "I gather from TV cop shows that the . . . the blood spatter pattern . . . can have a significant story to tell."

She stopped to breathe; it had hurt her to say those words, but she had to continue. "Miguel gave me a copy of the police report. We should keep that secret, I think—that he gave out the information. If Miguel is an ally, even a half-ally, we need to protect him too."

"Losoya is a good man," Ken agreed. "And a brave one, apparently—willing to take risks. We'll keep this piece of information just between the two of us. But what does the report say?"

Ava nodded. "The reporting officer wrote that there wasn't . . . wasn't much blood . . . in the Escalade. We need to find out exactly what he meant. And that means that we need to see the vehicle for ourselves.

"I realize that may be a fruitless effort, since Losoya said that Will had called Biohazard for a cleanup. But if that group is as haphazard as everything else around here, we might be able to find *something*."

Ken blinked. Even though Ava had stumbled over the hard words—how much blood, spatter pattern—she had proved herself capable of a cold analysis.

"I'll get the VIN for you," he said. "Depend on that."

Ava nodded. "Thank you. Also, I keep thinking of Byron Hendley, because of that fight that he and Charley had. Were you there when it happened?"

"No," Ken said. "Rick and Brooke were, though. If this investigation is going to be up to you, then it's a job for all of us who were Charley's friends. So ask Rick and Brooke to tell you everything they can remember about the fight."

"I will," she answered. For a moment or two, Ava was silent. Then she said, "Ken, can you think of any reason why someone might *murder* my son?"

Ken answered without hesitation, "Revenge comes to mind. And Byron Hendley's name pops up first, because of that fight you just mentioned."

"But Byron was the one who started the fight," Ava countered. "If anyone had a score to settle afterward, it wouldn't have been Bryan. Charley was the injured party."

Ken thought about that for a minute. "You're right, of course," he said. "Except that you and I both know that it wouldn't be like Charley to try to get even. My guess is that Byron might have continued to harbor some sort of a grudge about whatever had led up to the fight. Or maybe someone else had a beef with Charley."

"Charley had enemies? Who?" Ava could not imagine such a thing.

"I wouldn't say he had *enemies,* in the usual sense," Ken clarified. "But our local drug lords—they call themselves the Consortium—get real edgy when their territory is infringed upon. They wield a lot of power on island."

"Oh, come *on!* Charley was not the kind of man who would be involved with drug dealers! That makes no sense to me."

Ken agreed. "I'm not suggesting that Charley was a user. I'm thinking that the Consortium might have suspected that he was a whistle-blower on some occasion, simply because our bud, Rick, is with the DEA. So now we need to keep an eye on the Consortium—that's all I'm saying. And Ava—you should realize that there's nothing unusual about that. Everybody on island always keeps an eye on the Consortium."

Ava sighed, shaking her head. "I'll remember. Now, maybe you'd better tell me more about Rick and his work with the government."

"I don't know Rick very well," Ken answered, "and I would assume that he won't be here for long. The U.S. government brings young eager-beavers here for training on a revolving door basis—one of the more unusual applications of our local 'Don't Stop the Carnival' theory."

"Don't stop the carnival?" Ava echoed. "Now what do you mean by that?"

"*Don't Stop the Carnival* is the name of a novel that Herman Wouk wrote, about half a century ago. The book is still a bestseller here, because it describes the dreaming and scheming of island life—our 'sucker born every minute' mentality."

"I still don't understand," Ava said. "Tell me more."

"Well, from time to time, a bunch of nuts come to the island and throw money around on some scheme that just won't work here," Ken explained. "Or they can't manage their employees, because they don't understand island people. When these entrepreneurs go broke, another bunch of nuts arrives to take a different tack. Round and round they go, you're up and then you're down, in your seat on the carnival Ferris wheel.

"The real island people are the only winners. They don't often win big, but they always survive when no one else does," Ken shrugged. "They ride one carousel pony and then another. The carnival never stops for them; it's their bread and butter. So: Don't stop the carnival!

"Recently, the U.S. government has decided that this island is a good location for teaching the spy business to young government agents. Aspiring James Bond types sign on with one agency—let's say ATF, for example—Alcohol, Tobacco and Firearms—and those recruits hope to progress to a prestigious job in a more glamorous agency like the FBI or the CIA, back in the States.

"Apparently, our duplicitous island is a perfect training ground for these neophyte agents—especially in drug-traffic control. The trainees move on from here to Colombia and the Dominican Republic. Or whatever the main hot spot of the moment turns out to be. Like Mexico, for example."

"Yes," Ava agreed. "Texas hears plenty about that. And I live only three hours from the border."

She sat silent for a while, pondering Ken's information. Below them, surf crashed onto rock. Beyond the shore, Ava saw graduated shades of blue, then sea and sky merging at a dim horizon. A stiff breeze lifted some spray and speckled it across the Tahoe's windshield. Ken turned on the vehicle's ignition and ran the wipers.

As he steered onto the highway again, Ava spoke at last. "Well, it's clear that we have our work cut out for us. I'll talk to Rick and see if his ATF experience sheds any light on our mystery. Now tell me something about his girlfriend, Brooke. Who is she, and how does she fit in?"

"Brooke moved here from the U.S.—Kansas, I think—a number of years ago. She was, and probably still is, one of those 'follow a dream' girls who drifts around," Ken said. "I think she was working in one of the boardwalk shops when Rick met her.

"My wife, Sandi, worries that Brooke will turn out to be just another lost woman in our island carnival. Too often, women from the States end up badly here, passed from one man to another. Fillies on a carousel, getting older, less attractive, more desperate. Brooke's a nice girl, but very young, very naïve. Sandi hopes that Brooke will make a go of it with a good man like Rick. If not, she should return to the States before her options diminish."

"Don't stop the carnival," Ava echoed.

They rode in silence for a while, and before long Ava recognized the road to Antillean Auto Sales.

As he turned into the car lot, Ken said, "This drug business probably isn't anything you need to worry much about, in terms of Charley. But it's just one more thing that you should be aware of, to understand the full picture here."

Ava got out of the Tahoe and walked around it, making a final inspection. "I appreciate the car," she said. "I just wish it had On-Star, in case I get lost."

Ken laughed. "You won't get lost. Find a beach road. If the Caribbean is on your right, then keep it there. You'll eventually come full circle on this island. But in case you do have a problem, consider me Ken On-Star. Make me a quick-dial on your smart phone."

When she had climbed into the car and fastened her seat belt, Ken bent over and gave Ava a boyish peck on the cheek.

"Thank you," she said—and almost added "Son."

Ava headed back toward her hotel, tensely focused on keeping to the left side of the road. When she saw a Burger King ahead, she stopped there, relieved to have found something familiar. Inside the shop, a man sat at a table, eating, while he balanced a live cockatiel on one shoulder and a parakeet on the other.

Welcohm to de islan', Mom, Ava told herself.

Between the hamburger shop and her hotel, Ava spotted a small grocery store. She went in, thinking that it might be good to have a few items that she could snack on in her room.

Then, with bread, sandwich meat, wine, cola, chips, a can of black beans, a can opener/wine opener, and three fresh mangos in a plastic bag, Ava continued on down the road.

She found her hotel and its parking garage with no trouble, checked the floor for centipedes when she got to her room, kicked off her shoes, poured a glass of wine, and went out to sit on her gallery.

A curious little lizard—a gecko, Ava supposed—crept along the railing. Ava had thought of geckos as ordinary cousins of the skinks that inhabit South Texas gardens. Now, watching this one, she had to admit that the Dos Marias variety was much more entertaining.

The gecko stopped, seemed to look at her, evaluating, cocking its head one way and the other. Ava chuckled, thinking of the insurance company cartoon gecko on TV. Then, as though this lizard had determined that Ava was a non-threatening species, it leapt, startling her. The lizard landed on the glass-topped table where Ava had propped her elbows.

The inquisitive green reptile and the woman contemplated each other for a while, the lizard inching closer to her, across the table. It came very near, so near that Ava felt again that the thing was examining her, evaluating her.

Then, as abruptly as it had appeared, the lizard made another prodigious leap—sideways, this time. It disappeared into the branches of a Ginger Thomas tree, where thick clusters of bright yellow flowers made a perfect camouflage for the creature.

Ava smiled, a bit ruefully. That gecko seemed to be the epitome of her experience on mysterious Dos Marias: Each time she seemed about to make some connection, it vanished without a trace. As Ava continued to stare into the yellow blossoms beyond her gallery, she reached out an arm to set her wineglass on the table.

The glass teetered and almost spilled before she caught it. With an un-thinking gesture, she brushed aside the stray item that had tipped her glass. It clattered to the deck and rolled to a stop against her toe. Ava bent over to look closer.

Another lump of sea glass. She frowned, uneasy. She shook her head, a reprimand. She shouldn't imagine meaning into every meaningless thing!

This piece of sea glass was milky white, and more triangular than the one she had received from the boardwalk bum. Ava pulled the greenish piece from the pocket where she had put it as a good luck charm, and set it beside the white one. Both were about the same size.

Ava saw them as a wave and a sail. She toyed with them a bit, rearranging their relative positions, turning them over, until the sail was a boat, cresting a wave on the sea. Strange, her mind persisted, to have two pieces of sea glass turn up under such different circumstances. Strange—and significant, maybe?

She chided at herself then. Of course the occurrences weren't strange! There was nothing unusual about them at all. She'd met a pan handler hoping for money, and some tourist had left a souvenir on the gallery, forgotten. There was nothing more to it than that. Ava sternly reminded herself not to let this island's aura get to her.

After a while, she put her shoes back on and went down to the hotel dining room. As she ate her dinner, Ava noticed a lending-library bookshelf on a side wall. When she had finished her meal and paid the check, she wandered over to look at the books.

She found a well-thumbed copy of *Don't Stop the Carnival*, the book that Ken had mentioned. She put a finger to one of Jimmy Buffet's books that Charley had loved, then pulled out a small, quaint volume, *Divers Information on the History of Sugar*. When Ava realized that it was the story of sugar mills, she took the book upstairs to read.

Sugar cane, which originated in Southeast Asia, now flourishes at tropical latitudes around the world. Christopher Columbus introduced it to the Americas on his second voyage, in 1493—the voyage that took him to St. Croix, now one of the U.S Virgin Islands. A British planter introduced the first stalks to the island of Dos Marias, but it was the Danes who most developed the sugar industry on the island.

Wherever cane grew, most of the labor fell on the backs of African slaves. They planted, they cultivated, they cut the cane. Slaves carried the cane to mills powered by oxen, mules, horses, or wind. Wooden rollers extracted the cane juice.

Ava studied a drawing of a mill, and the three upright iron-plated rollers inside it.

The middle roller attached to the blades of the windmill; the outer rollers attached to the center one with cogs. Slaves fed sugar cane stalks between the first and second rollers. Then a circular framework turned the cane, feeding it back between the second and third rollers. When the cane came out of the rollers, it had been squeezed almost dry.

Ava put the book down, imagining the slaves as they fed cane to the rollers—how they might struggle to force it all the way in. In so doing, a slave might find his own fingers, or his entire arm, caught in that awful press.

Ava imagined herself like the cane—squeezed dry, depleted, empty.

She thought then that her Charley was as much a captive as those long-ago slaves: He, too, was caught in Will Mattison's mill. But Charley would not be there forever! Ava would not let that be.

She shook her head sharply for "No," and then shook it gently, a few more times, to dispel difficult thoughts. She picked up the book again, to read more: The slaves transferred the expressed cane juice to a fire-heated copper kettle maybe six feet in diameter.

Ava knew something about those "kettles." She put her finger in the page of the book, and smiled a bit as she remembered. Some of those huge copper bowls graced the grounds of old sugar plantations south of Houston. When Ava and her husband were building homes in that area, some of their clients—especially those who planned quasi-antebellum homes—had coveted the kettles for their yards. Ava had gone on many a wild goose chase, trying to buy one of those prized sugar kettles.

Her clients would never have imagined—or cared about—the work that had gone on beside the kettles in the early plantation days. As the sugar melted, scum formed on the top of it. The slaves skimmed the scum off and sent purer syrup flowing on through a series of smaller bowl-shaped kettles. When syrup in the smallest kettle began to crystallize, slaves transferred it to wooden troughs. The syrup cooled there for about a month, to complete crystallization. After that, it wasn't a far stretch to the sugar bowl on the slave-owners' table.

The dark, un-crystallized residue of sugar production, drained away, found a market as molasses, the basis of rum. The plantation owner kept some molasses, mixed it with crushed coral, and used it as mortar for more mills and for other stone buildings that lasted for hundreds of years. In the end, the difficult and drawn-out process of sugar-making provided not only a small, sweet miracle, but also a surprising strength.

Slow as molasses. The phrase eased into Ava's mind like a healing whisper. It seemed to symbolize her arduous journey toward a gradual acceptance of her son's death. Ava did not look for recovery from grief—she could not imagine even wanting that. But the sweet miracle of remembrance would be strong enough to hold her life together.

Ava's little borrowed book went on to describe the rum distillation process, but she was not interested in that now. Maybe some other time.

She set the book on her bedside table and then lay down on her bed.

Much later, she awoke in the horror of a dream: Charley in the sugar mill, caught and crying. Herself, clawing at the mortar of the mill, trying to find a chink in its harsh strength.

DECEMBER 2

At last, daylight came. At last, Ava could dress and go downstairs for breakfast. But even as she did so, the dream preyed on her mind.

Back in her hotel room again, Ava turned the radio on, loud, and went out onto her gallery to look at the sea.

"WHDM Horizon Radio!" a deejay called out when the tune ended. "And I'm B.B. Bennack. Do you know what I love about this island? There's a horizon everywhere you look. We have horizons north, south, east and west, and even under water. Not many places on the continent can claim anything near what we have; up there, you see nothing but buildings. And clogged freeways." His voice took on a grim tone to indicate his abhorrence of heavy traffic.

"What horizon are you admiring now?" the D.J. continued. "Is it the sea, and maybe a sailboat on its way to a neighbor island? Is it our beautiful green hills? Wherever you look, isn't it wonderful here?

"We have other horizons as well," B.B. continued. "Dos Marias has horizons of opportunity. More EDC Corporations are coming in—investors eager to provide jobs for our locals. Cruise ships are including us in their itineraries. There are more and more favorable prospects for our young people. Horizons unlimited!

"I'm *glad* to live on this island, and I'll bet you are too. I'm so glad to live on this island, and to have Horizon Radio, that I dug up a real oldie for you. Jeanette MacDonald introduced this tune in the film *Monte Carlo* and she sang it again in the 1944 film *Follow the Boys*. See if you don't just love the sound of this:"

> *Beyond the blue horizon waits a beautiful day.*
> *Goodbye to things that bore me; joy is waiting for me.*
> *I see a blue horizon; my life has only begun!*
> *Beyond the blue horizon lies a rising sun.*

Ava quirked the corner of her mouth, remembering that old song, and the way that her grandmother had sung it. She was surprised that it would still be played anywhere, even on this little island. Still, she doubted that there would ever be, for her, a rising sun beyond a blue horizon.

Intruding on her sad thoughts, the radio's stream of commercials assailed Ava. A calypso song advertised a grocery store: *We got all dat you need.* The announcer for a dress shop mimicked the sly intonations of a one-time feature commentator on a network news show: *The store with the funky sign, and even funkier clothes.* A restaurant had opted for the old trick of involving the owner's kids: *My dad's fish smell fresher than his socks.*

Then the disk jockey came on the air again: "This is WHDM Horizon Radio, and I'm B.B. Bennack. Sea Breeze is on the air! Strap on your life vest and grab hold of the ship's rail. We're embarking on a breathtaking cruise!"

Ava decided that she would listen for a while. Maybe this program would offer some small clue that she needed. It seemed a silly thought, but incongruous things did seem to have meaning for her, here on Dos Marias Island.

"Caller Number One, go ahead please," the DJ was saying.

"Ah, yeah. Ah, is this B.B. Bennack?"

"Yes, Caller. You're on the air." Bennack's voice sounded weary.

"Ah, B.B.?" the caller said, still insecure. "Ah, well what I'm calling about is the telephone. I mean, we really have lousy utilities here. My phone is out more than it's on. I call and call and they promise to fix it, but they don't. And when I don't have a phone, I can't get on line either; I can't check my e-mail. Can you do something about that?"

B.B. chuckled. "Well, Caller, I thank you for your vote of confidence. I thank you for thinking that I can solve the world's problems. I'd like to believe I have my own small part in doing that, but I don't have a magic wand. Let's see if anyone else is having the same difficulty with phone service that you are. Caller Number Two, you're on the air with Sea Breeze!"

"Hey, B.B.! Great show you got going here. My problem is dog sh— I mean dog poop. Can I say that on the air?"

"You just did, Caller," B.B. answered, in a voice that almost betrayed his boredom. "Keep going."

"I have a little coffee shop close to your studio. You know, it's in that area where people like to walk their dogs. That's fine, but I wish they would just *walk*. I mean, you know? Why do those dogs have to stop right in front of my customers to do their business? I have people sitting outdoors—sidewalk café sort of thing, you know—and here comes a dog and poops right beside the customers. I'm losing business because of it."

"You have a bigger problem than that, Caller," B.B. said. "Dog waste pollutes the environment and causes disease. You'd better hope the Health Department doesn't shut you down."

B.B. chuckled then. "I'm just kidding, of course. We all know that the Health Department isn't going to get around to policing dogs, don't we? We know that they're too busy going on coffee breaks themselves." He chuckled again.

"I want to put up some signs," the caller persisted. "I want to warn people that their dogs can't sh— their dogs can't mess in front of my coffee shop. But my landlord won't let me put up a sign. Can I make him do that?"

"Let's think about it another way, Caller," B.B. said. "What happens when you put up a sign? Does it stop the bad behavior, or does it just advertise to everyone else that there's dog waste on your property? I'm certain you wouldn't want that!

"And as surely," B.B. continued, "we don't want to advertise to our tourists that we're a low-class third-world territory where people are so uncivilized that they don't know how to behave without signs to tell them!" B.B. paused to catch his breath after that long, run-on sentence.

"Caller, my whole switchboard is lit up now," he said. "You keep listening, and call back again if you need to say something more. Caller Number Three, you're on Sea Breeze!"

A timid female voice said, "Hello, Mr. Bennack," then went silent.

"Hello, Caller. Go ahead please."

"Mr. Bennack, I can tell that you're not a dog lover. I guess not everybody can be, but I'm sorry to learn that you're not," the gentle voice reprimanded.

"Oh, I *am* a dog lover, Ma'am. I am very *much* a dog lover. I have two dogs in my back yard. But everything has its place."

"Yes, it does, and that's my point," the woman persisted. "Like the bumper sticker says, *Shit happens.* I take that to mean, it's a natural thing to have to go, and we all do. For heaven's sake, let the dogs go too!"

"Whoop!" B.B. responded. "You almost got us bumped off the air there, Caller. I get your point, but–"

Ava turned the radio off. An idea was forming in her mind.

After a while, she phoned Craig Fahrenthold, Charley's best friend, and asked him to find time for a talk.

"What about now?" Craig suggested. "I'll come to your hotel. And I'll bring lunch with me. That'll be an easier way to talk, than in some restaurant."

"What is this Roti thing you bought?" Ava asked as they sat at her small balcony table.

"Easy meal for bachelors," Craig grinned. "*Roti* is a bread-like thing from India, wrapped around a variety of stuffings, most often spicy. Charley called the local variety 'island tamales'."

Ava laughed, and the sound startled her. Sad memory washed through her as she echoed the word "tamales." She sat up a little straighter, as if to shake off her melancholy.

"Craig, this is really too generous of you—on top of setting up the get-together at Pirates' Den." Ava reached out and took his hand. "I'm truly gratified to realize what a beautiful group of friends my son had!"

Craig grinned and shrugged, turning the compliment: "Charley had a way of attracting good people, because he was one."

"Tell me about you," Ava said. "I understand that you're a broker too? Where are you from? Are you married?"

"I'm a broker, yes. And I am married—sorta. My wife, Janice, isn't here. Like too many women, she just didn't take to this island. We have no shopping malls here, and there's not much of any place to go to wear fancy clothes. So my wife and my kiddies live in Atlanta, where we came from. She flies down with the kids from time to time; I get up there when I can." Craig shrugged, making a sad face.

"I'm so sorry," Ava said. "That's a difficult way to have a relationship. Do you plan to move back to Georgia?"

"Not any time soon." Craig shook his head. "I love this island. I *chose* to come here, for the sailing and the warm-all-year weather. I thought Dos Marias would be a great place for Janice and me to raise good kids. But it turns out that she and I just aren't the match I thought we were."

He wriggled in his chair, sorry he'd gotten off on that tack. "One of the reasons that Charley meant so much to me was that he loved sailing as much as I do. Since his wife Maura wasn't much into it, Charley and I buddied up together on my boat. But Charley wanted a boat of his own—a J Boat."

"Jay boat?"

"Charley wanted a racing boat, and J Boat is the brand he liked."

"He was actively looking for one of these J Boats?" Ava asked.

"I think he'd found it," Craig told her. "Charley said something about depleting a bank account."

"Oh!" Ava looked up in recognition. "That would explain something that Charley's banker said to me—about a large withdrawal. He tried to make it sound like something that I should be worried about. I think that was disgusting of him, now that I know the truth. But do you know where Charley's boat is now? I doubt that Maura would want to keep it."

"I agree that Maura would have no interest in a racing boat of the kind of boat that Charley wanted," Craig said. "He had a hard time accepting the fact that he and his wife turned out not to have a great deal in common. And that's sad, because Charley was such a family kind of guy. He imagined teaching his son to sail, as you taught him, and living aboard a ketch for weeks at a time."

Ava looked out the window, to the sea. "But Craig? I'm still wondering where Charley's sail boat is now."

Craig shook his head. "I don't think he had taken possession of it yet. I guess time ran out for him before he could do that."

Again Ava stared out to sea. She put a finger to the inside corner of one eye.

Craig took her other hand. "Charley talked a lot about you, Ava. I've been eager to meet you for a long time now. I just wished it hadn't come about like this."

"Thank you," Ava said, then pulled her hand away. "Subject change," she said. "Tell me about your own family—parents, siblings?"

"None. My father died years ago, and now my mom's gone too."

"That's hard," Ava said.

"Yeah. You and me, two drifters lost at sea." Craig deepened his voice in melodrama, "Lost in a sea of mystery."

Ava felt herself smiling a little. "You're not only a wise friend, but a clever poet too!" She made a quiet sound, something like a laugh. "Craig, I think we're going to be a solid team."

"Yes," Craig agreed. "I hope so. Tell me what you've been doing since I saw you last."

"I met with Miguel Losoya, the ADA, but he claims it's much too soon to know anything. And when I asked what the autopsy found, he said they didn't have time to do one."

"You're kidding me!" Craig snorted. "That's unconscionable."

Ava raised her hands in the *What can we do?* gesture that was beginning to be her habit. "Well, at least Losoya gave me the police report from that night. On the hush-hush, I think, so we should keep it to ourselves. And I doubt we'll get anything more from Miguel Losoya. I don't think he plans any further investigation at all." Ava's shoulders slumped.

"I'd say Losoya took a big risk in giving you that report," Craig told her. "Especially since there seems to be some kind of a cover-up. But since you have the information now, we can make our own investigation, more in depth."

"Yes. I agree," Ava said. "I'd like you to read the report for yourself. Take it with you, for when you have time."

She handed it to him, as he said, "It's not very long. I'll read it right now." He scrunched into a comfortable reading posture and propped his heels on the balcony rail.

Ava watched him for a while, and then asked, "Can I get you something else to drink? I have cola, or maybe I could order you something from the bar?"

"I'm fine with just water right now, thanks," Craig hardly looked up from the report. Ava sat, contented to watch him, and to watch that blue horizon. It steadied her, somehow. This island, for all its unsettling ways, seemed to give her a certain sense of balance. It smoothed away the sharpest edges of her grief.

When Craig had finished reading the ADA's report, he said slapped it and said, "This confirms what we already knew: Beyond any doubt, there's no way in hell that Charley killed himself. That's where we start. And from there, we can figure it all out."

Ava tapped an index finger to the tip of her nose, as if to say "You've got it." Aloud, she said, "If Maura saw Charley in the Escalade, as she told me, why didn't she try to get to him? Why didn't Will? Their hesitation, their negligence, is horrible—inexcusable."

"Maybe the 'excuse,' if you want to call it that, is that Maura and Will already knew that Charley was dead." Craig paused, thinking, then spoke again. "They would know that only if they knew a whole lot more that they aren't telling. They had to have seen something."

"My idea exactly," Ava said. "Losoya's fallback position is to try to convince me that Charley's death was an accident, if we won't accept the suicide theory."

"I'd consider an accident very unlikely," Craig answered. "Possible, of course, but very unlikely. Charley was a level-headed guy."

"Even if he and someone were arguing?"

"Even if," Craig confirmed. "And *if* he and 'someone'—read that as 'Byron'—were arguing, how did Charley end up in his car? Was there any damage to the car?"

"No damage was mentioned in the report," Ava said. "But there's another angle to consider. You won't believe it, but Charley's the Escalade doesn't appear to be on island now."

Craig made a disgusted sound. "Sht."

"Yes, I know. Ken has promised me he'll get the Escalade's VIN number and locate it. Then we get to the car and check it for damage."

"More time lost," Craig said. "I'm finding it hard to be patient with 'island time' right now."

"No more than I," Ava answered. "But we do have other things to consider, and maybe figure out. The other day, before the funeral, Maura told me her version of what happened. I'd like to hear another version. But didn't you say that you weren't with Charley that night?"

"Right. I wasn't there; that was one of Charley's evenings with the guys in *Maura's* group. And you'd have a snowball's chance in hell of getting one of them to tell you what happened."

"Yes," Ava said. "There's no question about that. So I'll just tell you what Maura told me.

"She was out with her girlfriends. After she and Charley got home, he took his guns out, and she asked him to put them away. He did that and then went out to his car, where she found him later. And then she called her father. That's the whole story."

Ava's sigh seemed to come from the bottom of her heart. "I can understand Will Mattison's wanting to keep our tragedy out of the public eye; I can see him taking steps to avoid the pain and embarrassment of public scrutiny. I do appreciate that. But you'd think he'd tell me—Charley's mother!—everything he knows about my son's death."

Craig nodded, and took Ava's hand again. "Mattison *should* do that. Of course. Since he didn't, I have to suspect that he's protecting someone. And naturally, Byron is the first person who comes to mind."

"That's exactly what Ken said," Ava agreed. "I've been speculating that maybe Byron followed Charley home for some reason. Of course Maura would invite him in. Charley had his guns out, and Byron saw them." Ava stopped, unable to say more.

Craig picked up the narrative. "Somehow, by design or by accident, Byron fired the twenty-two pistol. And Charley was in the way. Maura saw Byron shoot Charley."

Ava held up a hand, a stop sign, and she frowned. She had agreed with Craig's scenario to this point, but now he had gone too far. "Maura wouldn't protect Byron if he had shot at her husband!"

Ava doubted her own words as soon as she said them, no matter how much she wanted them to be true. "Maura wouldn't do that, would she?" Ava said again, much more plaintively.

"Regardless of how Maura felt about it," Craig answered, "I'll betcha that her daddy would want to protect Byron. I don't find it at all difficult to imagine that Will Mattison put Charley's body in his Escalade, so that the police could reach the desired conclusions. And Maura didn't say a word to stop him. *Then* Mattison called the police. After Charley was in the Escalade."

Ava only nodded. She picked up the pieces of sea glass and fiddled with them, wanting then to calm her as they had before.

Craig continued to theorize. "That scenario would explain why there was so little blood in Charley's Escalade. Even so, Mattison got Biohazard to the scene almost immediately. Why would he want to do that? Why would he think he *needed* them to do that?"

Craig was on a roll, the ideas, the words, tumbling out of his mouth as fast as he could form them. "I doubt that he got permission to call Biohazard when he did. Because the DA's office would want to see the vehicle first—before a clean-up job obliterated any possible incriminating evidence."

Ava looked up. "But what do you think, Craig? Would there be any chance, if we had the vehicle examined, that it might still show something? Even after Biohazard's job?"

"Well, it's fair to say that Biohazard, on this island, might be pretty sloppy," Craig said. "Still, I'll betcha that's why Will Mattison got rid of the Escalade. Because there wasn't enough blood in it. Because there might be fingerprints in it that Mattison had failed to wipe away."

Ava's piercing look demanded Craig's full attention. "Does Will Mattison have enough power to see to it that Charley's death will never be investigated, that no conclusions will ever be reached?"

"Oh, yeah!" Craig said, his voice grim. "Will Mattison *is* ultimate power here."

"He could have the District Attorney in his pocket?" Ava prodded.

"Without question. And as for the autopsy," Craig added, "Mattison could have strong-armed DA Naigle to waive that, because of what it might have shown—like gunpowder residue, or the lack thereof. With no residue on Charley's hands, we'd know he hadn't held the gun."

"Yes. It's not hard to understand why Mattison wanted to hurry the cremation," Ava said.

"Dammit!" Craig interrupted. "Maura and Will and Byron should have been checked for gunpowder residue and blood spatter as well. Far too late now, of course."

Quieter, he continued, "The autopsy would also have shown Charley's blood alcohol level. If he was sober—or close to sober—an impassioned argument, leading to a struggle and death, seems somewhat less likely."

Craig pondered for a moment. "Drugs in Charley's system would have shown up too," he said slowly. "Drugs might have been slipped to Charley without his knowing, so that he could be shot and killed. If Charley passed out after he got home, someone could have put the gun in his hand and pulled the trigger."

"Are you thinking of a professional hit?" Ava put a hand to her chest, feeling out of breath.

"It's worth considering," Craig said. "But, on second thought, a professional would be unlikely to use a small caliber weapon—unless he could get at very close range. In this case, I don't think he could do that; Charley had a lot of security around his house. Still, for the sake of argument, consider that a paid assassin gets past the security. He stands right in front of Charley, and—"

"My son—*my son!*—just lets an assassin aim a puny twenty-two at his chest?" An odd sound came from Ava's mouth, almost a laugh. "No, that isn't a believable scenario at all."

"You're absolutely right," Craig agreed. "And if there were a hit man who managed all that, you can bet he wouldn't be the kind of guy who would bother to lock the car door afterward."

"Unless he was very, very clever." Ava rubbed her forehead. "And if there was a hit man, where was Maura all that time? Craig, these hypotheticals aren't getting us anywhere."

Ava stood and walked across the room. "Craig, are you *sure* you won't let me pour you a glass of wine now—or call room service for a beer or mixed drink? Because I want to tell you something else that's on my mind."

"Yeah, it's time for the wine now. You know the slogan, 'We will have no wine before it's time'." The words were the closest thing to levity that Craig could muster.

When Ava returned with two glasses of red wine, she said, "We do make a good team, Craig. I'm more than glad you're on my side, because I'm certainly not the Miss Marple type."

"No, and I'm not Charley Chan," Craig said. "But there's an island proverb, *Any dirty water cool copper.* It means that when you make do with what's on hand, it's always enough to get the job done."

"Enough or not," Ava said, tapping the police report, "this scanty supply of dirty water is all that we have."

She sipped at her wine and said, "Now for my new topic: Do you ever listen to B.B. Bennack on the radio?"

"He's a character," Craig said.

"He is indeed! But I'd like to know more about him."

"Bennack does much more than the deejay stuff you heard," Craig said. "B.B. is the owner of the radio station. And sometimes his call-in show gets verrry interesting."

"What do you mean?"

"Bennack seems to want to slaughter sacred cows."

"Good!" Ava said. "The world needs a plentiful supply of sacred cow slaughterers. And this island needs more than its share. After hearing Bennack's talk show today, I got a crazy idea to go and talk with him."

"You want to go on his show?" Craig gave Ava a mock scowl.

"Oh, no! I do not intend to do that at all." Ava shook her head. "But Mr. Bennack does seem to have a finger on the pulse of this island. If I could talk to him privately, I think that he might have some suggestions as to how we should proceed."

"Good point," Craig agreed. "We need to get to the bottom of this; we need to make some sense of our speculations. Bennack might be the one who can help sort things out—a fresh, objective view, that sort of thing."

"I'll call him tomorrow morning and set up an appointment," Ava said. "But if he thinks I'll talk about it on the air, he has another think coming."

Craig smiled at her use of the phrase—one that he'd heard Charley use so many times. And with just as little likelihood that a situation would work out the way either of them might expect.

DECEMBER 3

Pick yourself up, dust yourself off, and start all over again, an exuberant chorus sang through Ava's radio the next morning.

Idly, she wondered where, and how, Bennack could dig up so many antiquated tunes. She wondered why the man played so few recent hits. Still, the words of the old song seemed an appropriate message for her this day.

Ava snapped her smart phone open, called Bennack, and made an appointment to meet him at mid-afternoon. Everyone else might operate on island time, she prided herself, but she was still capable of getting things done when they needed to be done.

She drove to Radio Station WHDM, housed in a suite of offices near the far end of the harbor. The modern business complex mimicked island colonial style, right down to its central courtyard. Ava climbed stairs to the second floor, found the door with a simple cardboard sign identifying WHDM, and knocked.

B.B. Bennack opened the door. He was a small, round man, with round glasses. A swirl of thin, grey hair failed to hide the gleam of his spherical, balding head. As Bennack greeted Ava, he said, "The office isn't much—we don't need much—but we have a gallery overlooking the courtyard. Come sit out there with me."

When they were settled, Bennack asked, "What brings you to Dos Marias?"

"My son lived here. He worked for one of the Economic Development Centers, and he was married to Will Mattison's daughter."

"Yes, of course. Collier. I should have made the connection. I've met your Charley. He's a fine young man."

B.B. watched Ava shake her head. She seemed sad, and that puzzled him. *This is going to be interesting*, he thought.

Aloud, looking directly at Ava, B.B. said, "As you must already know, Mattison is very big, very powerful, on this island. I can't believe you'd need anything from me, when you have him for an ally."

"I wouldn't call him an ally," Ava answered. "Quite the contrary, actually." She wondered when Bennack would ever let her get to the point.

"I guess you need to start at the beginning," B.B. said, "without my questions blocking your way. Tell me what you're looking for, and what you think I can do for you." He leaned forward, anticipating Ava's response.

B.B.'s demeanor surprised Ava and relieved her too. "My son is dead," she told him.

It was B.B.'s turn to look surprised. "I'm so sorry! How did I miss this story in the newspaper?"

"I think that there was nothing more than a small obituary notice," Ava answered. "That's the only thing I've seen. If there was a detailed article, no one has shown it to me."

B.B. frowned. "Don't you think that's odd? After all, your son was a notable in this community, in his own right, and he was a part of one of the most prominent families—Will Mattison would have us think *the* most prominent family—on Dos Marias."

"I hadn't given that any thought," Ava said, "but you're right. Maybe I should check the old newspapers to see if I missed it."

"I can have my wife do that," B.B. offered. "She knows how to get along with the newspaper people, while not tipping her hand."

"Good," Ava replied. "I'd appreciate that."

"So," B.B. said, "begin at the beginning, and tell me the full story."

The generally-loquacious man listened quietly as Ava outlined her perplexities regarding her son's death. B.B. expressed sympathies with a few succinct words, occasionally asked a brief question, and often took notes.

Ava ended her narrative with the meeting at Pirates' Den, the night after Charley's funeral.

B.B. consulted his notes again and tapped a pen against his note pad. "This Assistant District Attorney, Losoya, seems to be a good man. Do you agree?"

"Well, *maybe*," Ava answered. "He made it abundantly clear to me that the DA's office will make no investigation of my son's death. They didn't even perform an autopsy."

"Unconscionable!" B.B. exclaimed. "So you're investigating on your own?"

Ava nodded. "You might say so." She summarized the more recent events, and again B.B. listened closely, taking careful notes.

When Ava finished her story, B.B. said, "*Welcome to the Hotel Dos Marias. We are all just prisoners here, of our own device.*" He chuckled. "The Eagles wrote that song, you know, about Hotel California, but I think of those lines often in connection with this island."

He held up a hand and ticked off on his fingers the main points that Ava had made. "Your son is dead under mysterious circumstances. The newspaper didn't report on it, and the DA won't investigate it. The Mattisons won't speak to you. Maura is no longer pregnant, and no one will reveal what happened to the baby. Why do I think I smell a rat?"

Ava raised both hands and cocked her head in agreement. "There you have it. B.B., I think you can understand why I'm asking for your help. I believe that you know Dos Marias well, and I suspect that you understand the politics of this island—I mean the real, beneath-the-surface social politics that make this place run. Tell me: What do you think I should do now? Do I hire an attorney who can file suit to have the case opened? And if so, can you suggest someone?"

"You could do that, I guess," B.B. said with some hesitancy, "but I can't think of any attorney on island who would dare to touch this case. And I suspect that anyone from off island would find it impossible to pull the strings required to get to the resources that he or she would need."

B.B. stood, walked the length of his small gallery, and leaned over the rail. He spoke toward the ground, his back to Ava. "I'm wondering if you might consider this a subject for my call-in show."

"I was concerned that you might suggest that," Ava answered. "It's not what I want to do at all. And it's certainly not why I came to see you."

Bennack heard the wariness in Ava's tone and turned to face her. "The listening public is our best ally," he said. "Someone out there knows something. And we have a saying on this island: *When de hurricane blow, all skin one color.* That means, we help one another when times are hard."

Ava did not answer him right away; she mulled over his suggestion. Then, in a tentative voice, she said, "Well, I guess I could consider being on your show, if you think that's our only solution."

Bennack nodded. "I understand the serious nature of your concern. We may be playing with fire, Ava. I don't want to flim-flam you about that. If Will Mattison is involved in a cover-up or something worse, he'll continue to do whatever it takes to protect himself."

"I agree, B.B.," Ava said. "And I don't want to put *you* in a difficult position either—much less a dangerous one."

B.B. spread his arms wide. His flushed face broke into a wide grin as he said, "That's what journalism *is*, dear lady! That's why I'm in this business. I haven't had a good crusade in years, and I'm more than ready to take this one on!"

Ava's sigh seemed almost a groan. "How do we begin?"

"Slowly. Carefully," Bennack cautioned. "Give me some time to do a little undercover work—a couple of days should be enough. Then I would very much like to have you on my show, if you can gird yourself up to do it. We'll invite my listeners to share their knowledge . . . and their theories."

"Interesting," Bennack said again, when Ava had left his office. His eyes fell on the threadbare carpet, the scuffed desk, the pile of unpaid invoices atop it. This meeting with Ava Collier might lead to the break that he had been hoping for.

Bennack was not unaware of how the public saw him: a foolish man, out of date, tilting at windmills. But he'd played with the big boys, once. He knew Madonna, and Ringo. He knew Kenny Chesney, who had a home over on St. John. Kenny had given him a demo album, and Bennack was grateful for that; his budget didn't provide for much new music.

And now, out of the blue, this Ava Collier walked through his door. Of course Bennack felt sorry for the woman's plight, but he also saw great potential in it—a terrific boost in his listenership. That should lead to a boost in advertising, which would lead to funds, and new music, and more listeners. His spiral was moving upward now; B.B. could feel it.

He pulled the Chesney CD for good luck and played "Don't Blink."

Ava Collier, listening on her car radio, paid careful attention to the words of Bennack's selection: *Don't blink. You just might miss your babies growing like mine did, turning into moms and dads . . .* And that hurt.

After she returned to her hotel room, Ava telephoned Rick Rowland. "I need to talk with you and Brooke," she said, "as soon as possible."

"I can't get away till about five," Rick responded. "But in the meantime, I'll contact Brooke. We can all meet at Falling Down, a beach bar and restaurant on the west end of the island. It's quieter than our boardwalk hangouts," he explained, "and Falling Down has live steel pan music with one of the best men in the business. Brook and I should be there by about five-thirty."

"Falling Down sounds extraordinarily appropriate," Ava told him. "That's pretty much how I feel these days."

The hotel desk man told Ava how to find the place. His instructions took her onto a cliff-hugging two-lane road heading west. Falling Down, a pleasant but unpretentious outdoor eatery, occupied a rocky point softened by a sprinkling of sand. The rock ended in a three-foot drop to a narrow strip of beach where wavelets splashed. Farther out, breakers curled across a long reef, sending a soft roar shoreward. Beyond that, at this hour, a glaring sun inched toward the horizon.

The people Ava saw seemed more like locals than a tourist crowd. Those sitting at the U-shaped palm thatch bar seemed to be regular customers; they joked with the bartender that way. A few early diners watched the late-afternoon sun from a scattering of wooden picnic tables. Ava did not see Rick and Brooke, so she chose a small, umbrella-topped table, as near the water—and as far from other customers—as possible.

She watched Steel Pan Sam unpack his island-style percussion instruments. Just as he began a loud and lively version of *The Tide is High*, Rick and Brooke arrived and sat down with Ava.

When they'd completed a standard "how are you?" routine, Rick nodded toward Steel Pan Sam and said to Ava, "The guy makes his own pans. They're pieces of discarded oil barrels. He does some kind of fancy heat-and-hammer work on them to get the sounds he wants."

Rick squirmed and looked behind him. "But the problem here is for *us* to get the drinks *we* want. Nobody waits tables here half the time."

He stood up. "I'm going to the bar to put in our order. Brooke, what do you want?"

"Mai Tai, sweetie."

"What are you drinking, Ava?" Rick asked then.

"I seem to have an affinity for something that comes out of a sugar mill," she said. "So you might order me some sort of rum drink—a *light* one."

As Rick walked away, Ava turned to Brooke. "I'm glad that we have a few minutes alone. I want to ask you some girl-questions."

"Okay," Brooke said, sounding unsure. "If I know the answers."

"Do you have a close relationship with Maura?"

Brooke giggled, "As *if!*" She shrugged her shoulders in a childish way. "Maura has her debutante bunch. And they think they're different. Better. Just because they were born here. They certainly wouldn't have anything to do with someone like me. Really, I think it's a wonder that Maura married Charley."

"What do you mean?"

"As a transplant, Charley had friends like himself, guys new to the island. I mean, like Rick and Craig, and the others you met at Pirates' Den. The EDC people he worked with and stuff."

"Didn't Charley and Maura have any friends in common?" Ava asked.

"Well, sure. I didn't mean that they *didn't*," Brooke said quickly. "Of course they went around with her bunch as a *couple*, and of course *Charles* got together sometimes with the people Mr. Mattison wanted him to be friendly with—the people who never used his nickname." Brooke had twirled her hand in the air when she said "Charles."

"But when *Charley* was on his own," Brooke continued, "he had truer friends. He had *us*, and we called him what he wanted to be called. Of course we were always happy to include *Miss Maura*, but we sure weren't bosom buddies with her." Again, the flighty hand signal.

Ava suppressed a smile at the obvious sarcasm in Brooke's intonations of *Charles* and *Miss Maura*. "So I guess there's no reason for me to think that Maura would have confided in you regarding her feelings about their pregnancy?"

Another giggle from Brooke. "Duh!"

"Were you with Maura and Charley on the night of the fight with Byron Hendley?" Ava asked then.

"Unfortunately." Brooke flicked her thumbnail against a front tooth. "Rick and I both were there."

"Tell me about that."

"We went to the Keg Wharf," Brooke began. "We can always count on seeing someone we know there, so it's almost always where all of us go. That night, I remember, we were all thinking of things to toast. Of course, we offered a toast to the bartender, and then one to his dog—he has this really *ugly* dog. We toasted the girl who served our drinks and we insisted that she sit down and have a drink with us. Later, Byron offered a toast to Maura's baby."

"You say that he made a toast to *Maura's* baby? Not *Charley's and* Maura's baby?"

"Well that's *Byron*," Brooke answered. "I'm pretty sure that's how he put it, but it seems a long time ago now."

Rick returned with the drinks, interrupting Ava's questions and necessitating a round of clinked glasses and casual conversation. Steel Pan Sam played an old Belafonte song, *Island in the Sun*. As he put his playing mallets aside, the bartender clanged a ship's bell.

"Falling down!" he yelled. "The sun is falling down!" Waitresses worked through the tables, offering the guests free Cruzan coconut rum shots as the sun slipped below the horizon.

Brooke, Rick, and Ava clinked glasses. "To better days," Rick said.

"To answers," Ava amended. She took one small taste of her very coconut-y rum shot and then returned to the business at hand.

"Rick, Brooke was just telling me about the night of Byron and Charley's fight at the Keg Wharf. From what I'd heard before, I was surprised that Byron was with your group."

"Oh, he didn't come with us," Rick said. "People just show up, on the boardwalk. I suppose Byron stopped at our table because he saw Maura there. I think Ronald Huffington may have dropped by for a while too, with some new girlfriend. Even Andy Flanagan came by, alone."

"That's true," Brooke said. "But after a while—thank God for small favors!—it was just Rick and me, and Maura and Charley. *And* Byron." Again, Brooke tinged her tone with a sort of disgusted sarcasm.

Ava ignored it, asking simply, "Was Byron there with a date?"

"Huh-uh." Brooke rolled her eyes and shook her head *no*. "He has a regular girlfriend, Donalee, but he said that she was working at the Casino that night. Donalee is a cage cashier. The Casino is a pretty classy, but still . . ."

"You don't like Donalee much?" Ava prodded.

"Oh, I like her okay. I mean, she's an all right girl, but kinda *coarse*. You know? And not someone of Byron's *stature*, not someone his *family* would approve of. I can't imagine that Byron and Donalee had much of anything in common. Except, you know . . ." Brooke mimed a huge extension of her own bosom.

Ava let that go. "Several things about Byron don't add up for me," she said. "If Byron represents 'the next generation of leadership on Dos Marias,' as Mattison claims, where are the stellar young ladies who should be eager to share his life?"

Rick made a derisive grin accompanied by a nodding of his head that grew to include a rocking of the entire top half of his body. "The nice mamas on island don't want to risk their darling virgins to the embrace of Byron Hendley. He is a stag in rut—completely out of control. Everybody assumes that Byron will grow up some day, but as long as he's intent on sowing wild oats, the social elite will keep their daughters away from him.

"That means that when Byron wants a little nookie, he has to go slumming to get it. Donalee is marginally acceptable, someone that he can be seen in public with—for the time being, at least. I suppose his parents look the other way."

"And this had something to do with the argument that night?" Ava asked.

"Well yeah!" Brooke responded. "It had *every*thing to do with it. "Rick started ragging Byron about Donalee not being there, about Donalee having to work nights. Charley jumped in, and off they went, teasing Byron. They are always doing something like that, just to watch Byron get mad. I'd guess you'd say they like to bait him."

"That sounds dangerous," Ava said. "Isn't it true that Byron is known to have a temper?"

"Yeah, and that's why people bait him," Rick answered. "He's makes such an idiot of himself when he goes ballistic. Watching him is something to do, some entertainment."

Brooke tried to explain. "You know, there's not a lot of variety on this tiny island, so we have to make our own fun." She set her mouth in a grim line then. "But that night Byron was drunker than usual, and he turned meaner than usual."

"What exactly did he do?" Ava prompted.

Looking up toward the stars, Brooke began, "Byron said something like . . . um . . . not everyone could have a Maura, not everyone could marry the richest, most desirable girl on island. And then he stood up and tried to turn the table over. Charley stood up too, to try to hold the table down. But he was drunk too, so he sorta tripped or something. He fell against Byron, and Maura tried to help him—help Charley, I mean. And the next thing I knew, *she* was falling down. And the table went down on top of her. Charley plunked back into in his chair and Byron stormed out onto the boardwalk.

"I couldn't see where he went from there. Somebody got Maura up and she told Charley that she needed to go home—right away. She looked really bad. But she managed to walk with Charley, around the corner to the parking lot. Byron was waiting for them there. He took one swing at Charley, and he fell to the ground."

Ava interrupted Brooke. "Who fell? Byron or Charley?"

"Charley."

"How do you know this? Were you in the parking lot then?"

"Huh-uh." Brooke shook her head. "Not at first. But Maura told me, after Rick and I walked up a minute later. We were there when Byron started kicking Charley. He kicked him in the ribs and in the jaw. Charley was just lying there, and we tried to protect him."

"I helped Maura get Charley in the Escalade," Rick said. "We put him in the passenger seat. Maura had to drive home, even though she wasn't looking all that good, herself—doubled up, like she was in pain."

Ava had put her hands over her eyes during this recital. Now she looked directly at Brooke, and then at Rick. "Did this sort of thing happen often—Maura driving Charley home?"

"Well, not because of being *beat up*, but yeah, I'd seen it before—Charley being a little too sloshed to drive."

"Would you say Charley had a drinking problem?"

Brooke cocked her head. "Is that what it sounds like to you? It's just island behavior. Look at the tourists, for godsakes. And yeah, Charley was shit-faced *some* Saturday nights, but Byron *always* was. I guess we all drink too much, at one time or another. It's just such a small island."

Brooke stood then. "I've got to go to the ladies' room. You should see it, Ava." She put a coy hand to her mouth and giggled.

"I mean, you don't have to see the ladies room, exactly, but you should see right outside it. They have the cutest washbasin, a real conch shell, pouring water in to a huge clam shell. It's out where the men can use it too."

As soon as Brooke left, Ava asked Rick, "Do you think that Charley and Maura had a good relationship?"

"Your son wasn't the sort of man who would talk about things like that," Rick said. "He and Maura were very private. Charley wasn't the type to be all over his wife in public, but they seemed as happy as any married people I know. And hey, he got her pregnant, didn't he?"

The words cut at Ava's heart, but she could not bring herself to tell Rick that Maura had lost the baby. She wondered, now, if Maura's fall on the night of the fight had caused that.

Then she asked Rick, "How did Charley feel about the pregnancy? Did he seem excited, or burdened?"

Rick grinned. "You'd think he was the first man in the history of the universe to father a child. I'd never seen him so happy."

When Brooke returned to the table, Ava quickly directed a question to her, forestalling another spate of babble. "Brooke, I know that Byron had dinner at Charley and Maura's home, just a week after the fight. Does that seem strange to you?"

"Not really," Brooke said. "I mean, Maura and Byron have been friends like fur-EV-errr. Like, I mean, they were 'special friends'." She made little quote marks in the air as she said the last two words.

Ava turned to Rick. "Do you agree?" When he nodded, she continued. "All right. Now I want you to tell me about the night that Charley died. Who was in that group?"

"Actually, I wouldn't call it a group," Rick explained. "Maura was going out with her girlfriends that night, so Charley tried to get the guys together. But I was the only one who could make it."

"Really?" Ava said. "Maura told me, the day of the funeral, that Charley was with Byron and Parker and Ronald that night."

"Maybe that was what *she* wanted to believe," Rick shrugged. "Or maybe Charley wanted Maura to think it."

"What do you mean?"

"Maura kept trying to force a relationship between 'Charles' and her friends—like he shouldn't be able to choose for himself who he enjoyed and trusted. So sometimes he let her think he was with the people she wanted him to be with."

Ava frowned. "That doesn't sound like a couple with a good relationship."

Rick reached out and patted her hand. "Naw, they were okay. And at least he was only sneaking around to see some guys, not another woman."

Ava forced an acknowledging smile. "Was Charley drinking heavily that night?"

Rick laughed, raising his hands as if to shield off an attack. "Hey! It was guys' night out. We all tossed down a few."

Ava did not smile. "And Charley's consumption was about normal for him?"

Rick straightened up. "Yes ma'am, I'd say so." He made his answer brisk and respectful, realizing that Ava was in no mood for flippancy.

"By the end of the evening," Ava continued, "did Charley appear drunker than usual? Or did he appear to be drugged in any way?"

"Hell, no!" Rick said, now angry. "Nothing like that. "It bugs me that you keep leaning so hard on Charley as a drunk or a druggie. No way he was anything like that. I can't understand why you think he was on drugs."

"Not *on* drugs," Ava said. "But I was thinking that someone might have slipped him a mickey. I'm just trying to explore every possibility." She decided to take another tack. "Can you describe Charley's mood that evening? Did you sense anything unusual?"

Rick shook his head. "He was in every way normal and light-hearted. I assure you that Charley was not drugged. That's why we have all wanted to talk to you. Because absolutely nothing about that evening, or any other evening, pointed to trouble. And certainly not to suicide."

Although that was the confirmation Ava had been hoping to hear, she wouldn't allow herself to accept an easy answer. She made a gesture in the air and spoke in a sardonic tone. "Charley hadn't a care in the world."

"I didn't say that."

Ava just nodded. "I talked with Ken Leland a few days ago. He thinks that revenge might have been a motive, if Charley was murdered. Can you think of anyone—one of Maura's friends, one of Charley's clients, or even a business associate—who might have had a reason to want him dead?"

"No," Rick said, in a voice that would accept no argument. "No way. Charley and I were pretty tight—almost as tight as he and Craig. If Charley had any problem, I'm pretty sure I would have known about it. So I can tell you that there was no problem. Not with anyone that I can think of, for sure."

"Good enough," Ava said. "New question: Miguel Losoya, the Assistant District Attorney, claims that Charley was talking on his smart phone late on the evening he died. Is that correct?"

"Gee, I don't think so. He might have, but I don't remember it."

Ava cocked an eyebrow, thinking: *So Miguel was trying to throw up a smoke screen?*

"Mrs. Collier," Rick said. "Brooke and I have talked this thing through and through. If we have to point a finger at anyone, it has to be Byron. His mood swings are hair-trigger violent—like the night he fought with Charley. And the Mattisons are protecting Byron—they will always protect Byron."

"Are you suggesting that Will Mattison—or Clio—might have a special reason to protect Byron?" Ava asked.

"I don't know of one. But that class—those people who have been on this island for so many generations—they always protect each other. They form a solid wall that no one can get through."

Ava nodded. "It's hard to accept the idea that the Mattisons may be protecting my son's murderer," she said. "He's my son, but he was their son-in-law, too. How could they go against him that way?"

She stood up then, shaking her head in dismay. "I hope that you will forgive me, but I've had enough for one day. I do thank you for sharing, and for understanding that I just can't take any more right now."

Brooke, who had been silent throughout Ava's last, long interchange with Rick, hopped up. Giving Ava a hug, she said, "Of course we understand. Just call us when there's anything else we can do."

"Mrs. Collier," Rick said, "you can think of me as your son." He hugged her too.

As Ava walked to her car, Steel Pan Sam's rendition of *Have You Never Been Mellow* taunted her. "Oh, Sam," she sighed to herself, "I don't think so. I haven't felt mellow in a very long time. And maybe I never will again."

DECEMBER 4

Sunday was a long day. Too quiet.
Late in the afternoon, the phone rang, and Ava welcomed that as a relief.
A man's voice asked her: "Okay, are you ready to take the plunge?"
Ava puzzled over the question, trying to recognize the voice. Then she remembered—B.B. Bennack!
"Have you completed your investigation?" Ava asked, putting a hand to her chest. She felt somewhat surprised, and certainly rushed. She wished that she could put off, for just a little longer, the terror of going on B.B.'s radio program. Temporizing, she asked, "Are you sure that you have all the information you need?"
"Far from that," B.B. told her. "Far from that! My friend John Ciardi wrote that *a good question is never answered*. He also observed that good questions *lead not to answers but to new questions, and the new questions to others, and they to others yet*. That's where I am now, Ava; that's where you and I both are. Every new question that we ask leads to more new questions."
Ava blinked. This was a side of Bennack that she had not seen before. The man's sophistication and intelligence impressed her—and relieved her too. She felt a flicker of hope that some good might come from her ordeal on WHDM radio.
Bennack continued, "I want to spend a full week on the cover-up of Charley's death, but I only need for you to be here

on the first day. Beyond that, of course, you're welcome to come to the studio any time you want."

Ava just nodded.

"But before we get started," B.B. continued, "I need some 'back story' on you—some personal information, for color. Could you fill me in now?"

"Certainly." Ava moved out to the lounge chair on her balcony, with its comforting view of the water.

"Is this your first trip to Dos Marias?" Bennack asked.

"No, I visited my son here before his marriage, and of course I was here again for the wedding."

"Where are you staying now?"

"At a hotel. And I've rented a car," Ava said.

"Because your investigation into your son's death is going to take a significant period of time." B.B. intoned the words as though practicing the way he would speak them on the program.

"I guess you could say that," Ava answered. "I think I'll be here for more than a few days."

"When you were here before, visiting your son, what did the two of you do?" Bennack asked. "Did he show you the sights?"

"A little, on my first trip. We sailed out to at El Niño Cay—isn't that the name of the little island out there? We picnicked and snorkeled, and I was amazed at the beauty I saw under the water! Charley was proud that he'd taken me some place that I enjoyed so much.

"My son had sought employment here because he wanted to sail and snorkel. He always intended to take up scuba too . . ." Ava's voice trailed off.

B.B. changed the subject, asking her about her career. As she told the story of her development as a woman in business, B.B.'s comments showed that he was impressed. And that made Ava smile. She began to feel more comfortable with him, and with the idea of what lay ahead.

"Good," Bennack said, when Ava concluded her story. "That's the kind of angle I was looking for. I have to be on air in just a few minutes, so I'll cut this short and just plan on seeing you here tomorrow morning, no later than eight a.m. That way, I can have you briefed before the show begins."

DECEMBER 5

When Ava arrived at the radio station, B. B. Bennack gave her only a quick orientation, a glass of tap water, and an almost-comfortable chair. She sipped at the water, her heart pounding.

Too soon, B.B. pointed to the clock, put a finger to his lips to remind Ava that silence was now necessary, and assumed his on-the-air persona:

"This is WHDM Horizon Radio! And I'm B.B. Bennack. What horizon are you seeing now? Is it overcast or clear? Can you make out the other islands today, or are they obscured by cloud? Sometimes things are not what they seem in this beautiful Territory of ours.

"If you're a regular listener, you know that Mark Twain is one of my favorite all time writers. I collect his more intriguing quips, the way some people collect seashells or beach glass. Try this one on for size: *There isn't a Parallel of Latitude but thinks it would have been the Equator if it had had it's rights.*

"Isn't that a doozy? Doesn't that describe our island?" B.B.'s voice dropped dramatically. "And doesn't it describe some people you know?

"We're going to be talking about Latitude this week—about how some people push their limits, and about how they try to limit other people. We invite you to join in our conversation. But first, as the old cliché goes, this message."

B.B. clicked a button and a commercial played—B.B.'s own voice, prerecorded. Ava observed the operation with fascination; it seemed to confirm what she had already surmised: that B.B. did almost everything that needed to be done at the WHDM radio station. While B.B.'s taped voice enthused about new homes for sale on island, the man leaned forward to speak with Ava.

"As soon as we're back on air," B.B. said, "I'll introduce you. Think of this interview as slow dancing. All you have to do is stay relaxed, be yourself, and let me lead."

Ava smiled at that, and nodded. Nervousness arose in her throat, and B.B. noticed. He nudged the water glass closer to her hand. The commercial ended, and B.B. spoke into the microphone.

"You're listening to WHDM Horizon Radio, I'm B.B. Bennack, and Sea Breeze is on the air. Strap on your life vest and grab hold of the ship's rail. We're embarking on a breathtaking cruise!

"My friends, I have a visitor to our island here with me today, name of Ava Collier. She is a most interesting woman.

"Ava, during the commercial break just a minute ago, you heard me telling our listeners about some new houses going up on our island. You know something about that business too, don't you?

"Yes I do," Ava said, surprised at the angle from which B.B. had chosen to approach this interview.

"Are you a decorator, or something like that?"

"Well, I do some decorating," Ava said, "but my main interest is in building homes."

"Not with your own *hands*!" B.B. sounded aghast, and that made Ava smile.

The smile came through in her voice as she said, "No, of course not, B.B., though I do know which end of a hammer is which. I own and manage a company that builds luxury homes and small cottages in a seaside community in Texas. We can provide everything from an architect to the final touch of paint and flowers in the yard."

"You said *We*," B.B. continued, "so I guess your husband is your co-partner."

"My husband died some years ago. During his lifetime, he did take the lead role, and I learned a lot from him. So, after his death, I felt competent to handle the building business on my own. Of course, I have a staff to support me, and they're the reason I said *we*."

"Wow," B.B. said. "Just wow. I'm speechless. I'm *flabbergasted*. All you people listening to this conversation can't see this pretty little lady, as I do. She looks delicate as a mimosa blossom, but Ava Collier is a woman as competent as they come. I'll betcha she knows how to be tough as nails when that's called for. I gotta confess that I wish that she'd join us here, and build some beautiful homes for our island—beyond the great ones we have, that is.

"Now, now—I know what you're thinking: 'Here goes B.B., off on another commercial.' But that's not it. That is not it at all. Ava Collier has come here today to Ask. Us. For. Our. Help.

"Yes," the timbre of B.B.'s voice deepened a bit, "Ava Collier has encountered a difficulty on our island that none of her vast experience or expertise can help her with. I want all of you good neighbors to help me look at this problem with her. She is here with us today hoping that we will share our thoughts and our concern. She hopes that we can shed some light on a mystery that is troubling her."

B.B. glanced quickly at Ava before continuing. "Ava Collier came to Dos Marias because her son died. Her son—her only son, her only *child*—died in a most dramatic way. But our esteemed local newspaper didn't see the need to write about it!"

B.B. adjusted the volume of his voice, higher, and more shrill. "Don't we have to wonder about a newspaper that doesn't report the news? Here is the way I would have written it, if I worked for that newspaper instead of running this radio station."

B.B. lowered his voice again to continue. "Dos Marias lost one of its most promising young businessmen last night. Charles Collier, known to his friends as Charley, and recognized as the husband of Maura Mattison, died of a gunshot wound. The police investigative report was strangely brief, but included this sentence: *Mr. Will Mattison told us that the wife of the homeowner, Maura Mattison Collier, was in her residence, indisposed. He denied us access to her for questioning.*

"Indisposed?" B.B.'s voice rose to the level of drama and kept on rising. "The wife of the deceased is too indisposed to talk to the police? Sure, she's distraught by what has happened. She's horrified, and she is deeply grieving. But aren't those the very reasons that she would *want* to talk to the police? Wouldn't she want to help them find the person or persons who had done this awful thing? And wouldn't her family try to encourage her to cooperate?" B.B. paused after each question, letting it sink into his readers' minds.

"So let's say that a good newspaper reporter begins an investigation," he continued. "Here are some of the things that he or she would learn."

As B.B. Bennack talked on, Ava Collier tuned him out. She knew the story too well, and found it too painful to hear from another person's lips. She understood that it was necessary for Bennack to lay the groundwork, but she also understood that she didn't have to listen. Ava did not return her attention to Bennack's voice until he was wrapping up his summary of her story.

"So this is all we know," Bennack said. "Charley died, and someone is covering up ugly truths. We're hoping that some of you listeners have information that could shed light on this mystery. Maybe you were at the restaurant where Charley and Byron Hendley had their fight. Maybe you saw Charley on the last night of his life. Maybe your cousin was paid to transport Charley's Escalade just before it disappeared. Maybe your sister's best friend works in the District Attorney's office and remembers hearing something that never made it into the official notes. Maybe you know a very brave Someone who works for Will Mattison and is willing to tell what he or she knows."

With each "maybe," B.B.'s voice rose in volume and fervor. Then he paused, settling down. In a deeper tone, B.B. said, "Think about how you can help, while I try to sell something to pay the bills."

Bennack reached out to punch the button that made a commercial play. By the time it was over, red lights gleamed on all three phone lines. Bennack pressed the button on the first one.

"Ahoy there, Sailor!" he said. "What's your Sea Breeze?"

"Aw, man," a male voice drawled. "Don't stir up this stuff. Just don't do it man."

Bennack clicked him off with a brisk "Thank you, caller" and opened the next line. "This is Sea Breeze. Who am I talking to?"

Bennack heard a feminine whisper and turned up the volume: "I won't give you my name, but I used to work at the Keg Wharf. Where Charley and Byron had the fight?"

"Yes?" Bennack urged. "Were you working that night?"

"No, but I know what happened. Everybody in the kitchen was talking about it. Byron made a toast to Maura and her baby. Then he said something about wishing it was his baby. Then Charley jumped up and hit him. And then the brawl started."

"Caller, can I transfer you to another line? Off the air? Would you give your name and phone number to my secretary so that we can talk privately?" Bennack used his most beguiling voice. "I'm switching you now."

He reached to the phone lines. "Caller number three. You're on the air."

"That last girl was full of shit, man. Kitchen help never know anything. They get it all second hand. I wait tables. Byron was *boasting* that nobody would ever know the baby was his. That's when Charley hit him.

"Charley was really in a rage. We saw him that way a lot. Maura tried to protect Byron, and then Charley punched *her*. In the stomach. But not on purpose . . . I think. Maura sat down hard—on the ground. I helped her up, but she was doubled over, hurting. The whole bunch of them left pretty soon after that. Didn't leave much of a tip, either."

Again Bennack solicited the caller's name and number, then went to a commercial break.

As soon as the advertising tape began to play, Bennack turned to Ava and said, "This is terrible for you. I'm sorry it's going this way. Don't believe any of it. People call in to say the damnedest things." He moved his head in a slow arc, like a searchlight seeking a sign.

"I don't know. I guess some people get their sick kicks that way. Or maybe . . ." B.B. squinted his eyes in contemplation. "Maybe someone is trying to throw up a smoke screen."

Ava didn't answer him. She just sat, her head in her hands.

"I can shut this down if you want. Right now," B.B. offered.

Ava looked up at him. "No," she sighed. "I can handle it. I'm more than willing to endure the pain, because some of the things they're saying add to other things I've been told. I can't imagine that this can get any worse. And who knows? The next caller may say something that will be truly helpful to us. Let's just go on." She straightened her shoulders as though girding for battle.

B.B. thought Ava looked like Margaret Thatcher as he went through his usual on-air rigmarole. He chastised callers for providing speculation rather than fact. He urged knowledgeable listeners to present—on or off the air—hard information, or subtle details, even, that might lead to helpful conclusions.

"Yes, Caller," he said then. "You're on Sea Breeze."

"Hi. Ahhh. Ah, you might say this is Dave?" The caller's voice went up at the end of the sentence, as if he were asking a question, and he continued that pattern. "Well, I don't know anything about the white fight on the Boardwalk? But would anybody be interested in hearing about another fight with some of the same cast of characters?"

B.B. leaned into the mike, as if to reach for the man who had spoken. "What do you mean, Caller? What night are you talking about?"

"Well, the night Charley was killed? I just happened to be driving by his house, and I thought my tire was going flat? So I stopped the car and got out and went to look at my tire?

"Charley and Maura's house has a big stucco wall on the road side of it? But that doesn't keep sound from coming over the top? I heard loud voices, so I stopped? Maybe there was a problem, and I should, you know, help?"

The caller paused, and B.B. filled the dead air space: "Yes, Dave. It's good to know you're a responsible citizen."

"Well, yeah? What I heard was some people arguing? And then I decided I'd better get out my smart phone? To make a recording of what I was hearing? I thought, you know, that maybe it would land me a big deal on national T.V. from the States? People do that all the time? You know the shows I mean?"

B.B. was getting impatient. "Yes, Caller, I do know. Consider this your audition for the big time. Tell us what you heard."

"I heard somebody say 'I'll kill Byron, so help me I will.' A girl—I guess it was Maura?—she was begging somebody to stop? To give her the gun? There was a lot of yelling? I heard some *bam-bam* like something thrown around? And then I heard the gun go off. A big, loud gun. And Maura started screaming."

"Yes, Dave?" B.B. prodded. "And then what? You rushed to their aid, right?"

"No, man! I didn't want to get shot too? But I got it all on the tape? I started up that old car of mine without even worrying about a low tire. I just wanted to get out of there as fast as I could? But I got it All. On. Tape."

B.B. interrupted again. "Caller, how many voices did you hear that night?"

The lights in the studio dimmed, brightened, dimmed again. And then the room went black.

"Damn!" Bennack said. "Ava, we're off the air. The power's gone."

"Mattison can't do *that*, can he?" Ava tried for a light tone, but failed.

Bennack answered in a calming voice that did not convince Ava. "Power goes off here all the time. That's Ilwic for you."

"Ill wick?" Ava echoed.

"Island Light and Water Commission. I-L-W-C. We often use the acronym as a cuss word, *Ilwic*."

"How long do you think the power will be off?" Ava asked.

"Our emergency generator should click on, any second now," B.B. said, glancing at his watch. "Should have come on already, as a matter of fact. This outage could be just our building, or this division, or it could be the entire island. The power could come back on at any minute now, or stay off for hours. But it's unusual to be without power for an entire day. Unless, of course, we had a hurricane.

"Ah!" The lights came on with blinding intensity. But the three red buttons on the phone lines did not glow.

"WHDM Horizon Radio," Bennack boomed. "Can anybody hear us out there? Was our power outage the supreme editorial comment, the supreme response to our topic for the day? And, if so, is the power about to go off again?" His chuckle seemed a weak attempt.

"I hope our last caller is still listening," B.B. continued. "If you are, Dave, please give your name and number to my assistant. I'm switching you over to her right now. In any case, folks, it's almost news time, so we'll end our discussion for the day with this quote from poet John Ciardi:

It takes great courage to engage a confusion deeply. It is at least a ponderable proposition that the courage to engage it is better than is that order of conviction that can survive only by refusing to consider seriously those questions an inquiring mind must find unavoidable.

"End quote, and amen! Thank you, callers. Thank you, listeners. Let us hear from you tomorrow or the next day. Call in any day, on this topic, or any other. We welcome your courageous and inquiring minds on Sea Breeze!"

Bennack punched buttons, then leaned back. "Over and out," he said glumly, to no one but Ava. "Let's go get a drink." He paused to pick up a crumpled envelope. "Where the devil did this come from? It has your name on it."

Ava opened the envelope and found a slim dagger of bright red sea glass. "About that drink," she said. "Let's make it Painkillers. And I'm buying."

DECEMBER 9

Ensuing days attracted many callers to Bennack's talk show, but Ava avoided the program. She did listen, with intense gratitude and interest, to tapes of the show that Bennack gave her. Fast-forwarding through commercials and idle chatter decreased the duration of Ava's pain. Stopping and starting the tape allowed her to make careful notes for future investigation.

She dialed Craig's number on her cell phone. "When can we get together? There's a lot to talk about."

"You won't believe this," Craig responded, "but I was just about to call you. I can't stay on land another day in this excellent weather. Would you like to go sailing with me tomorrow?"

DECEMBER 10

Ava stood in the hotel's porte-cochere, so when Craig drove up, they were soon on the way to their adventure. The day seemed far too warm for late autumn, Ava thought, but optimal for sailing.

Traffic near a school slowed them almost to a stop. Smiling people stepped out from curbs, waving and holding posters that represented a variety of political candidates.

Booths lined the road, two blocks before and after the school. At each booth, a half dozen or more ardent citizens supported various candidates. Several of the campaign workers shoved pamphlets through the car window and into Ava's unwilling hands.

"Do you vote here?" she asked Craig.

He shook his head no. "Even if I did register to vote in the Territory, I couldn't vote in a Presidential election—no citizens of U.S. territories can do that. They're allowed only to vote for a Congressional representative who does not have a vote in Congress."

"What does a representative to Congress do, if he can't vote?" Ava asked.

"She," Craig corrected. "The current rep is a woman. And I gather that basically she's a lobbyist, presenting our opinion on issues pertinent to the islands."

"And do the people here actually give the Representative their opinions?" Ava asked.

"I don't know that they're any better about that than a lot of people in the States," Craig said, "but I have the impression

173

that, on the local level, this Territory's people take elections very seriously. There's a lot of talk about corrupt island politics, but when I see a turnout like this, I want to believe that some people care very much about the system."

Ava looked around her. "I hope so. And I hope that someday soon someone who cares will call in to the radio station to report something helpful about Charley's death. I hope that someone in the DA's office will be brave enough to ask the right questions. I guess I'm hoping against hope, that I will somehow resolve the mystery surrounding my son's final hours."

Just at that moment, she saw a dark woman on the curb, holding the hands of her two small children. An instant later, a dark hand reached through Ava's car window, shoving something into her chest.

Instinctively, Ava fought the hand away. Later, when her panic subsided, she read the innocent flyer that the woman had left. It simply advertised a political rally and fund-raiser:

QUADRILLE
&
GRAND FOOD SALE

Seafood & Regular Kallaloo
Roast Pork, Roast & Stew Goat, Salmon Balls
Barbecue Chicken, Conch in Butter Sauce, Fry Fish
Souse & Potato Salad, Bull Foot & Red Peas Soup
Johnny Cake, Banana Fritters, Veggie Lasagna, Veggie Goat Water
all Trimmings included

Ava read it aloud to Craig, and then said, "I think I can figure out terms like 'fry fish' and 'stew goat' but what in the world is 'bull foot and red peas soup'?"

He laughed. "Your guess is as good as mine. And that 'veggie goat water' is something I'd just as soon forget."

"Yes," Ava chuckled. "And I'm wondering how lasagna, of all things, got on this island menu. It seems to me that there's a very strange and intricate blend of cultures here."

"Indeed." Craig slowed the car as he approached a turn off from the main highway. An arrow-shaped sign indicated the direction to Spanish Cove Marina. Beyond that, brush and flamboyant trees crowded a winding road.

"Except for those beautiful flowering trees," Ava said, "the brush reminds me of South Texas."

"Charley always said the same thing," Craig answered with a pleased chuckle. "And I told him what I'll tell you: Islanders call that brush tan-tan."

The road through the tan-tan ended in the marina's parking lot. An old man ambled out to meet Craig and Ava.

"Good morning, Winston!" Craig said. "It's good to see you again. How have you been? Family okay?"

"We doin' jus' right, Misteh Craig, jus' right."

Craig climbed out of the car and went around to open Ava's door. "Ava," he said, "meet Winston Watley, who was your son's good friend as he is mine."

Ava stepped forward to shake Winston's hand, and she remembered to say "Good morning."

"Winston has a repair yard here at the marina," Craig told her, "and he also looks after those of us who have boats in these slips." Then, turning to Winston, Craig asked, "Is our food ready?"

"Soon come," Winston replied. "Alma walk wit' it."

"We'll carry our gear bags down to the boat," Craig told him, then spoke to Ava. "My boat's half way out the dock there, on your right, stern to. You'll see her name, *Priorities*."

"Nice name," Ava smiled. "First things first."

"Yep," Craig answered. "I try to keep in mind the most important things in life—like sailing with a lovely lady on a beautiful day."

When Ava had stowed her gear in the cabin and come back on deck, she saw a woman as old and stooped as Winston, struggling with a large hamper.

Ava stepped onto the dock to help, saying, "Good morning. Are you Alma?"

"Good mornin'," the older woman responded. "Yes, I be Alma. And dis be yo food fo today." She set the hamper on the dock and proceeded to touch each item as she ticked it off her list: "Two jerk chicken wrap, bottle wine, two plastic glass, bottle opener, chips, home-made cookies, paper napkin, watta." She pointed to an unlabeled quart bottle, filled with clear liquid, presumably water.

"Anyt'ing else yo need?" Alma asked.

"This looks great." Ava spoke with delight and enthusiasm. "Thank you. Let me pay you for this now."

By the time they had completed their transaction, Craig arrived to free the dock lines. They motored away from the marina, then hoisted sail.

Craig took wide, lazy tacks in the general direction of a small island. "El Niño Cay," he told Ava, pointing.

She nodded. "According to my Tex-Mex Spanish, *el niño* means 'baby boy.' Historian Clio Mattison probably has a story about that little cay."

"Yeah," Craig chuckled. "Something about the *dos Marias*—the two Marys—and the baby. Maybe another island power struggle—who gets the baby."

Ava made a small smile to show that she'd heard him, but she could not think of a reasonable response. And she emphatically did not want to think about Maura's lost baby—her own lost grandchild.

Instead, Ava looked out across clear water that changed from pale glass green to bright turquoise to dark azure, with infinite shades in between, depending on the water's depth, the clouds, and the composition of the sea floor at that particular spot.

White sand reflected brightest, while coral reef growth made the sea appear darker. The deepest water glowed with a most intense indigo blue.

Ava said, "Charley and I came out here on one of the charter cruises, the last time I visited on island. A woman aboard admired these water colors so much that she asked the captain if he would please stop at each place where the color changed, so that she could bottle a sample to take home."

"She really thought it was the water that changed?" Craig hooted.

Ava nodded and grinned. "Tourists make strange assumptions, I guess. Especially those who've never seen salt water before, maybe."

Then her voice turned grim. "It's easy to laugh at the tourists, but I should remind myself that I'm one, as well. And certainly I need to be very careful about making assumptions."

In silence, Ava and Craig watched the shore slip by: new condo complexes, crumbling Danish walls, remnants of sugar mills, a luxury hotel or two. Sloops, ketches, powerboats, and Sunfish accompanied them toward El Niño Cay. On the horizon, other sails gleamed.

Craig approached the cay, circled to choose a spot, and set his anchor fairly close to shore. "What say we snorkel and then have lunch?" he proposed.

"Sounds like a plan," Ava agreed.

Almost before the words were out of her mouth, Craig pulled off his shorts, revealing the Speedo beneath them. He reached for his mask, snorkel, and fins and handed another set of gear to Ava.

"Let's get wet." An instant later, Craig was in the air, and into the water with a splash.

Ava had worn a swim suit under her shorts and shirt as well, so she slipped out of them quickly to join Craig in the water.

The sun brightened a spectrum of delights, a living rainbow of fish and corals. Above a carpet of red and orange encrusting sponges, two-inch yellow circles—juvenile fish called tangs—flashed blue flirtatious eyes. Larger fish—greenish-blue queen angels—trailed yellow fins like the trains of royalty. Above their yellow faces gleamed crowns of neon blue. All around the angels and the small yellow tangs, lacy purple sea fans, six feet wide, formed a backdrop or a curtain that swayed slightly in the current.

Making simple surface dives, Ava peered into cavelets of coral, almost touched the arm of a small octopus, found clusters of marine alga called sea pearls. She swam into the shallows and waded ashore on El Niño Cay. Ava had collected a few small shells when she heard Craig's shout.

"I'm hungry! What about you?"

She nodded and he shouted again, "Beat you back to the boat!"

Ava didn't accept the challenge; she simply waded into the water and took long, easy strokes, until she arrived at *Priorities*.

While she and Craig enjoyed the lunch that Alma had packed, a yellow-breasted bird, four inches long, flew in to watch them from a safe spot in the boat's rigging. The bird's back and wings were dark, but she had a white throat and belly, a conspicuous white stripe at her eyes, and a red crescent by her beak. As crumbs fell from the picnic meal, the bird fluttered down to the table and began to peck at the bounty.

"Birder books label her a bananaquit," Craig said, "but locals call her the sugar bird, or sugar thief. She eats nectar from flowers in gardens, as hummingbirds do. And she'll come right onto a dinner table to rob the sugar bowl. That's why she's watching us now."

"How fascinating!" Ava said. "I've become rather interested in a sugar thing myself." She launched into the story of Charley's incarceration in Mattison's mill, then asked, "Craig, do you know anyone who can help me get my son out of there?"

"Haven't a clue, Ava. Sorry." Craig's grim face showed his frustration and concern. "I'll keep an ear open for that. But tell me what else has been going on. I heard you on the radio with Bennack. Did you get anything from that?"

"A lot of heartache and anger," Ava said. "Bennack felt it too, I think. I didn't get any real leads, but there was some corroboration of the events on the night that Byron and Charley fought."

Craig nodded. "I heard the guy who said he taped an argument in Charley's yard, the night Charley died. What do you make of that?"

"I don't know what to think," Ava answered. "It could have been someone bragging, just to hear himself on the radio. But the story does complement what we already know, so it's frustrating that the station went off the air just after B.B. asked the caller how many voices were on the tape."

"He did describe an argument, and he did say that he heard a gun go off," Craig said. "That's significant."

"Yes," Ava agreed, "but his story leaves me with as many questions as it answers."

"We need to get that tape," Craig said, "and we need to know if it was coincidence that Bennack's power went off exactly when it did."

"When we solve that mystery, we solve Charley's as well." The words might have seemed optimistic, but Ava's tone betrayed hopelessness.

Craig had watched her mood change. For a while, she had seemed to be a normal, relaxed person, enjoying the day. Then, through this conversation, Craig saw Ava settling back into her gloom.

"We *are* going to solve both mysteries," Craig said, making his voice calm, assuring Ava. "Just not today. Today's priority is R&R. Let's lift the anchor and hoist the sail."

On the other side of the island, a telephone rang. A dark young man named Treacle just looked at it over the smoldering tip of the joint that he held between his fingers. He took a deep toke before he lifted the receiver. Took the toke . . . and held it . . . and exhaled slowly . . . before he said hello.

"Good day, Treacle," a familiar voice said into his ear. "How yo feel 'bout makin' a buck? Yo up fo dat?"

Treacle inhaled again. "Oh yeah," he said in that slow, seepy grunting tone that went with breath holding. "Ah beginnin' to wonder when Ah could afford to buy some good shit."

"De Man have a package fo yo to deliver. A big package. Ah gotta meet yo to tell yo where to take it. Yo wanna go fishin' tumorrah?"

"Fishin's good," Treacle grunted. "An' de package be waitin' fo me at de usual spot?"

"Yeh. I'll tell you 'bout it while we fish. Vehicle park in de usual spot, wit' de package inside. An' afta de job, yo money be in de usual spot too."

Treacle grinned as he contemplated his thin, twisted joint. Nothing, absolutely nothing, was so fine as blowing things up and getting paid to do it.

December 11

Treacle saw that the package *was* big—it filled the whole passenger seat of a nondescript pickup, and the floorboard there too. Treacle had no idea how the Man could get hold of explosives like that, and he didn't want to know. It was enough to feel certain that the Man would always supply what a job required, plus a little extra. And he paid good, too. On time.

Late that afternoon, Treacle jingled the pickup's keys in his cupped hand, then eased into the cab. He maneuvered the main Dos Marias highway with careful attention—didn't want to miss the steep road that would take him up Mount Lookout.

Once on that road, Treacle rolled slowly past locked gates protecting the estates of wealthy white men who only lived on island part time. He scowled. *Hard to imagine havin' dat much money, an' leavin' dat much to waste. Maybe one o' dem men owns what Ah about to blow up. Well, dat man deserve to lose it.*

Treacle eased the little truck along a rutted road, climbing toward the ridgeline of Dos Marias Island. The farther he drove, the narrower the road became; it seemed little more than a trickle of sand. Treacle passed the turn-offs to several more estates, fancier.

The road became rough and rutted, and home sites along it grew sparse. Treacle slowed almost to coasting, quieting his vehicle. He made a flowing right turn to follow a ridgeline through the tan-tan and realized that he'd oozed himself down behind the steering wheel. Huh! As though that made him less conspicuous, as though somebody wouldn't see the truck before they saw him.

By the time he reached his destination, tan-tan scraped the sides of the truck cab. The road appeared to end at a turnaround, so Treacle stopped, looking for the continuing trail described in his instructions. He spotted it and scanned it for tire tracks. Seeing none, he followed the trail around a bend and came into a large, clean parking area that surrounded the base of his target.

He saw two new air-conditioners alongside the control building and guessed that the installers had mowed the whole area to make their work easier. Made seeing him easier too and he didn't like that. But Treacle saw no signs that any work was going on now; he didn't expect he'd be interrupted, or even noticed. And he sure didn't want to be.

What he did want was a closer-up look at the tall structure. He pulled almost into the brush at the edge of the lot, opened his door and slid out of the truck. He eased the door shut then, slow, careful not to let the latch click into place.

He looked all around a massive tripod; he leaned back to see up to its top. A triangle of three skinny legs formed each of the tripod's big legs. Heavy beams, set slant-wise, braced each of them against the other two. Treacle figured that he'd have to disable two main legs.

No reason not to start with the one nearest him. Easiest. He ambled to it and ran his hand along it. Smooth. Three plastique charges on each of the skinny legs, plus charges at the first diagonal beam, should do it. He'd just sticky the charges on with duct tape.

He had plenty of that. Whoever supplied this job had the wherewithal to do it right, and the smarts to supply it right. And he knew that Treacle was the man with the skill to do it right—slow, steady, and just so. Wouldn't take long at all.

Treacle set to work. One package at the base of the near leg, another up higher on it, at the first joint. He went over to the next leg and did the same thing. A couple more packages at key joints just for the hell of it. Because he had plenty.

Treacle sauntered back to the truck, feeling a little cocky now. He checked the remote devices. Sweet. He slipped in behind the wheel and stretched a lazy hand to the truck's ignition.

Nice o' De Man to gimme dis remote trigger, Treacle thought, fondling it as he drove away. He'd be glad to be down, off the hill, before the tripod blew. There might be some consequences that even the Man couldn't foresee or take care of.

Treacle eased onto the main road, heading for a favorite beer joint and listening to WHDM radio. Not his kind of music. Continentals' music. Jimmy Buffett crooning that it had been a lovely cruise. Shit.

Treacle pulled off the side of the road to light a cigarette. He picked up The Man's remote with a gesture so gentle it seemed almost like love. With a look of adoration in his eyes, Treacle pressed the remote's button.

No more shit music after that. Just a satisfying, deep roll like thunder coming down off Mount Lookout. Treacle grinned, a wide, slow grin. And then he changed his radio back to a good island rap station.

Ava was listening to WHDM when it happened. At first, she thought the break was just another power failure. But then her smart phone chimed, and she heard Bennack's voice.

"Ava, my transmitter on Mount Lookout has been destroyed, blown up. I can look out my window and see the smoke. You and I both know who did it, even if we can't prove a thing. Even if we don't dare say another thing. But Sea Breeze is off the air, dear lady. WHDM is off the air. I had always operated on a shoestring, and there's no way that I can recoup from this blow."

Ava moaned, a sympathetic sound.

"I fear it's a rogue wave for you too, my friend," B.B. continued. "Now, I have no doubt of Will Mattison's power. It is so far reaching that an honest investigation into Charley's death may never be possible."

"Yes," Ava sighed. "But I must keep doing whatever I can. Right now, however, the issue is You, dear friend. I'm responsible for getting you into this situation, so I need to know what I can do to help you through it."

"Oh, I'll make out," Bennack said, his voice hearty. "I always do." He made a small noise that might have been a sort of laugh: "I guess this brings new meaning to the old phrase, *It just goes with the Territory.*"

"We will stay in touch, B.B. I care about you, and you have been so generous to me. I cannot thank you enough, and now I wish I could undo all that has been done."

"Chin up, Fine Lady! Everything comes 'round."

And then Ava heard only the buzz of an empty phone line. She felt lost, utterly lost. Where could she go from here? Where might she find answers now?

Ava left her hotel room and went to sit on her favorite bench, looking at the harbor. She studied the crumbling old sugar mill, thinking of the stronger one that still held her son imprisoned. *Now is the time to free Charley from that jail*, she resolved.

Ava's mission was clear: she had to do it *now*, in retribution for all of Will Mattison's destructive deeds—hiding the facts of Charley's death, locking Charley in the sugar mill, and now blowing up B.B. Bennack's transmitter.

Then, as though she had willed it, as though she conjured him up, the Boardwalk Bum appeared.

"I heared yo on dat radio show," he said. "Yo soun' real good. I hope some good come of it."

"That hasn't happened so far," Ava said, making a sad face as she looked up at him.

The Boardwalk Bum returned her sad gaze, while patting his pockets, looking in his ammo belt, and finally hauling out a piece of bright green sea glass. "Maybe dis mek yo feel betta."

She took it without saying a word, pocketed it, looked up at the Boardwalk Bum with a tremulous smile.

"You need some time off from all yo troubles," he said. "I bet yo haven't even seen all dis islan' yet. I bet yo haven't lift up yo eyes unto our hills."

"Well, no, I guess I haven't done that," Ava admitted. "But what I most need now is some information. You seem to know a lot about what goes on here, so maybe you can help me."

The Boardwalk Bum shuffled his feet to show his discomfort.

"I want to find someone who can get something for me," Ava began.

The look on his face did not offer her much encouragement, but she persisted. "I want this to be done with no one learning—not ever—that the item I want has been taken. Would you know of such a person?"

The Boardwalk Bum nodded. "Like I say, Mom, lift up yo eyes to the hills. Hatuey live deh. Hatuey know many things. An' he know de man yo need to fin'."

With a wave of Boardwalk Bum's hand, a taxi appeared. "Bernard, dis nice lady need to go visit wit' Hatuey. But take her de pretty way. Show her our islan'."

Ava climbed into the cab. She gave no thought to her safety; that didn't seem like much of an issue. The mission was simply to free Charley from Mattison's sugar mill.

This cabbie, Bernard, seemed as silent as the one who had met her at the airport almost two weeks ago; he was nothing at all like the talkative one who had driven her to Iron Will's mansion.

Bernard followed the main highway to a road that led inland. He turned there, and the road began a steady climb into the mid-island hills. He turned at a sign pointing to a Scenic Drive.

A highway marker, Route 59, lay at an acute angle, almost in the dirt.

The road became a rutted trail. Grasses and tan-tan grew so high that Ava could see no vista at all. She began to feel panicky.

The taxi came to a dead end and stopped. "Yo might want to look aroun'," the cabbie said. Ava noticed stones, almost obscured, and got out of the taxi to investigate. She saw a battered sugar mill, still standing, though the top seemed to be caving in. She looked around for other structures, but nothing else stood. Tan-tan and vine ate at the last crumbled stones of an old plantation.

Ava stood a little straighter, inspired by the endurance of that mill. She turned, walked a few steps, and came to a cliff where the shrubbery had fallen away. She looked down a green hill and across a glade, to a hidden cove with a white sand beach. She imagined that she had found a paradise that no one knew existed. A paradise that even Iron Will could not defile.

After she returned to the taxi, Bernard followed one road and then another. Ava accepted his meanderings; she felt at peace, for the moment, in the hills.

After a while, they came to another sign, pointing up a narrow, winding road: *Devil's Backbone*. It appeared to be just that crooked, and that knobby. Ava imagined that the taxi bounced from one vertebra to the next along Satan's bent back.

Trees arched overhead; lianas dropped from branches forty feet above the road, down to a creek bed running beside the pot-holed tarmac. Here and there, huge termite nests bulged in the branches of towering trees. A great blue heron swooped across the road, alighting at the edge of a small marsh. Motionless, it stared into the water, awaiting prey.

Bernard drove on. He slowed, turning onto a rocky trail; he followed it for a mile or two. The lane ended at a frame bungalow built on piers, simple, but carefully tended. A man on the porch stood as Bernard braked the taxi to a stop.

Bernard got out and opened Ava's door. She stepped out beside him. The dark, stocky man on the porch ambled to meet them. "Good afternoon."

Ava said "Good afternoon" back to him.

"I am called Hatuey. The coconut grapevine told me to expect you. Welcome, Ava Collier." He held out his hand.

Ava suppressed a shudder. How could he know her name?

She looked into the man's unfathomable brown eyes. Deep lines crinkled the skin around those eyes and across the breadth of Hatuey's forehead. Soft curls sprouted behind a receding hairline, and a thin mustache ran into a bit of curling beard at the base of the man's chin. One hint of a smile twitched Hatuey's mouth as he shook Ava's hand with his stronger, broader one.

She hardly heard the taxi back away.

HATUEY'S STORY

The story of a grain of sugar is a whole lesson in political economy, in politics, and also in morality.

—Auguste Cuchin

DECEMBER 11

"Welcome," Hatuey said. "Welcome to my Lodge."

He watched Ava make a small smile. It seemed partly for him and partly for pleasure. Hatuey's deep, resonant voice had warmed her, and now he smiled too.

Ava groped for something to say but heard it come out trite: "This is beautiful country." She made a broad gesture then, as though to take in the trees, vines, hills, rocks—everything.

"I am glad that you came to enjoy this place with me with me." Hatuey's voice was deep, resonant, and confident, his tone sincere. "The land you stand upon has belonged to my people since the beginning of time." He took Ava's elbow, steering her onto a trail that led toward a small cluster of buildings.

"I don't know much of the history of these islands," Ava said as they walked.

"You would know more, if you had been here for my presentation on October 12."

"I guess I got here as fast as I could," Ava said, using a joke that Northerners often used, when they moved to Texas. "Was October 12 some sort of local holiday?"

Hatuey stopped walking. He turned to look at Ava as a teacher looks at a failing student. "We did not celebrate," he said sternly. "The Italians celebrated in New York City. The whole Catholic world celebrates that day, I think, in celebration of the vast opportunities that proceeded to them from that date. The Spanish and Portuguese could certainly celebrate, and perhaps the Danes. But we, who have always lived here, have no reason to rejoice on October 12, or commemorate that date.

"For us, October 12 is a day of mourning—a day of mourning and reflection. On that day, in the year now known as 1492, Christopher Columbus landed his ships at one of our islands."

"Yes," Ava answered. "Of course I know that Columbus discovered America. I guess I just wasn't thinking about how the October date applied here. Now, it seems to me that you have quite a story to tell about it."

"I do." Hatuey nodded solemnly, looking Ava in the eye. "But not now. Perhaps later I will tell you *our* story about that Columbus. The islands, that he thought *he* discovered, were ones that *we* had discovered, and settled, long, before that Italian navigator was born. Long before."

Hatuey drifted off in thought for a moment, then quickly said, "But first, of course, I should answer the question that brought you here. And even before that, you should have the opportunity to learn where you are." As he talked, Hatuey had steered Ava into a compound composed of half a dozen simple structures. "Would you like to look around this small piece of my land?"

Ava saw other buildings, half-hidden in tan-tan, and intriguing. "Yes," she said. "I would like a tour of your place, if you have the time to show me."

Again Hatuey half-frowned at her, teacher-like. "Time is not something that we own, or save, or spend, Ava Collier. Time simply *is*. We offer you a cabin in our lodge, for as long as you would like to stay. Our rates are quite reasonable. If you decide to spend the night with us, I will be happy to show you around tomorrow morning. If you choose not to do that, Bernard's cab will come back when you are ready, and return you to your fine hotel."

"No, don't call him. I would like to stay here." Ava took a step back, hearing her words, feeling that her tongue had betrayed her. But she did not take a second step back; she sensed that she was safe, and she wanted to believe that she was where she was supposed to be.

Ava slipped a hand in her pocket and grasped the shard of leaf-green sea glass that the Boardwalk Bum had given her. That had been little more than an hour ago, but now seemed somehow part of a time quite removed from the world where the taxi had deposited her. Ava had an odd sense that she had been lost, but now was found. She felt inexplicably cared for. And she frowned at herself for imagining that.

Hatuey's voice called her back to attention. "First, you should determine where you will sleep." Then the strange man, whom Ava had found so eloquent, surprised her by lapsing into island dialect: "Tek look 'roun' dem dwellin'." He made a vague gesture, encompassing a wide swath of land.

Ava would have liked to believe that Hatuey's change of dialect was a sign that he had accepted her. Her more suspicious mind suggested that the man was probably just going through a well-rehearsed sales routine, regularly aimed at gullible tourists. Since she had no way of determining which interpretation of Hatuey was the true one, she decided that it really did not matter.

"See which one o' dem habitat yo like de bes'," Hatuey continued. Then he pointed. "Up top o' de hill deh yo fin' showers an' de toilet. We get hot wadda from a solar thermal flat plate collector. It mek lotta hot wadda; we keep two eighty-gallon super-insulated tank full.

"Yo got runnin' wadda in yo cabin, a rechargeable lantern, and propane fo cookin' coffee an' what evah. But since yo didn' know yo was comin' to spen' de night, Ah 'magine yo don' have food. So yo can tek meals wit' me and my lady, if yo like."

"I would like that very much," Ava answered. "Thank you."

"I'll have de boy bring yo some bed linen an' towel when yo d'cide where yo wanna to sleep. He walk wit' a cooler o' ice, too. Now you go—go anywhere, poke aroun', den tell me what cabin yo decide on." Hatuey made a brushing-away gesture to get Ava moving.

She wandered past a few of the cottages. Each seemed somehow like a ship—a land ship that displayed the true craft of a master shipbuilder, more than mere carpentry.

A glimpse of grapevines on old stones drew her down the hill to an improvised habitat created within crumbling walls three feet thick. Its front porch served as a rudimentary kitchen and dining area. From the porch, Ava walked into a sort of sitting room that revealed the cabin's split-level design. Floor-to-ceiling windows led to a gallery.

Upstairs, Ava saw a broad, rustic bed. Its headboard, made of a polished slice of wood, followed the natural curve of the tree from which it had come. Small mahogany cabinets flanked the bed, and a soft mat of woven palm lay beside it.

Ava walked out onto the gallery, where a cathedral canopy of leaves filtered the waning sunlight. When she looked down, she discovered a colony of land tortoises foraging within a low stone enclosure.

"This is the one," she said aloud, believing that only the tortoises would hear her. But Hatuey's 'boy' had apparently followed her, with the promised bed linens. He placed them on the bed, neatly folded.

Ava set her purse atop the sheets, and then, when the boy had left her, she took a few moments to freshen up. She frowned and shook her head at her mirrored reflection—a remonstrance to the impulsive girl that she had somehow suddenly become. She had no change of clothes, no toothbrush, even. But then she laughed at her reflection, tossed her head, and headed back to the central grounds of Hatuey's lodge.

A young boy stood at a spit above glowing coals, slowly turning a whole hog. Ava sat down at a nearby table.

Soon a woman appeared, offering Ava a glass of cold water with a little ice. "Good night," she said.

Ava fought against looking at her watch as she responded, "Good night." It wasn't dark yet, and the phrase still seemed to her more a goodbye than a greeting. But since it seemed to be the island way, Ava tried to become accustomed to the strange wording.

"I'm Geena, Hatuey's wife," the woman said then. She stuck out her hand to Ava in the brash manner of a woman from the western U.S. Her wildly curling light brown hair framed a pale face dotted with dark freckles, and Geena had the slim, sinewy body of a long-distance runner.

Ava would have imagined a different sort of woman for Hatuey, and she scolded herself for that assumption. She should know, by now, that Dos Marias marriages were often multi-hued. Still, she could not help asking, "Where did you come from?"

"Berkeley," Geena answered. "But I've been here for five years now. I can't imagine ever leaving. This place grows on one, I think. I see that you've moved into the Schoolhouse Bungalow. That's a good choice for you."

Ava's eyebrows went up with surprise. First, because Geena presumed to know what Ava would like, and secondly, because of the bungalow's name. "That's what you call it?" she asked. "Schoolhouse Bungalow? I'd have thought Tortoise Town, or something like that."

Geena laughed in appreciation. "The Danes put up those stone walls in 1841, as one of the schoolhouses in the island's first school system. It's said that the building was the school for slaves, but I'm not certain of that."

She shrugged, letting the subject go, and then added, "The South American red-footed tortoises that you saw there are part of our successful captive-breeding program. Hatuey started that twenty years ago, way before my time here."

"Where did the tortoises come from to begin with?" Ava asked.

"Well," Geena answered, "some think that immigrants brought the tortoises here long, long ago. That could be true—but it could refer to earlier immigrants than most people imagine. Hatuey's ancestors arrived here by canoe, a long paddle up from South America. Doesn't it make sense that they would bring hearty food—like tortoises—along?"

Without waiting for Ava to answer, Geena continued, "However the turtles got here, I love them! They're mellow, friendly, slow moving and very curious. You might try feeding them hibiscus flowers, fruits, and vegetables. They'll love you for that."

Ava smiled. "And I think I'm going to love you for those luscious scents coming from the kitchen—if you're the cook."

Geena made a small shrug. "Everybody cooks here. Tonight, Claudio is responsible for the roast pig."

"From its size," Ava said, "I think you must be expecting quite a number of guests."

"Not tonight," Geena laughed. "We've only you, unless someone else happens by to surprise us. But high season is just around the corner. We do weekly pig roasts then, and sometimes the demand exceeds our supply. This fat hog is part of a plan to help us get ahead of the game.

"And right now—" Geena stood as she said it— "I'm the bartender. Perhaps you might like to try my famous five-rum tonic, soothing and deliciously spicy?" Without waiting for a response, Geena headed toward the bar.

Ava continued to sit at the picnic table, content to do nothing more than watch chickens chase invisible bugs. She thought that she glimpsed a peacock once but considered the idea incongruous, impossible. Tree frogs tuned up. And the sweet scent of innumerable trees surrounded her.

Ava felt quite certain that Will Mattison would never come to a place like this. She wondered if Charley and Maura ever had. She ached to think that her son might have missed such spots—little Edens that now seemed to Ava to hold the true essence of Dos Marias. She ached at not knowing more details of her son's life on this island. She ached from the realization that this "never-to-know" pain would remain an unshakeable part of her from now on.

Hatuey came, bearing a platter of sliced pork. The boy, Claudio, followed with a big bowl of something that looked like potato salad. Geena brought tomatoes, napkins and utensils. Hatuey raised the pork platter high.

> "Praise the Creator of all things.
> Bless the stewards of all things.
> May we be safe and may we be strong
> for the day that will come."

"Amen," Ava echoed, surprising herself with the appearance of a long-forgotten habit. They began to eat.

"Wonderful potato salad," Ava said after a while.

Geena laughed. "That's breadfruit you're eating. Glad you like it."

"You just go into the bush and pick this?"

"Of course! Breadfruit trees are among the easiest to spot, because of their broad, raggedy leaves. But I do cultivate a variety of other vegetables, using natural methods. We have traditional Caribbean root crops, leafy greens for salads and stir-fries, and ordinary things like cucumbers, tomatoes, okra, string beans, pumpkin, carrots, beets, peppers. And I grow my own herbs for cooking and for bush teas."

"Well!" Ava said. "I'm totally in awe—of both of you, and of what you have done with this place."

Hatuey shook his head. "It's not so much what we have done with the place, but what the place has done for us. The Taínos and Caribs called this island *Choreto,* meaning 'abundance' in their language, Arawak.

"I don't think I've ever heard of that language," Ava said.

"Most people think that," Hatuey agreed, "but you use Arawak words all the time. *Barbecus*, for example, is our word to name smoked meat. Our *hamaca* is a fine resting place—a swinging rope bed. We call our long boat *piragua*, and a small one *canoa*. You will recognize in those words the Cajun word *pirogue* and the more widely-used *canoe*. We named the sea cow *manati*, and the fierce tropical storm *hurakan*—your hurricane. There are many more examples, of course, but you get the idea.

"Our Choreto, our Island of Abundance, can be just as bountiful today, as it was in the time of naming these things. For example, our massive West Indian almond and mahogany trees provided the woodwork in your bungalow."

"And," Geena added, "I'm experimenting with tobacco, using seeds from plants we find growing wild, a holdover from colonial cultivation. Maybe someday we'll make our own cigars!"

Ava gasped. "How did you learn to do all this?"

Geena gave a self-deprecating shrug. "After Berkley, I joined up with CARE to do outreach work in sustainable hillside farming and soil conservation programs. When I came here, I soon realized that I'd have to adapt everything I had learned—the Caribbean climate, pests and soils are so different. I use plant association, crop rotations, mulching, terracing and composting."

Geena stopped, looking closely at Ava. "But I think I've given you much more than you need to hear right now. You must be tired."

Ava glanced at her watch. "Yes, I guess I *am* tired. And your school house cabin is luring me to that beautiful bed. Thank you, Hatuey, for a wonderful afternoon and evening. You are a superb host. And Geena, you are a gracious hostess!"

"Let me refill your drink, so you can take it to your room, Ava," Geena offered. "Or would you rather have something else?"

"I think I would enjoy another five rum punch," Ava smiled. "And maybe some water to take to my shelter?"

"It's already there."

Ava took the rum tonic and started down the dusky hill to her temporary home with the slow tortoises. She stripped out of her clothes and slipped between the sheets naked. She felt very natural, native, and, oddly, at home.

DECEMBER 12

Hatuey's conch shell horn woke Ava. That, and a glance at her surroundings, reminded her that she was in Choreto, the land of Abundance. Ava stretched; she smiled. She walked out to speak to her tortoises. She felt like Eve, about to explore Eden.

And she remembered that she was naked. Ava went back inside to pick up the clothes that she had thrown down beside the bed. After she put them on, she stepped into her sandals and started up the hill to Geena's kitchen.

Hatuey sat there, drinking bush tea. "We should get an early start," he said to Ava, "while the day is cool."

Geena set a plate before Ava—typical American bacon, eggs and toast. Ava raised an eyebrow and smiled up at her new friend.

Geena smiled back. "I still speak the kitchen language of Continentals, as well as that of Choreto." She added a soft chuckle.

Shortly after breakfast, Hatuey and Ava started down a path through the rainforest. From time to time, Hatuey snapped a twig or picked a berry to show to Ava. Once or twice, he stopped to dig out a root. Always, he named the specimens and told Ava something about them.

"Most of the plants here came from somewhere else—as did you and I. They came from Africa, India, Australia, South America, South East Asia, Malaysia, Java, and Madagascar. A few of the growing things are true natives—the calabash, white frangipani, kapok, ginger Thomas trees, cashew, papaya, sapodilla, manchineel, cordia, sea grape, and cabbage palm.

They live together in harmony—an example for the more mobile species, which are not always so skilled in getting along."

Hatuey winked, as though suggesting that he and Ava knew something about the difficulties of getting along with others.

A ferret-like fur ball dashed across the path in front of them. Watching that mongoose disappear into the brush, Ava asked, "Hatuey, what's the plural of mongoose? Is it mongooses or mongeese?"

"Nothing like that," Hatuey chuckled. "We say *two mongoose dem*. They're the reason we don't have snakes on this island."

Ava nodded. "I remember the Riki-Tiki-Tavi mongoose story. In the end, he gets the snake, doesn't he?"

"Indeed he does," Hatuey answered. "And you may get yours, as well."

Ava frowned. *How would Hatuey know that she was on a quest?*

As they walked on, Ava recognized the easy things—banana trees and coconut palms. Hatuey pointed out a mango—a tall, sturdy tree with graceful, slender leaves—and then a carambola.

"Carambola?" Ava questioned. "I thought that was the name of a golf resort over on St. Croix."

"Well of course it is," Hatuey laughed, as they walked on. "They named the resort for the tree. Its yellow fruits have longitudinal ridges, so when you cut cross sections, you get a star shape. Hence the name you probably know it by—star fruit. I suspect that Geena will throw some into your salad tonight."

Soon he stopped again. "Calabash tree. See the big round seedpods? They get made into bowls," Hatuey said. "The Latinos use them for maracas, a musical rattle. And some tourist shops sell ladies' small handbags made from calabash."

In a clearing large enough to allow a wide-spreading tree, they stopped beneath it. "Rain tree, you would say," Hatuey told her. "We call it *saman*."

Looking low as well as high, he pointed out a sweet potato vine, several hibiscus plants, and even a coffee bush with berries just beginning to turn red. As they hiked down a steep chute heavy with trees, Hatuey pointed out teaks and black olives and cacao trees.

Ava listened to a faraway call that Hatuey identified as a mangrove cuckoo. A nearer mournful cry, from a streambed, was the deep forest Barbary dove, he said. Ava told him that sound reminded her of South Texas.

"I hear that your South Texas also has fruit orchards," Hatuey replied. "Here, we've planted close to 250 fruit trees. We have soursop, genip, guavaberry and mesple—many varieties that most people from the Continent would not know. Some trees are giving us fruit already; over the next few years, we expect to have much more. On your way home, ask the taxi driver to stop where you can buy soursop ice cream. Soursop season is over now, but since the ice cream is our island specialty, the shop should still have some in the freezer."

Hatuey walked on, and Ava followed, listening to him. "Some people call the mesple tree 'naseberry'; others say 'sapodilla', which you might recognize." Ava just looked at him quizzically, so he continued. "That small brown fruit is one of the sweetest in these islands—and it only has two smooth, black seeds. Find one, take it in your hand, and just enjoy!"

"Sapodilla . . ." Ava struggled to make a connection. "I thought that had something to do with chewing gum, chicle."

"Yes! Of course!" Hatuey grinned at her like a teacher who was proud of his student. "Most Continental people just think of the sap, and not of the fruit. But good trees produce good things from many parts. You should remember that."

Hatuey's admonition seemed to hold yet one more hidden message that Ava could not fathom. They walked in silence for a while, before Hatuey said, "Everything comes around." He pointed straight ahead. "Here we are back where we started."

Geena had their lunch set out. When they had finished eating, Hatuey told Ava that he had work to do all afternoon.

"I'm sorry you have to work," she told him. "It feels like nap time to me; I find that I'm really tired. I guess your hilly terrain demanded too much from the calf muscles of a woman who's spent her life on a coastal plain."

Hatuey just chuckled, but Ava knew she'd need to pace herself here, and if she walked more tomorrow, she'd carry water along.

Ava undressed, rinsed out her underwear, and hung it to dry. Then, enjoying the freedom of nudity, she rested in her cabin, watching the tortoises. Two of Hatuey's sentences rang in her memory: *Good trees produce good things from many parts.* And *Everything comes around.* Ava felt that Hatuey had intended her to derive special meaning from those words, but she was too drowsy to think about them right now. She dozed . . .

And then it was dinnertime. Geena had prepared a fresh grilled tuna. With it, she served chayote. She had cut the mild, squash-like vegetable into thin slices and cooked it in butter with scallions and nutmeg. Just before serving, Geena added a sprinkle of cheese. And as Hatuey had promised, bright yellow carambola stars twinkled in Geena's salad of mixed field greens.

As they ate, Hatuey said, "It might be time for another history lesson, if you are interested."

"Everything here fascinates me, Hatuey," Ava said. "Even your name. Tell me about that."

His nod seemed almost a bow. "I have taken the name Hatuey to honor a great Carib leader at the time of the Invasion. And to demonstrate that our tribe is by no means extinct."

"Invasion?" Ava echoed. "You mean the Columbus thing?"

"No, after that," Hatuey said. "Columbus was nothing more than a temporary visitor. Later, many Europeans came—a full invasion of them. Their descendants may call that coming The

Conquest, but we never will. The Europeans committed terrible atrocities in these islands. They decimated our people." Hatuey paused.

"But they did not conquer us." He gave Ava an intent look, commanding her attention. "We were not the Europeans' only victims, of course. They also traded with unscrupulous Africans, buying human beings, ripping them from families, transporting them across the sea to serve as slaves.

"Some of those poor souls escaped. We took them in, mixed our blood with theirs and created a new race, the Garifuna or Black Caribs. You must understand the importance of this. Blacks have built this hemisphere as much as have the Whites, and in some important ways, they have contributed much more. Not only did they perform backbreaking labor, they brought cuisine and plants and language and costume and custom.

"And of course, nature being what it is, other blendings of blood occurred. Simone Beranger is a beautiful physical example of that, a testament to the fact that we are all one people. Our intermingled heritages are a thing that we honor— that all peoples, everywhere, should honor. None of us is purely one thing."

A chill ran through Ava. *How does this man know that I know Simone? Have I found a witchdoctor, or a seer, here in the brush? Or is Hatuey a part of a plot that Simone has orchestrated?* Ava shivered at a hint of foreboding.

Hatuey continued in his friendly, conversational tone. "Some of us have been here for so long that we think of ourselves as natives. How we got here is a tale best told under the stars. If you have finished your meal, let's walk over there, to the edge of that hill. Geena will bring us rum punch."

Geena's presence, and her punch, calmed Ava. She wanted to trust these people and this place. She wanted to learn the secret of their serenity, a quality that she knew she would need in the bleak years that lay before her.

Ava sat and listened to the silence, until Hatuey began to talk.

In the magical time before *if* became *is*, the People were always walking. When they reached shorelines, they made boats. With their boats and their walking, they made great migrations.

When the People arrived at new places, did they find the land empty? We do not know. Perhaps they encountered other People who had always been there.

Once upon a time, very long ago, a group of Caribs left mainland South America, heading north along the chain of tropical islands. Traveling in kayaks that held ten people or more, one generation followed another, moving up the archipelago. They traveled as slowly as snails, bringing with them only what they could not do without.

The first explorers traveled alone, without families. Those who arrived on this island found Taínos, who spoke Arawak, as they did. The Taínos had come from the same place, at an earlier time, and had named this island Choreto. The Caribs killed most of the Taíno men and married their women.

The settlement prospered. It got so large that a new village began, and then another, and another. In time, the People built a great many towns. Some of them liked living in the valleys, where they grew cotton and cane. Others liked living on the shore, where they caught fish and collected clams. Everyone liked the days of trading, when cloth might buy dolphin fish, or seashell jewelry might pay for pottery. Also, on these days, or for special observances, the People loved to gather by the shore for a kicking and bumping game with a huge, hard ball.

In time, all of the islands around here filled with a People who believed in a God that they called Yokahú. One day Yokahú came to visit a woman called Anakawna and her husband, a man called Huhaloó.

"Where are you, Huhaloó?" the god Yokahú said, looking right at the man.

Why does Yokahú, who knows everything, ask this question? He asks because he wants to examine Huhaloó, to determine Huhaloó's understanding of his role in the grand scheme of things.

What Yokahú is really asking is, "How far have you come along your road, Huhaloó?"

Huhaloó feels guilty right away. He realizes that Yokahú knows that he has done the one forbidden thing. He has eaten the fruit of the tree of the knowledge of good and evil. Now Huhaloó knows everything that Yokahú knows.

Or at least he thinks he knows it all.

"Well, Huhaloó," Yokahú says. "Since you are so smart now, there's no reason for you to stay in this perfect place. You must be feeling as cooped up as an animal in a cage, knowing that you have a whole world to explore out there. So go on—go on out from of Choreto. Learn all the aspects of having the knowledge of good and evil."

Well, after that heavy message, Huhaloó and Anakawna decide that it's time for a swim. They want to get a little bit weightless, you know. So they walk down to the perfect beach in that perfect paradise. They frolic in the waves for a while, trying to wash away the ominous feeling that came with Yokahú's words.

Huhaloó and Anakawna sit in the sand, and as it happens, because of the particular curve of that beach, and because in those days they had perfect and all-seeing eyes, just like God, Huhaloó and Anakawna can see all the way to Haiti, and all the way to the island of San Salvador. But of course, those were not the names of those islands then.

With their ability to see so far, Huhaloó and Anakawna look out across the sea and through the trees and around the mountains and into coves where three ships lie at anchor.

Those three ships are unlike any that the People had made in Huhaloó's perfect world. The three strange ships are as big as the islanders' largest piraguas. And these boats have something new and different—huge white wings that help them fly across the sea.

"We are seeing evil," Huhaloó says to Anakawna. "We are seeing the world beginning to change. I fear that Choreto may never be the same again."

Anakawna cries, "I want to go back to the way things were before."

Huhaloó takes her hand, and together they run back through the fruit trees and the food vines, and the crying birds. Running and running, they look for Yokahú. But Yokahú has gone from them, leaving them to fend for themselves, now that they have knowledge of good and of evil.

Anakawna weeps. Huhaloó comforts her. "I think that we have two choices," he says. "We can change with these changing times, or we can be satisfied as we are."

"You are right," Anakawna replies, "but either way, we risk disaster."

"That is the story, as I like to tell it," Hatuey concluded. "There are other versions, of course. Because we all have different knowledges of the Good and the Evil. But the history books agree on some things:

"It was only a matter of time until the ships with wings came closer to Choreto. They arrived first at Ay-Ay, an island with a name that evokes images of a river that then flowed, but flows no more, through the cleft of steep valleys. Columbus named it for the holy day on which he first saw it. That was the Feast Day of the Holy Cross—in Spanish, he said *Santa Cruz*. It was the French, later, who changed the name to their language. And now the people of the United States pronounce a strange combination: 'Saint Croy'." Hatuey said "saint" to rhyme with "ain't," and he made a face as he said it.

"Well," he continued after the digression, "Columbus' ships anchored in a deep estuary on Ay-Ay/Santa Cruz/Saint Croy. The estuary was not far from one of our ball courts. Twenty-five European sailors rowed ashore there.

Four of our men and two of our women jumped into a *canoa* and paddled out to see what was going on. A fight ensued. Our men killed one of the Spanish sailors and wounded another. Then Columbus' sailors rammed our *canoa* and overturned it.

"The invaders returned to their boat after that, and they told their Admiral Columbus what had happened. Later, he named that point of our land *Cabo de Flechas*, by which he meant 'Cape of the Arrows.' What a joke! Such subtlety in a name, to cover up their defeat.

"The people of Ay-Ay would have chosen a name that suggested victory, a name that would forever honor the place where we first showed those invaders that we did not want them. And maybe Columbus' name does that for us: We drove them away with our arrows!"

Hatuey's tone deepened then, and his face darkened. "That little skirmish was the beginning of a long, slow siege. We were then, as we are today, a loving people, but the invaders' acts of force and violence and oppression taught us to conceal our foods and our families. The invaders would not understand the meaning of our rituals—like eating the hearts of defeated rivals—so they called us cannibals. They used this misinterpretation as an excuse to drive us out, so that they could take our gold and silver, our land, and all of our resources.

"Throughout the islands of the Caribbean, people fled to the mountains to avoid attacks and beatings. The most powerful ruler of the islands saw his own wife raped. Many women suffered that fate. Mothers saw their babies smashed into the rocks. Wives heard soldiers betting as to who could split their husbands in two with one stroke of the sword, or spill out his entrails with a single jab of the pike. The invaders burned some of our people alive. From that time on, we sought for ways to throw those evil people out of our lands.

"But we contracted European diseases for which we had no defenses, and those diseases almost wiped us from the face of the earth. Many history books will tell you that the Europeans destroyed us all together, but you can see that this is far from true." Hatuey looked sharply at Ava, waiting for her to nod in understanding.

When she had done that, he continued. "What is true is that by 1901, only thirty-seven Carib families continued the old ways, living on the island of Dominica. And a few of us, on other islands, do what we can. Puerto Rico has an active group of people with Taíno blood.

"To this day, Yokahú continues to challenge us, as God challenges all people, with one simple question: *Where are you?*

"*Where are you, Hatuey?* He asks me. And I have to think how far I am along the journey of my life. I have to ask where and how I have strayed from my path, and what good I have accomplished.

"*Where are you, Geena?* God asks again, of this woman whose path has led her to be my wife, so far from the life to which she was born.

"Our war with the invaders will never be over. Because there is no way that the Europeans can give back the world that we have lost, the life that we have lost."

And my battle with Will Mattison will never be over, Ava thought. *Because there is no way that he can give back what I have lost, either.*

Hatuey read her musing. "The Great Soul asks you, Ava, *Where are you?* I know that you are on your path, most certainly. Seek your answers, and you will find them. *If* becomes *is*. *Is* becomes *if*."

He stood up. "Sleep well this night, Ava." And then Hatuey was gone.

Ava stirred in the middle of the night, believing that she heard bagpipes. That should seem strange to her, she thought, but now it didn't. Somehow, nothing seemed strange or out of place in Hatuey's world.

The bagpipes played *Amazing Grace.* Black voices sang along, and Ava recalled that those words had been written by a man who had once captained a slaving ship. Perhaps he had even brought slaves to this island.

"I once was lost, but now I'm found," the voices sang. As Ava had been lost, but now, somehow, was finding her way. Her Charley was lost still. But she would find a way to free him, too.

Good trees produce good things from many parts. Everything comes around.

DECEMBER 13

Ava awoke with the sun in her eyes. She started to stretch, then winced—her neck was stiff and sore. *I must have slept crooked,* she thought.

Coffee. The word, the idea, came into her mind as she picked up her clothes, now thoroughly soiled. She put them on with distaste, glad that at least she had rinsed her underwear clean.

"Coffee," she said aloud when she sat at the table, and Geena set a cup between her hands.

Ava rubbed her neck, complaining.

Geena said, "I can fix that," and reached into a brown paper bag. She pulled out a pale, knobby root, broke off a small spur of it, put it on her chopping block, and diced it into fine bits. She scooped the pieces onto the blade of her knife and tapped it in the center of a terry washcloth, arranging the dice in a line there. She folded the cloth pharmacist style, then popped it in her microwave and pressed the *one-minute* button.

That step startled Ava; the rest seemed so primitive, and the microwave seemed so out of place. But it was fast and efficient. All at once, scent told Ava what the chopped root was—ginger.

Geena wrapped the washcloth in a hand towel before offering it to Ava. "Be careful," she said. "It's very hot. Pull away the outer insulating layers of towel one at a time, as you are able to stand the heat, and as the cloth begins to cool."

Ava pressed the bundle to her neck and in no time at all, her pain eased. Some time later, when she happened to think of it again, she realized the soreness had left her entirely.

"What do you plan to do today?" Geena asked her. "Do you have specific things in mind, which you would like to see while you are here?"

"I want to smell, and hear, and feel," Ava answered. "I want to come upon surprises."

Geena laughed—a bird trill of a laugh. "Then you are definitely in the right place."

"Which direction should I head in?"

"Heed an ancient proverb," Geena advised. "*If you don't know where you're going, any road will take you there.* But if you go kinda catty-cornered from here, you should come to one of the old factories. You'll recognize its yellow brick, that came here as ballast in a ship. The factory will give you a starting and finishing point, so that you can get back here for my pumpkin soup at lunchtime."

It was Ava's turn to smile. "I'm certain that will lure me back promptly! But if I'm not here by dark, send someone to find me." She laughed, and Geena echoed.

Feeling freer and more relaxed than at any time on Dos Marias, Ava hiked farther than she had anticipated. She stopped then, fearful that she might have missed the ruins that Geena had described. Ava swatted at the no-see-um gnats that gnawed her ankles, and she reminded herself to carry bug spray the next time.

When she came to the ruins, she was surprised to see that they still stood tall, though a blurred keystone date seemed to suggest the late 1700s. Although the site covered considerable ground, no machinery remained—nothing to reveal what work had been done there. Just impressive walls, and mystery.

Ava found a trail behind the factory and followed it. Before long, she heard a humming sound, a drone, as of a faraway engine. She turned to look back at the factory. *No, impossible,* she thought—though nothing seemed impossible in Choreto. Here, even ghost machinery might run.

The drone persisted. Ava walked a few feet one way, and then another, until she localized the sound. It came from one old tree—a bee tree. Ava had found honey the way a Taíno would, or even an old Dane.

Ava recognized a mahogany tree, amused that its leaf pattern resembled that of the Texas pecan. *And why not?* she thought; pecan wood made beautiful furniture too.

Eventually she found her way back to the factory ruins, and from there to the Lodge. For lunch, Geena had prepared more than just pumpkin soup—and even that had been enriched with goat meat stewed into it. With the soup she served green banana *tostones*—a sort of fried chip—a tossed salad of greens and herbs from her garden, pan-roasted cassava bread, and a pitcher of bush tea.

They were just finishing the excellent meal when Ava startled at a loud crash behind her.

Hatuey laughed. "Jumbi walk," he said.

Ava made a face and looked around again.

"You know about Jumbies, don't you?" Hatuey asked. "The good spirits? No? They're part of African folklore. Any time we hear an unexplained noise in the *tan-tan*—in the bush—we say 'Jumbi walk,' meaning that those spirits are abroad."

"But what was this noise?" Ava asked. "I thought I heard a tree fall."

"Eggs-ackly," Hatuey laughed. "We're clearing a small piece of land. A tree came down. Yes, yes." He gave Ava that look that she could never understand.

"Lotta choppin' down happen in dis islan'," Hatuey said then, slipping fully in to DM dialect. "Alla time, from slave day to now, certain Big Rich White People believe dey have de right to chop down whatever get in dey way. Trees, people—whatevah get in dey way."

Ava frowned. "I think you're talking to me in some sort of code, Hatuey. "Please don't do that. I'm tired of games. If you are hinting that you know something about my quest, just tell me, straight out."

Hatuey nodded. "Well-chosen words, Ava. Words that I was wishing I might say to you. I have been waiting for the asking and the answering of our question."

He stirred his tea and sipped it.

Abashed, Ava sat silently, thinking how to begin. She made a grim movement with her lips, tasting already the words that felt so distasteful in her mouth. But she felt no hesitation in saying them to Hatuey. Because she trusted him.

"My son died here, on this island, seventeen days ago. He was married to Will Mattison's daughter, Maura. Will has told me that my son committed suicide, but I cannot believe that. I would like to learn the truth about my son's death."

"All Ah know," said Hatuey, studying a twig that he picked off the ground, "is dat de las' rat at de hole leave he tail out." He made a circle of his thumb and fingers and pushed the twig through it, then jiggled its end to simulate a tail.

Ava closed her eyes and shook her head in short twitches.

"That's an old proverb," Hatuey explained, dropping his patois. "It warns us to get out of a situation before it's too late."

Ava arched an eyebrow at the swarthy Carib. "Are you saying—to use a proverb of my people—that I should leave well enough alone? Is there a danger that I should know about? Or do you think that my son's murderer is going to get caught—with his tail hanging out of the hole?"

Ava stopped then, breathless, exhausted from saying so much, that was so difficult.

Then she said at last, "Hatuey, if a person wanted someone to steal something, and it was necessary that this be done with not one other person learning of the theft—not ever—could that be accomplished?"

Hatuey sipped his tea again. "The Person would have to tell more. One would need to know the value of the thing to be stolen, because that always affects the outcome. One would need to know the location of the prize, since that affects the planning. Then one would have to be acquainted with a person who would have the ability to get to the prize in its location. And some moneys would change hands, of course."

"Of course," Ava nodded, appreciating Hatuey's full abandonment of the patois, but still irritated by his evasions. "I do expect to pay for this service."

The two of them sipped their bush tea.

Looking straight ahead—not at Hatuey, not at the trees, not at anything—Ava said, "Will Mattison had my son cremated, and the ashes put in a golden urn. He put the urn in the old sugar mill at Estate Clary, and he had the door and windows barred. Now the time has come for me to get my son out of the jail where Will Mattison has locked him up."

Hatuey craned his neck, looked all around. Slowly. "People aroun' here know yo always gotta watch out fo' deh cowfoot woman."

Ava felt more puzzled than ever, and more than a bit irritated.

"Cowfoot woman," Hatuey explained, "is a bush jumbi who steals children."

"And in this situation, I'm the cowfoot woman?"

"Some might see it that way."

Ava nodded. "So you're warning me that some people on this island might become aware of my plan?"

"Around here, people say *What' don' meet yo, don' pass yo*. That means, there's not much you can do about what yo don' know."

Ava nodded. She meant it only as a sign of moving on. She did not mean to indicate that she understood, or agreed. "So, if I'm willing to take the risk of getting caught, is there someone who might be willing to help me?"

"Anole," Hatuey said.

Ava shook her head. "I don't understand."

"You need Anole."

Ava frowned. She'd come to the hills, to the rainforest, in a trusting frame of mind. Now, just when she thought she might find answers at last, Hatuey offered her nothing but the same vexation she often felt with island people.

"But what is a nole?" she said, letting the irritation show in her voice.

"There's *an* anole, right in front of you," Hatuey enunciated carefully and pointed at a lizard on a tree trunk.

"That gecko?" Ava said. She felt even more lost now, and more annoyed with the Taíno's manner.

"That is no gecko," Hatuey said, patient as a schoolteacher with a slow student. "Geckos have suction cup feet. Our native lizard is called an anole. He has tiny claws for gripping." Hatuey looked at Ava with an intensity that demanded her understanding.

But Ava only looked at him, puzzled, so Hatuey continued. "On this island, a certain man is also known as Anole. The man has the ability to climb like our native lizard. We value the grip of his strong claws."

Ava raised her eyebrows, and her voice lifted in expectation. "This Anole is a man who could reclaim Charley's ashes for me?"

"He could, beyond question," Hatuey said placidly. "And I think he might be willing to do that. But you will have to find him and ask him."

Grateful as she was to have some information at last, Ava still could not react to Hatuey's mysterious nature with amusement. "How do I find Anole?" she asked in a tone to show that she meant business now.

Hatuey sighed, but responded in the speech pattern of Continentals. "Go to the circle by the boardwalk, where all the taxi drivers wait for fares. Look for a pale green taxi. You know how all the taxi drivers have painted their taxis' names on the windshields?"

Hatuey stopped, waiting for Ava to nod. "On this pale green taxi, you will see the name 'Smoothest Ride.' You will go up and wish the driver good day, and then you will aks him if he is Regional Delaney."

"Are you saying Reginald?—R-e-g-i-n-a-l-d?" Ava asked.

"Could be," Hatuey responded pleasantly, adopting the island patois once more. "Could be Reginald, but his momma write R-e-g-i-o-n-a-l. When you aks dis man if he be *Regional*, if he say yes, yo say Ah sent yo. If he say no, yo say *t'ank yo* an' go away an' go back to try again anuddeh day."

"Then this project may take some time." Ava made a grim line of her mouth.

"Time takes time," Hatuey agreed. He smiled and nodded as he said it.

"But I am feeling eager to move on." Ava realized that she sounded like a petulant child as she said it; she felt that she was wasting time. And now she wanted to end an encounter that had been out of her control from the very beginning.

She found Geena, thanked her, and settled her bill. "Can you call me a taxi now?" she asked.

While Geena made the call, Ava walked back to the Schoolhouse Bungalow, said goodbye to the tortoises, and carried her purse and Geena's linens up to the main area.

By then, Ava had regained her composure. She found Hatuey, working at a woodpile. "Thank you," she said. "You are a remarkable man. I hope that we may meet again."

Hatuey shook her hand and gave her another of those long looks that Ava could not interpret. She turned, walked toward the road, and saw a taxi approaching.

Hatuey shouted to her. "One last t'ing! I almos' forget t' give yo dis. From yo frien'."

He caught up with Ava and placed in her open palm another piece of sea glass. This specimen was amber in color and again triangular, but so notched along the edges that it resembled a flint point.

Ava gripped it tightly, nodded a sort of "Thank you," and climbed into the taxi.

The cab retraced their previous route, passing once more the marshy area where Ava had seen the great blue heron. The bird was there again—or still. It stared intently into the water, poised to strike.

AVA'S STORY TWO

Patience.
The windmill never strays in search of the wind.

—Andy J. Skivlis

DECEMBER 13

Back in the comparatively commonplace world of Dos Marias, Ava Collier focused on the business of freeing her son.

She got her little rent car out of the parking lot and drove to a bank with an ATM. When she had secured the cash in her handbag, she drove to another parking lot, nearer the boardwalk. Once there, she walked to Paradise Burger, a café close to the taxi stand. Ava ordered a Presidente beer, a Texas Burger with jack cheese and sliced jalapeños, and tostados on the side. It bemused and comforted her to find a Texas treat on Dos Marias. She supposed that many of the St. Croix refinery workers hailed from her home state, and visited Dos Marias, creating a demand for their particular brand of comfort food.

While Ava waited for her meal to arrive, she watched the taxi stand. Most of the cabs that she observed, as she munched on her burger, bore blue or white paint. A pale green cab pulled away just as she got her order, but its name showed clearly: *Envy Me*. A shabby taxi carried the name *Hand 2 Mouth*. Then another green taxi arrived and parked at the curb. On it, Ava saw the name that she had been looking for—*Smoothest Ride*.

Ava counted out more than enough money to pay for her meal and a tip, set a salt shaker on the bills to keep them from blowing away, grabbed her purse and hurried toward the taxi circle.

A wiry old man sat at the wheel of *Smoothest Ride*.

"Mr. Delaney?" Ava asked.

"Good afternoon." The man tucked his chin down and pursed his lips, shaming Ava for once again forgetting island manners.

"Good afternoon," Ava echoed. "I'm wondering if you might be Regional Delaney. A friend of mine described a taxi like this and said that Regional was the driver."

"Regional is," the cabby nodded. "Who tol' yo to look fo' him?"

This wasn't going quite the way that Hatuey had described, but Ava decided to take the plunge. "My friend Hatuey told me that Regional Delaney, who owns a taxi like this one, could help me find a man that I am looking for."

"Hatuey say dat, do he?" the old man asked. "Well den, yo might as well stop standin' in de sun and get in heh. Ah be Regional. Sit in de front wit' me, if yo want to."

Ava opened the front passenger door and slid into the seat beside him. "Regional," she said, without indulging in more formalities, "I am looking for a man called Anole. Can you take me to him?"

"No, Ah cannot take yo to he, but Ah can take yo to a place where yo might find he. But den yo have to make yo own way back home. Ah couldn' be waitin' deh. Ah might lose too many fare."

"Oh," Ava assured him. "I would be happy to pay for all of your time."

"No," the dark cabby said with obvious concern. "Ah might lose too many fare if I be seen waitin' deh—fare fo' many a day."

Ava considered what that might mean, looked around, and glanced at her watch. There would be many hours of daylight still ahead. "Okay then, take me as far as you can, right now."

Regional looped his taxi through the narrow one-way streets of the historic Danish town and came out onto a somewhat broader road. He followed it to a sort of fishermen's village where he weaved his car between nets sunning in the street and over-turned battered skiffs receiving new bottom jobs.

Ava could not stop staring at Regional's neck, dark and wrinkled and moist like the brownies her mom had baked when she was a girl in Somerville, Texas. Ava felt embarrassed to be thinking that Regional's neck looked good enough to eat, but somehow she thought it did. And somehow, that communicated to Ava that this was a wholesome man, a man whom she could trust.

Regional drove across a narrow bridge and through a caliche parking lot. At the back of the lot, Ava saw a tipsy shack made of unfinished tree limbs. A rusty pipe guided smoke out through its palm and corrugated tin roof.

"Ah can see by de fire dat Paulus has started supper," Regional said. "Yo might get a good meal o' conch if yo want to wait aroun'. Yo might find Anole at a game o' domino in de back right corner o' dat shack. He won't aks how yo foun' him, and Ah don' want yo volunteerin' no information."

"Of course," Ava agreed. "I understand."

Regional reached across Ava to open her door, so that she got an even closer—and almost tempting—look at the man's chocolate brownie neck. "How much do I owe you?" she asked.

"Fi' dolla do it. When yo ready to leave, follow de road back 'cross de bridge and up a little hill. Yo fin' a marina behin' it, and some taxi deh to take yo home. Good luck to yo."

Ava fished from her purse enough money to cover the fee and a tip, and handed it to Regional. "Thank you. Thank you very much. And have a good day."

Ava stepped from the cab, even more filled with trepidation than when she had stepped into it. She approached the shanty with slow and hesitant steps. Dozens of chickens—hatchlings, pullets, hens, and roosters—scurried from her feet. A few lazy mixed-breed dogs moved sullenly, only a token inch or two out of her way.

Ava could not see into the dark shack. She took a deep breath, stepped inside, and waited for her eyes to adjust to the gloom. Gradually, she was able to make out three rickety card tables and an odd assortment of chairs. At the far right, in the back, four sets of eyes stared at her. The dark faces around those white eyes blended into the shadows of the shanty.

Ava cleared her throat. No eye blinked. "I ah," she began, and coughed a little. "Good afternoon."

Four voices chorused, "Good afternoon." Another voice echoed from behind her, somewhere near where the campfire smoke rose. The cook named Paulus, Ava supposed.

"Good afternoon," Ava said again. "I am wondering if one of you men might be Anole, or might know where I can find him."

"Who want to know dat?" a somewhat antagonistic voice said.

"Well, I ah, I am Ava Collier, and a friend of mine suggested that I should talk with Anole, about a problem that I have—ah, some business that I need to transact."

"An' who might yo frien' be?" another voice challenged.

"Hatuey sent me. Regional drove me." Ava hoped that her voice did not sound quarrelsome. Or frightened. And she most devoutly hoped that she had not betrayed her benefactors, Hatuey and the taxi driver.

"Dat Regional. He never will stay fo' a brew," an older voice cackled. "Yeh, yo foun' Anole. He de only one heh what ain't spoke yet. Yo and him betta walk down to he camp to do yo talkin'."

Ava's eyes had finally adjusted to the dark just enough for her to see a lithe young man rise and move toward her. Instinctively, Ava stepped back.

"C'mone," Anole said with a slight jerk of his head.

Ava followed Anole out of the shanty and along a rutted caliche trail. The man had his hair done up in dreadlocks—short, spiky ones. *A punk rock Rasta?* Ava wondered.

Anole turned right, onto a faint path between flamboyant trees now without their brilliant red blooms. Seedpods clacked in the breeze, and the lacy leaves of the trees half-masked the crudest, simplest camp that Ava had ever seen.

The site was pretty, at the crook of a meandering lagoon, but Anole had nothing more than two scraps of lumber, nailed between trees, to serve as a table. Ava saw a scattering of rusty pots and dented cans beside a small, battered shipping crate that might be the boy's sleeping quarters. A one-gallon cooking oil can held a seedling hibiscus. That was all, except for some garbage.

"Yo can sit," Anole said, pointing to a five-gallon cooking oil can. He dropped abruptly into a yogi position on the sand and cocked his head at Ava. "Hatuey say dey sump'in' Ah might do fo' yo?"

Ava nodded. "I am looking for a man who would be willing to steal something that was taken from me. Although this item is very precious to me, it has no value to anyone else. If you are the man for this job, you need to understand that you may be at some risk in trying to retrieve this thing that I love."

"Somebody else don' want yo have dis t'ing what b'long to yo? Who be dat somebody?"

Ava took a deep breath and looked Anole square in the eye. "Will Mattison."

"Aw, man!" Anole seemed to make a sort of sideways hop, like his namesake lizard. "An' I guess dis t'ing yo want be at Estate Clary, too?"

"Yes," Ava nodded. "It is." At the look in Anole's eyes, she added quickly: "But not in the big house. Just out on the property."

"Yeh, well." Anole ran a spike-nailed finger along the length of the side of his nose. Then he scratched his head, first behind his right ear, and then across the top.

"Heh how we go 'bout it," Anole said finally. "Yo tell me eggs-ackly wheh to go. Ah go an' look. Ah figure it out. If Ah haf to go a second time to figure mo', yo pay mo'. After Ah figure it out, Ah meet wit' yo agin. We set up de whole plan. Dat sound copasetic?"

The closing word startled Ava—a word that her grandfather had used, after his service in World War II. "We've got a plan," she said to Anole. "Shall I pay you something now?"

Anole shook his head side to side. "Ah wanna look fust, my own look, no obligin'. Den Ah tell yo what yo owe an' when. Now—where eggs-ackly be Ah goin'?"

Ava described Estate Clary and the sugar mill's location, about a half-mile from the main house. She described the bars bolted across the mill's windows and door, and the placement of the urn. "That urn is what I want you to bring to me," she said.

Anole shook his head. "Ah spec Ah fin' mo' den bars holdin' in dat t'ing now." He rubbed his hand across his mouth. "Tell yo what. Yo go home an' wait. Yo don' try get a-holda me no how. Ah'll find yo when Ah'm ready. Won't be long."

Anole popped up to a standing position. "Now, yo folla dat path like yo was continuin' on, not goin' back de way we come. De road make a loop. Yo won' have no trouble findin' de bridge, or de hill, or de marina where yo can get a ride back to whateva fancy home yo come from. Go on along now, 'cause Ah got a domino game waitin'."

DECEMBER 15

Two nights later, when Ava still had heard nothing from Anole, she fidgeted. She itched with impatience for resolution; she longed for a break from the tedium of waiting. She ached from the tension of imagining where Anole might be and what he might be doing. She called Craig Buchanan, told him about Hatuey and how that meeting had let her to Anole.

"What a woman!" Craig said. "I'm proud of you, Ava. I don't know how you accomplished all that, but I sure do admire you for it. Can I pick you up around six and take you to dinner?"

"I'd love to see you, but we could just eat here, on the Boardwalk."

"No," Craig said. "You need a change of atmosphere. I'm treating you to some authentic French cuisine—at Restaurant Niçoise."

Craig drove Ava to the far side of the island, where he said that most of the working-class people lived. Seeing the shabby surroundings, Ava was inclined to feel uneasy about the quality of their meal, but she needn't have worried.

The restaurant owner greeted them. "Craig," she said, with a strong Gallic accent, "it is so nice to see you again. And who is this lovely woman you have?" The sixty-something restaurateur looked Ava up and down, then smiled. "I am Marie," she said.

"*Enchante*," Ava responded, hoping to please her. "*Ma appelle Ava.*"

"Ah, *Madame,* for your words in my French language, I will lead you to my best table."

Ava and Craig followed Marie past an antique mahogany bar and down a few steps to a flagstone patio. Framed posters—Moulin Rouge, the Eiffel tower, a sunset at Nice—decorated the walls. Candles flickered on the tables. Ava and Craig sat on wrought iron chairs, beside a fountain. Recorded French tunes, featuring an accordion, played in the background. "Bring us a bottle of very good red wine," Craig directed.

"*Mais oui.*"

When Marie had left them, Ava said, "I continue to be amazed by the cultural blend here. I had no idea that Dos Marias held a restaurant so authentically French."

"But of course," Craig said, echoing Marie's intonation. He laughed, then returned to his Midwestern accent and continued. "Marie and her husband opened this place some thirty years ago, and I'm told that it was an instant success. Marie is a widow now, but she found a good chef, and with her charm as hostess, the restaurant's popularity continues."

Craig raised an index finger. "I just had a thought! There's a French plantation over on St. Croix that you would enjoy, called Whim. I go there for the music, because they bring in excellent classical musicians from the continent—from several continents, actually. The audience sits in a stone room, where a huge chandelier and some wall sconces glimmer with beeswax candles. *No* electricity is used at all, except for one small light on the piano. You feel like you're going back in time—hearing the music of that time, in a room built during that time. It's pure magic."

Marie returned with the wine, interrupting Craig's reverie. He ordered two onion soups. Ava took one sip of the wine and found it excellent.

After a few more sips of wine, and attendant casual conversation, Ava asked Craig what had been going on in his life.

"Not a whole lot," he said. "Just business. I do have one piece of information for you—but it's not a good one, dammit."

"Well," Ava said, "I guess we have to take the bitter with the better, as they say. Maybe *any* information is better than *no* information. What have you learned?"

Craig leaned forward, a grim look on his face. "We have proof positive that Byron went straight to the Casino after he and Charley and the other guys split up on the night that Charley died. Casino Security keeps an accounting of everyone who comes in and out the door. Byron was hanging around Donalee's cashier booth from about ten p.m. until the Casino closed at two a.m. So Byron couldn't be the one who shot Charley."

Ava exhaled a sigh like all the wind going out of an inflatable dingy. "So now what?" She shook her head.

"I don't know," Craig said. "If we'd found that tape, we'd know how many voices were on it, and we might be able to identify them all."

"Yes," Ava agreed. "We've been assuming that Byron's voice was there, but if not, it may be that my son—." Her voice had weakened; she could not finish speaking the awful thought.

Craig saw Ava shudder. He reached out a hand to her shoulder. "I'm working on this, Ava. I promise you that I am. Don't torture yourself with things that *are not true*." Craig took her hand, and his eyes begged hers to believe.

Ava looked down and away. "I know, I know." She took a deep swallow from her wine glass.

"Just hold on, until we have the facts," Craig admonished her, and then sought for another topic. "What have you been doing? Have you found some way to occupy your time and your thoughts?"

"Someone suggested that I'd enjoy a look at the rainforest," Ava said, "so I had a taxi take me there. I met the strangest couple, at a place that does pig roasts."

Craig grinned. "Durn it, I should have thought to take you there myself! Hatuey and Geena are famous around here. Did you enjoy your visit with them?"

"Yes, I stayed overnight—two nights, actually. Hatuey has interesting stories to tell."

Ava did not intend to say anything more about it, so she was relieved when one of the bus boys walked up to her.

"Mrs. Collier?" he said. "Domino." He pressed something into Ava's palm—something about the size of a domino, but irregular in shape. Ava knew that it had to be a piece of sea glass, and she guessed that it was a message from Anole.

She slipped it into her purse quickly, but not before arousing Craig's curiosity.

"What was that?" he asked.

Ava shook her head. "Nothing. Maybe something we can talk about later."

She didn't want Craig to know about her meeting with Anole; that was her business, and hers alone. If any adverse outfall resulted from the contract she had made with Anole, Craig should not be implicated.

Ava assumed that the sea glass, and the words with which it was given, meant that she was to meet Anole again at the domino shack. She assumed that she was not expected right away, but on some other evening, soon. She would keep this night for relaxation, and she needed that. She suspected that another stressful day awaited her.

Ava took a sip of her soup. "Excellent! I could make an entire meal of just this. Shall we just put my quest on the back burner?"

DECEMBER 16

Ava did not look at the sea glass until the next morning. It was dark blue, and it might have been a narrow triangle, except that the apex was missing. Without that point, the shape seemed to resemble a sugar mill, Ava thought. She toyed with it, toyed with interpretations, and spent the day in utter frustration.

At last, as the sun dropped toward the horizon, Ava headed for Anole's lagoon. She crossed the bridge and stopped her car not far from the domino shack.

Anole popped out from nowhere. "Cool ride, Mom!" he said. "Take me somewheh!" The boy jumped in without waiting for an invitation or even an okay.

"Drive anywheh yo wan', jus' not too touristy," Anole directed. "Drive west maybe, or central. In de country. Jus' win' aroun'. Yo can't get lost 'cause Ah'll get yo home. Dis be a good way fo' us to talk."

So Ava drove—a bit nervously—as Anole reported on his survey. She concentrated, hard, trying to catch the meaning of every word.

"It not hard to get to dat mill. Ah come by wattah, quiet boat. Mistah Will t'ink highly o' dat gol' vase t'ing. He put Plexiglas or like in all de window, and inside de bars at the door. Ah t'ink it not to keep me out, but to keep bird from getting' in and shittin' on de vase, yo know? O' bat, maybe. Bat guano shuh stink.

"But de good news be, Mistah Will put wood on de top o' de mill. Mon, dat s'prise me! Mos' folk jus' got de rock, yo know? Just de ol' rock wall o' de mill. But dat Iron Will done it right. He put in de paddle, an' what look like de box what hol' de paddle."

Ava took her eyes from the road to turn her head and look at Anole quizzically. As hard as she'd struggled to interpret the boy's accent, now his words themselves confused her.

"Paddle?" she asked.

"Yeah, Mom. Paddle." Anole raised his right hand, the fingers splayed and the thumb tucked into his palm, and then he rotated his hand a bit. "Fo' fan blade, yo might call it. Wood t'ing on de top o' de mill hol' dem blade what catch de breeze an' turn de grind what mash de cane."

He said it singsong, bouncing in his seat. Settling down, Anole said, "An' dem paddle *big* . . . BIG!" He popped his eyes, to indicate how large. "Dem paddle almos' touch de groun'. Sump'in' to look at, Miz Collier. Yo oughta go see."

"I've already been there," Ava said simply. She did not need to explain to this boy.

Anole hopped and turned in his seat, peered out the window, and then continued. "Dem paddle don' turn. Will didn' make 'em to, an' dis boy be glad. Mattison make my job easiah, not hard. No machinery at top, far as Ah can see, an' no cloth on de paddle, just dey ribbin'. So de win' can't mek 'em turn—not even a big blow! But wit' wood all 'roun' up deh, Ah know Ah can get in."

He twisted sideways in the car seat. "Ah b'lieve it be safer go in t'ru de top. Not likely anybody look up dat high. An' anyway, Ah like to climb, yo know." Anole cocked his head and gave a boyish grin that did not inspire Ava's confidence.

"Ah gotta climb up dat sugah mill fo' to see how to get in t'ru de wood. Gotta see how to get it open. You will pay me fo' dat. Den yo will pay me fo' de supply Ah decide Ah need. An' yo pay me de las when Ah put dat vase in yo han'."

"No," Ava said. "I don't want the urn. The urn—the vase—must stay where it is. I want Will Mattison always to be able to look at that urn in full confidence that it's just as he left it."

Anole's eyes widened. "You don' want dat gold urn? Dat t'ing wo'th lotta money, Mom!"

"What's in it is worth much more to me," Ava said. "I just want you to bring me what's *in* the urn. If you take the urn, our deal is off, and I will turn you in to the authorities as a thief."

Ava paused, her eyes firmly meeting Anole's wide-eyed stare. "Take a plastic bag with you," Ava instructed. "A gallon-sized zip bag, I'd say. Empty the contents of the urn into the bag, being very careful not to spill a thing. Be *very* careful. Treat the contents with respect, the way you would treat your mother or your best girl friend."

"How heavy dis bag be, when I get it, Mom?"

Ava paused, remembering those few precious moments at the funeral, when she had held Charley's urn in her hands. She made a quick calculation. "Your plastic bag will weigh about six pounds, I would guess," Ava said. "Maybe the weight of a newborn baby. Handle that bag as carefully as you would handle a baby."

Ava paused a moment, then added, "Come to think of it, I want you to refill the urn with sand or something, so that it weighs about the same. Just in case somebody picks it up later on."

"Well, firs' t'ing firs', Mom. One t'ing atta time. We ain' up deh yet. Right now, Ah need yo firs' payment. My hazard pay, yo know, fo' climbin' up deh an' lookin'. Den we get togeddeh to work out de full plan."

He watched Ava nod, and his eyes brightened. "Hey! Yo like de way Ah sent yo de message 'bout meetin'? Yo pretty cool, figurin' dat out. Nex' time Ah may do it diffrent, doh."

"When do you plan to make your survey?" Ava asked.

"When Iron Will ain' home!" Anole laughed, craning his neck upward, displaying a large Adam's apple. "Ah been aksin' 'bout dat. Yo know Jump-Up? Dat be tomorra night.

"Iron Will be in town den—he got a big do at dis Jump-Up. Means Ah can do my checkout den. No moon dat night, too!" Anole laughed again.

"Afta dat, mo' plannin', and Ah pick up yo treasure de night o' Coterie."

Ava had no idea what Jump-Up might be, or Coterie, but she assumed that Craig could explain them to her.

Anole looked around, pointing out landmarks to Ava. "Yo know where yo be? Yo know how get home from heh? Good. Den Ah be gone. Bye."

With that, Anole was out of Ava's car and out of sight. She blinked. She looked around, and at last recognized a green and yellow striped tavern that she had seen before. It marked a turn toward a shopping center, and from there, she would be on a familiar drive home.

DECEMBER 17

Right after breakfast, Ava called Craig and asked if they might go to the Jump-Up together.

"What a wonderful idea!" he laughed. "You keep thinking of things that I should have thought of myself. But how did you hear about Jump-Up? And do you know what Jump-Up is?"

"B.B. Bennack mentioned it to me," Ava said—a small white lie. "And no, I don't know much about it, but I became curious. And then I thought I would enjoy it more if you would go with me."

"Of course!" Craig responded. "I wouldn't want you there alone, in any case."

Ava thought that he sounded like a concerned and dutiful son. Then Craig's tone lightened: "What if I told you that Jump-up is a pagan festival involving men fifteen feet tall and the slaughter of baby goats in the streets?"

"I'd hope you were teasing me," Ava replied.

"Well, I *was* joking about the baby goats, though I'm pretty sure that at least one booth will be selling stew goat," Craig said. "And I can guarantee that you *will* see Mocko Jumbies—lots of them, and all very tall."

Ava raised her eyebrows. "When I visited Hatuey in the rainforest, he said something about Jumbies—*Jumbi walk*, I think. Is this what he was talking about?"

"Hatuey may have been referring to the historic Jumbies that Africans believe in," Craig answered. "You won't see them—and probably no one else ever does, either! The Mocko Jumbies at

Jump-Up are men and boys in costume, but they're awesome enough."

"And are they really fifteen feet tall?" Ava asked.

"Tall," Craig hedged. "Varying, I guess. They're on stilts and in costume. You'll see."

"Everybody does this?" Ava's voice showed her doubts.

"Oh, no," Craig responded. "You have to be *trained* to be a Mocko Jumbi. They practice on a regular schedule, to keep up the skill. The ones you'll see are a semi-professional part of Jump-Up, which is a street festival designed to boost the local economy. Our Mocko Jumbies serve as a lure for tourists and Continentals. Shops stay open late, with good bargains. Steel pan and other bands play on almost every corner that doesn't have someone hawking local foods. And then the Mocko Jumbies come stalking down the streets."

"That really does sound too good to miss," Ava said, smiling. "Does the date have any significance?"

"Not that I know of, but considering the season, I guess you could call it our answer to the Macy's parade in New York City. The festival gets everyone in the Christmas shopping spirit."

"Don't say the 'C' word." Ava turned instantly somber. "I don't want to think about the holidays!"

"Of course," Craig responded. "I do understand your feelings. We'll just focus on Jump-Up as a crazy island event. This one, every year, launches the Debutante Season on Dos Marias."

"You have *debutantes* on this island?" The implausible idea lifted Ava's thoughts away from her serious concerns.

"*They* do," Craig corrected. "The old settler families, and some of the new rich. They do debutante-ing up big, island style. There'll be nothing in it to trigger painful memories for you."

But every day does that, Ava thought, though she did not speak the words aloud.

Craig held the silent phone to his ear for some moments. He made his voice cheerful when he spoke again: "This Jump-Up may be bigger than usual. You know that block behind the wUnderWorld dive shop? The one where everything around it was closed up?"

"I didn't notice."

"Will Mattison bought the whole block, had some refurbishing done, and got his agents busy leasing space to shop keepers and other enterprises. According to the newspaper, he'll be at the gala opening of the Mattison Mini-Mall during Jump-Up. It's a thing very unlike Mattison, who ordinarily avoids the common throng."

"Good strategy," Ava said, and then bit her tongue. She hoped Craig would think that she had meant that Mattison had planned well, but Ava was thinking of Anole's wisdom in choosing that date to break into the sugar mill. He seemed somehow too bright a boy to be living in a packing case.

"So we're going?" Craig prodded.

"Oh, yes!" Ava agreed. "What time should I be ready?"

"I'll meet you at your hotel no later than five o'clock," Craig told her. "There'll be such a crowd that I'll have a hard time finding a parking place even that early. Wear good walking shoes. And be sure you have plenty of money!" he laughed.

Craig circled many blocks before finding a parking spot for his truck. He walked past darkened office buildings on the way to Ava's hotel and the bright lights and happy noise of Jump-Up. Ava waited for him in the hotel lobby and stood when he entered, ready to head out onto the street. They heard the steel pans before they saw them: Some thirty children, in their madras plaid school uniforms, played *Amazing Grace*.

"That's not the kind of music that I expected to hear on steel pan," Ava said, surprised.

Craig chuckled, "I guess the teacher doesn't want the kiddies playing *Red, Red Wine*. In any case, you'll hear a lot of variety tonight. But right now, let's see if we can find the Road Kill girl. She always sets up her booth a block or so from here."

"Road kill?" Ava made a face, somewhere between perplexed and disgusted.

Craig laughed. "Road Kill is a very popular hot dog stand." He pointed ahead, toward a long waiting line near a push cart beneath an umbrella. Ava recognized some of Charley's friends there—Ken and Sandi Leland, Rick Rowland and Brooke Randolph. A little off to one side, B.B. Bennack licked mustard from his greasy fingertips. A petite East Indian woman—presumably his wife—dabbed at more mustard on the front of his shirt.

"I should have told you another of our island truisms," Craig chuckled. "Always pay attention to whom you meet on this island, because you'll always see them again, and sometimes in the most unexpected circumstances."

The friends greeted them with hugs and laughter. Sandi showed off a gold bangle bracelet that she'd just purchased for less than half the usual price. Bennack told them that he was on his way to handle the DJ responsibilities at a corner music spot.

"That's just for kicks," he explained. "I'm working on a new deal, something really big. In the meantime, this keeps me in the public eye. That's important in my business, you know."

Ava offered B.B. her congratulations—hoping that the 'new deal' was something real and not a vanity excuse.

Craig was still in the Road Kill line, so Ava drifted away, looking for something to drink. For a second, she thought she saw Geena, but before she could determine if Hatuey was with her, Ava lost the woman in the crowd. Ava passed up a Painkillers booth and found beers, then walked back to Road Kill, where Craig still had not made it to the front of the line.

When finally they had their grilled bratwursts with sauerkraut—and chili, Ava had insisted—they ambled past booths selling East Indian rotis, Spanish-inspired sauces and

African-like handicrafts. Next to the History Alliance booth, an impassioned group urged passers-by to Stomp Out Domestic Violence.

Yes! Ava thought, then she shook her head in self-reprimand. Everything here seemed to have meaning, to speak to her too personally. Even the ironies.

She turned her attention to street bands that offered blues, jazz, calypso. At one wide intersection, two men stood opposite each other. At right angles to them, two women stood. Near the two couples, musicians tuned up.

"This looks something like a Texas square dance!" Delighted surprise animated Ava's voice. "But we have one *couple* on each side of the square, not just one person."

"This Quadrille and your square dance probably share a common root," Craig answered. "Quadrille was the name of a dance that began in France in the late 1700s. Since it was much livelier than the minuet, the dance soon became the rage all over Europe."

"Craig," Ava laughed, "you are just a walking encyclopedia on more things than I could have imagined."

He shrugged. "It was the music that got me interested. I'm into all kinds of music, as I've told you. When I started looking into that, I learned about the dancers and all."

"So tell me more about the music," Ava prodded him.

"It's known as Quelbe, and the musicians are called a 'scratch band.' Apparently, that strange term came about because the early musicians had gourd instruments that they played by scratching them. Now guitars, flutes, and saxophones supplement old-time banjos and conga drums. I've even seen such creative innovations as automobile exhaust pipes! It's all part of the resourceful Quelbe tradition.

"See the guy by the microphone? He's the floor master—you Texans would consider him a square dance caller. The floor master is an essential member of the Quadrille group, because he gives the dancers and the musicians their spirit. The more dynamic the floor master, the more animated the dancers become."

Ava nodded. "The women's plaid dresses—and those head scarves—are pretty spirited too."

"My wife, Janice, got interested in that, when she was here," Craig said. "She is very into fashion and clothing design. So she told me that's not just any plaid, it's Madrás, brought to the Caribbean from India around the 19th century. It's a hand-woven cotton fabric that's soft and light, and that makes it ideal for the island climate. The Madrás head ties became a traditional part of Caribbean attire. Ladies always wore them to Quadrille dances and the Sunday market."

"The head scarves aren't all tied in the same way," Ava observed. "I suppose that has a story too?"

"Oh, yeah," Craig nodded. "Janice told me that a head wrap with one point extended means that the girl is free and interested. Two points show that she's engaged, but a daring young man could still try to attract her. Three points indicate that the girl is taken, but four points mean she's available!"

"How delightful—but confusing!" Ava laughed. Then the laughter itself turned her solemn once more. She wondered if Charley had ever attended a Jump-Up. He'd told her that Will Mattison avoided the common throng, so now Ava speculated that Charley had been pressured to do the same.

Ava tried to shake the thoughts away with a quick jerk of her head. There was too much she never know about her son's life on Dos Marias. Each time she discovered a new element, she had to struggle to put it behind her.

Ava walked away from the square dancers, looking for another distraction. She saw a booth offering fancy scented soaps in the shape of hibiscus blooms, palm trees, and mermaids. She noticed a glass blower, and behind him, in a closed display case, she saw what must have been his prime work of art: A coral reef, measuring several feet in each dimension, holding a wide variety of colorful blown-glass fish.

At the next corner, Craig and Ava spotted the approaching Mocko Jumbies. Crowds cleared the center of the intersection to make room for a troupe of the most unlikely characters that Ava had ever seen.

The shortest of them towered five or six feet above her head, and that Jumbi's head only came up to the waist of the tallest one. Unadorned boards formed the lowest part of their stilts, ending with small rubber pads to grip the pavement. Baggy pantaloons hid the upper section of the stilts and the walkers' real feet. Very short skirts, over the pantaloons, further amplified the effect of extremely long legs. The blouse of each outfit seemed an old-fashioned school-marm's bodice, and its long sleeves and gloves hid any hint of skin. Every dancer had swathed his face with cloth, leaving eyeholes; a few had mouth holes, too. A tall peaked hat, broad-brimmed, topped each head; feathers at the tip of the hat further extended the illusion of the dancers' overall height.

"Tell me about this," Ava said softly to Craig.

"I read up on it, just for you," he grinned. "We are watching a living African art form traceable to the 1200s, but probably much older. As I think you know, *Jumbi* is a West African term for a certain kind of 'spirit'—a very large one. The Jumbies' height represented the power and greatness of God. Their elevated vantage point allowed the good Jumbies to see evil spirits approaching African villages from afar. The Jumbies had plenty of time to warn the residents, and with their supernatural powers, they kept those evil spirits away.

"The stilt walker tradition emerged—members of the village, protecting their anonymity with masks and traditional clothing. As ersatz Jumbies, *mock* Jumbies, they moved through the dark African night, emulating the real Jumbi spirits, and striking terror in the hearts of those who had done wrong.

"Enslaved Africans, transported to the Caribbean, brought their religious traditions and observances with them—including the Jumbi and Mocko Jumbi. When European slave masters forbade those practices, the Africans transformed their rituals into a festive context, creating an effective disguise. But most islanders of African descent still respect the true religious meaning of Jumbies and Mocko-Jumbies alike.

"Oh! Look!" Ava's astonishment at the Mocko Jumbies' acrobatics interrupted Craig's talk. She'd watched the dancers' rhythmic gyrations as Craig explained their history. She'd seen the Jumbies form a line, grasping each other's shoulders.

And now a Jumbi extended one of his stilt legs high over his head. Another Jumbi performed a backbend, arching so low that the feathers of his hat almost brushed the ground.

"Imagine doing that on stilts—how high?" Ava asked.

"Ten feet, and sometimes more, I think," Craig answered. "It's an awesome art, isn't it!"

"Awesome, indeed," Ava agreed. Then the Jumbies' antics turned her thoughts to Anole's gymnastics and high reach, practiced at this very moment, some miles away.

As the Mocko Jumbies worked their way on down the street, Will Mattison strode into the intersection that they had vacated. He appeared, for once in his life, small and insignificant by comparison. Mattison stepped to the podium and began to speak the self-congratulatory words appropriate to his stature.

If he only knew, thought Ava. But she fervently hoped that Mattison would never know what happened on his property that night.

On the far side of the island, Anole trudged through the mangrove, toting a five horsepower outboard motor. He always kept a small boat and paddles near his lagoon campsite, but for this sugar mill job, he'd borrowed a motor. That would make the job faster, and not tire him out. He'd need his strength for the climb. Two climbs—one up, one down. And then two more climbs, on the next trip.

Anole stopped just short of the shore, waiting until the night was full dark. Then he eased into the boat and bolted his motor to the stern. Then he yanked the starter rope on the motor. It purred like a kitten. Anole guided his boat through the lagoon to its narrow neck, then under the bridge leading to the domino shack. Past that, his boat slipped through the night-blue water of the Caribbean with no sound louder than a soft purr. Anole turned right, following a familiar route that all fishermen used to get to the bonefish flats. He passed a particular point of land, turned right again, and shut the motor down.

As the forward motion of his boat slowed, Anole reached for an oar beneath his feet. He paddled his silent way to a tiny cup of hidden cove on the shore of Will Mattison's estate. Anole bent low, allowing the boat to slip through an overhang of shoreline mangrove. He secured his boat there and eased over its gunwale into the water, sighing with relief to feel that the wet came not too far above his knees.

Moving his feet slippy-slide, the way all knowledgeable fishermen do, Anole crept quietly ashore. Tan-tan gave him the handholds that he needed to mount a low rise of land.

He could just make out the top of the sugar mill, at the brow of a hill not a quarter-mile away. The Mattisons' home lay another half mile beyond that. Anole walked stealthily, alert for dogs or a watchman, but all he heard was a faint hint of music from the boom box at the domino shack. Sound carried far, when a man took the trouble to listen.

Anole reached the mill and stood before it for a while, just looking at the cone of rough rock that towered some forty feet above him. As he had done on his previous visit, he surveyed the mill's standard two long slits, like windows, and the arched doorway.

Question is, Anole thought, *did Mattison make a way to get inside? Seems he would. You'd have to think he would know that some bird or bat or rat would get in there and start messin'. You'd have to think he knew that the plastic windows and door covering would get dirty and need cleaning. And the gold vase would have to be polished from time to time, to keep Missus Maura Mattison Collier happy.*

Anole tried each sheet of Plexiglas and the welded bars across it; all seemed firmly attached. He knew it would not be safe to go in at that level, anyway. *Too obvious,* he thought. *Too easy to be seen.*

Running his hands along the wall, Anole carefully felt out the stones' identity. This mill was an ordinary, familiar construction—a hodgepodge of yellow limestone, blue slate, coral heads, and yellow ballast brick. Materials of convenience had served well enough for a Danish businessman whose goal was a tower of strength and productivity. Still, the mill seemed as sturdy today as three hundred years earlier, when slaves had mortared the stones together with a cement of ground up seashells and molasses.

The mix and irregularities of stone reassured Anole that he'd have all the footing he needed to climb up the mill to its summit. He tested out a toehold here, a finger ledge there, just enough to get the general feel of it. And then, lizard-like, Anole began to climb.

As he scaled the wall, he began to make a mental list: piece of pipe, rope, dark clothes with lots of big pockets, a flashlight. That zip-closing plastic bag that Mrs. Collier wanted, empty, and another one holding six pounds of sand.

About twenty feet up the tower, a little more than half way, Anole stopped. His left foot had found a projecting chunk of coral that provided a firm foundation; his right hand, flat on a horizontal surface of black slate, seemed reaching into the heart of the mill itself. In that secure position, Anole took time to breathe. More importantly, he took time to listen. And he checked for car lights, a possible warning of Mattison's return. He saw nothing, heard nothing.

Anole resumed his climb. Hand. Foot. Hand. Foot. Seeking to the left, to the right, a little higher, a little less high, for the next good hold. Soon enough he could see the top rim of the stone mill, clear as day. He was almost there—or he was almost to the next questions that mattered, anyway.

Two more moves and Anole established another firm foothold. From this one, he could study the doghouse-shaped wood structure supporting the wind blades. He could see now that it occupied only half the space on top. Anole crept sideways around the mill, checking it out from all angles. He could sit beside that doghouse, on wood planking, to think things out. Not tonight, though it tempted him. But next time, when he was dressed right. For now, he clung to the side, pressed tight against the old stones.

Anole eased upwards a bit more to look over the stone lip. Be damned if there wasn't a simple trap door with just a little hasp and padlock. The easiest thing for him to do would be to unscrew the hasp. Anole added penetrating oil and a screwdriver to his mental shopping list. He felt of the screw heads and amended the list—a small Phillips screwdriver was what he'd need.

He'd lay a piece of pipe across the opening, and attach a rope to it to haul out the bag of whatever was in than damned urn.

Easy, easy job. But he didn't want to make it sound too easy to Missus Ava Collier. And in any case, it was a dangerous job. It was a job that would stay dangerous, too. For a long time—months, maybe, or even years. Iron Will Mattison was known to have a long memory, and patience, and a long reach. He could grab you anywhere, any time. Like a Jumbi gone bad.

Anole shuddered.

Can't think that way. Think cold. Lizard-like, Anole looked all around from his high vantage point. He saw car lights, far off, not yet to the Estate's gate, but maybe going to turn in there. He'd learned all he could learn for now; he just had to figure out what he'd need for the surprises. There would always be surprises on a job like this.

Anole took another look around the wooden doghouse, made his way to the side of the mill that faced the shore, and started slowly down. He jumped the last eight feet, preparing the spring in his knees to land him agile and bouncy, and ready to slip into the tan-tan.

Anole skittered through the brush, and across the beach, and into his boat. He shoved off and let that momentum carry him until the boat found a current. He was hoping for the current to move him for a while before he began to paddle. He paddled for a very long time, it seemed, and then, so quietly, he pulled the rope just once to start the motor on his little skiff.

Will Mattison spent scant time on his remarks at Jump-Up— just the standard, pride-filled words required to describe his bold concept of what this mini-mall, this section of town, this entire island might become with just a little more work. He introduced each of the new shop owners, and each of them echoed his words. Once Will had cut the ribbon across the main entry, curious shoppers crowded in, leaving the streets of town unusually empty for a Jump-Up night.

Ava had no interest in buying anything—certainly not in Mattison's mall, but not on the street, either. Her mind was elsewhere. She looked at her watch, wondering where Anole was now. That was futile, she knew; it might be hours, days before she would learn anything about his reconnaissance.

To distract herself, Ava paused at a kiosk where a dark islander made specialty sandals. She tried on a pair with woven leather circling her big toe, and a wide strap of the same weave spanning her instep. They seemed as elegant as they were casual; she believed she could wear them all summer long in Rockport, Texas.

While the craftsman measured Ava's feet for a custom fit, Craig wandered outside and across the walk. He saw a man sprawled in the dirt, leaning against the corner of an ice cream kiosk. The bum looked up and tipped his cap. He grinned.

Craig recognized the man as Treacle, a sleazy character, and he realized that the cap-tipping gesture was not meant for him. He looked around to identify the intended recipient. And then he saw Simone. Craig ambled away from her, then quickly slipped behind a kiosk. From there, he could watch and listen without being seen.

Simone spoke angrily to Treacle, and he responded, "Aw, Honey, is dat any way to greet yo ol' man?"

"You have no reason to be hanging around here," Simone insisted.

"Perfect reason!" Treacle countered. "Ain't no reason mo' important than a man seein' his woman when he wants. I miss you, Baby." Treacle reached an arm toward Simone's waist, but she eluded him.

"I miss you too, but we have to follow the rules. You know that. Please, Treacle, just go away. NOW!"

Simone stomped off in a huff, and Craig retraced his steps to the sandal shop. Ava was ready to go.

As they left the shop, Craig again spotted Treacle, now lounged against the old sugar mill, watching the crowd.

Ava saw him tip his hat. "Is that sidewalk bum someone you know?" she asked Craig, joking.

"That's Treacle. I thought he was living down island now. I thought they ran him off of Dos Marias. I've never been sure of what he does, but I doubt that much of it is legal. Where ever that man is, something sinister transpires."

Ava looked up at Craig, her eyes full of sudden awareness. "Could Treacle be the guy who destroyed Bennack's transmitter?"

"Huh! You may have something there!" Craig sounded surprised and delighted by Ava's idea. "I think it's entirely possible that Treacle could have been responsible for that."

"And could he . . ." Ava's voice was more hesitant now. Fearful. Sad. And unable to express the suspicion that she was viewing her son's killer.

"I don't know," Craig said, his tone gentle as he intuited her unspoken question. "It never would have occurred to me that he might have murdered Charley. I mean—why would he? But the strange thing is, I saw Simone Beranger talking to Treacle a few minutes ago. They seemed to know each other very well. Treacle referred to Simone as his "Woman.""

Ava shook her head. "Even though I don't trust Simone, I still see her as a classy person. Certainly she wouldn't have anything to do with a creep like Treacle."

"Maybe she's leading a double life," Craig suggested.

Ava shrugged, unwilling to consider yet another duplicity, another treacherous friend. She looked at her watch again; and again realized how meaningless the action was. *Soon come,* she told herself; soon enough she would hear Anole's report.

Once more seeking distraction, Ava said, "Let's have a peek in that little shop over there. It looks interesting."

Ava walked straight to it, and Craig followed her into the shop. The counter displayed an unusual assortment of jewelry—earrings and necklaces mostly—and a few votive candleholders.

"It's chaney." Craig said.

Ava stared, mystified, frowning at small pieces of broken china, set like jewels in silver bezels. "I don't know that word. I don't understand what this is.

"*Chaney* is an old colloquial term for 'china'," the shopkeeper told her. "I'm Eula Mae Fletcher, and I own this store."

When she stuck out a hand, Ava shook it with a smile and said. "I think that what you've done with this . . . *chaney?* . . . is very pretty! But where does it come from? Do you smash up old china that you find in garage sales?"

"Not at all!" Eula Mae's tone sounded a little huffy. "I find authentic, antique chaney—or *china*, if you will—on the beach, washed up, perhaps, from antique, sunken sailing ships. I had begun as most people do, just picking up shells and seeking sharks' teeth in the sand, but I soon found that the things that were more rare—chaney and sea glass—interested me more. Over the centuries, people have thrown their trash into the sea, and the sea has returned it to them as jewels. That's why I call my shop Sea Gifts.

"I comb the beaches of Dos Marias every day of my life, looking for these treasures. Look at this," Eula Mae said, picking up a particularly pretty shard of pink china, set into an oval bezel. "This broken bit of porcelain once formed a part of a plate or saucer. Now it's a miniature work of art. I think we begin to appreciate design details more, in these broken bits, than we might have on the large, intact piece. It's easier to focus on the intricacy with which someone painted just one small flower—or in this case, a miniature sugar mill."

Ava's skin prickled with a sudden chill. She rubbed the back of her neck, to keep her hand from grabbing the chaney pendant. But she knew at once that she had to buy it. "Did you design all this jewelry yourself?" she asked. "You scavenge the shore, come up with ideas, and put the pieces together?"

"Absolutely. I work primarily in silver now, but as my business becomes more successful, I'd like to do some work with gold. Especially if the chaney is extraordinary—a full picture, or something like that. I put less significant chips on votive candles or other small decorative pieces." Eula Mae picked one up to illustrate her point.

Near the chaney votives, Ava noticed others, studded with bits of sea glass.

"That's another gift from the sea," Eula Mae told her. "It takes at least three years for waves, sand and tides to transform sharp shards of broken bottles into frosty jewels like these. I'm just fascinated by Nature's creative response to the waste we scatter on her shoreline—and directly in the sea itself. Again, I use silver to mount or link pretty little pieces for the tourists, but I do have some gold fittings on hand. When I find sea glass colors that are truly rare, I think they deserve to be set in gold, don't you?"

She held up a deep blue pendant and dangled it before Ava's eyes like a temptation.

"Why is that blue color so valuable?" Ava asked, thinking of the piece that the boardwalk bum had given her.

"Well," Eula Mae answered, "Heineken's and Presidente beer bottles give us plenty of green and amber, so those are the most common, and clear glass is only a little more rare. I'm always excited to find red, though sometimes that's just from car taillights. Then we have some lovely blues and aquas that are special treasures, just because we find them less often. Occasionally I even find lavender, and that is such a special delight."

"How would you know if red sea glass came from a car tail light?" Ava asked.

"The pieces are usually chunkier, for one thing," Eula Mae answered. "But the easiest way to identify tail light glass is its distinctive ridges—if it hasn't been worn down for a long time. See this one?" Eula Mae set a hexagon of brilliant red glass, crosshatched, upon the table. "Other markings can make a piece interesting, and therefore valuable, as well."

Ava picked up the red tail light glass, seeing that it was nothing like the slim dagger she received at WHDM Radio. Still, the tail light glass gave her a strange chill, as though it hinted at something that she needed to know.

Eula Mae interrupted Ava's reverie. "Would you be interested in some sea glass?"

"No," Ava answered. "But I do want the sugar mill chaney. And I have a small collection of loose pieces of sea glass that I'd like to take care of. I know that must sound silly to you, since the glass has been tumbled for a long time, but these pieces are special to me. I'd like to have a protective bag for them, if you have something like that."

"Certainly." Eula Mae laid a small leather pouch on the counter, and a few sheets of tissue for Ava to wrap her individual pieces in.

Ava pulled out a credit card and paid for her purchase. When she and Craig were out on the street, he said, "That's a beautiful thing you bought. I can understand why you wanted the sugar mill representation."

"Yes," Ava answered. She did not want to say more; she did not want Craig to know what had happened this night, perhaps was still happening, right now, at the Mattison sugar mill.

Now he nudged at her silence. "It sounded to me like you are pretty into the sea glass thing, too," he said. "I guess I didn't know that you had any more than the one piece that the boardwalk bum gave you. How many pieces of sea glass do you have now?"

"Six."

"Really! The bum gave all of them to you?"

"No, not all," Ava said. "The others just show up from time to time. It's eerie."

"So you are reading some sort of meaning into these strange arrivals?" Craig prodded.

Ava paused, mulling. "I don't know what to make of them. They seem to be symbols of Charley, somehow. But also, I'm thinking that they may be clues concerning my son's killer."

Craig started to ask her another question, but she stopped him, saying, "Not now. We can talk about all this later. I'm ready to go back to the hotel now, if you don't mind."

At the hotel entrance, Ava thanked him for the lovely evening, but she did not invite him in. Anole and the sugar mill were too much on her mind.

In her own room at last, Ava removed a Texas charm from the silver chain that she often wore, and she threaded in its place the chaney sugar mill pendant. She wore it when she went to bed.

She lay there, with her hand across it, as she stared into the dark. And when, at last, she slept, Ava dreamed of sea glass. She heard a phrase repeated again and again: *Red light break at the bottom of the sea.* And that made no sense to her at all.

December 19

Ava had waited for Anole to call all day yesterday. The phone did not ring, not then, and, so far, not today. She reminded herself that Anole had told her not to expect the same sort of contact as before. There was nothing that she could do but wait.

Finally, late in the day, the telephone rang. But it was only the girl from Sea Gifts.

"Mrs. Collier? This is Eula Mae Fletcher. I have just received word of a piece of chaney that might interest you."

"Oh," Ava interrupted. "I already have the piece of chaney that I want. It mean a great deal to me, but I don't have any particular interest in more."

Eula Mae persisted, "I'm brokering this chaney as a private transaction. The seller's emissary specifically asked me to contact you. He stressed that I should tell you that the chaney came from a sugar bowl. He said that you'd know how to find him."

Eula Mae stammered a little. "I'm not sure what all this means. I can't imagine how anyone would know what sort of a dish or bowl a small scrap of chaney came from. I hope this man's strange message makes more sense to you than it does to me."

"Well, as a matter of fact, Eula Mae, I think it does make some sense." Ava tried to ignore the prickles on her spine as she realized that Anole had sent her another coded message—an extraordinary and clever one.

"I will see the individual about the sugar bowl chaney," she told Eula Mae, "and you shall have your commission."

Ava hung up the phone and rubbed her shoulders, erasing the last of the prickles. What kind of network did these islanders have? Did someone shadow her all the time? Was it Anole? Or—the prickles returned—could it be Treacle? And if so, why?

Certainly Anole would be preferable, but even that thought gave Ava the creeps. She wished instead that there might be good Jumbies protecting her, keeping her from harm. Ava thought again of the boardwalk bum's phrase, the day she arrived on island: "Jah be watchin' yo."

She had taken the words as a comfort then, but today she wasn't so sure. Maybe she had misunderstood the boardwalk bum's meaning; maybe it had been more sinister than she thought.

Ava looked at her watch. She could easily to drive to the domino shack before dark, and that was her usual time for meeting Anole.

She put herself on guard as she walked through the hotel parking lot to her car, uneasy that someone might be following her. As she drove through the streets of Dos Marias, Ava watched her rear view mirror.

When she arrived at the domino shack, Ava peeked inside the door and called into the darkness: "Good night!" For once, she had remembered the proper salutation at this hour.

"Good night," a disembodied voice in the dark responded. "Anole be down to his place. Yo bes' park heh, roun' pas' dat tree, an' walk down to he camp."

Ava had little trouble interpreting the dialect now. She followed the instructions, though her apprehension increased. She told herself that she could find her way along the crooked little path. She remembered the row of conch shells that lined it. And she recognized the broken palm branch that pointed to a turn that she should make.

Ava found Anole perched on a fallen tree limb. "Sit," the young man said as before, offering the oil can stool.

Ava sat. "I hear that you have news about a broken sugar bowl—or was it a sugar mill break-in?"

Anole grinned, cocking his head lizard-like. "Yo sharp, Mom. Yo very sharp!"

"Well," Ava persisted, "how was your reconnaissance?"

"My look-over go good. Ah'm gettin' my list togeddah. Gettin' my plan done. Waitin' fo' de time."

Again, Ava noticed the cadence of his words, the way his body almost bounced as he spoke. Then the cadence stopped, and a serious, more adult Anole spoke.

"Ah need cash to do my shoppin'." He lifted his head alertly, as though checking a scent or sound.

"I brought some cash," Ava answered. "Let me see your list. How much money do you estimate that you will need?"

"Anole don' have no list wrote down. It be all.l.l.l up heh." He tapped his head. He waited for some response from Ava that did not come.

Anole cocked his head. "Yo need to write de list down or sump'in', so yo can compute de cost? Yo need to pull out one o' dem han' hel' add machine? Or mebbe yo smaht phone? Or can yo rememba, de way Anole do?"

Ava heard his words as a challenge; she sensed the hidden brag that although Anole might not read or write, he did have a good mind. Ava suspected that the boy's mind might be better than one lazily relying on the written word—or on a calculator. "Just tell me your list," she said.

"Coverall," Anole began. "Dahk grey coverall wit' lot o' zipper pocket. Dahk grey head rag. Fuel fo' de boat. Piece of pipe, rope, flashlight. Phillip screwdrive wit' t'ree head size. Reg'la' screwdrive too—a skinny little one. Penetratin' oil. A little towel. Work glove. Bottle Chiva Regal fo' afteh."

Anole grinned. "Got dat, Missus Collier? Dat be twenny-fi' an' fi'. Be t'irty, and twenny-fi' an' twenny-fi' be eighty. Say 'nuddeh twenny be even hunn-ed. T'irteen den. Two mo' twennys mek it one fitty t'ree. Mebbe ten, an' fit-teen. Den de t'irty-fi'. Ah b'lieve dat come to one seven eight. Roun' it off to one eight oh. Dat what yo mek it? Plus one twenny fo' my risk o' life an' limb. Even t'ree."

For the past week or so, Ava had worked hard to understand Anole's dialect, and she knew she was getting pretty good at it. When she heard "even tree," she knew, without having to think about it, that he was saying "an even three hundred." Now she looked him in the eye and said, "I think you left out the zipper bag."

"Two bag dem," Anole grinned. "One wit' six poun' san' an' one empty fo' what be in dat gol' vase. I didn' fo'get. I jus' plan on snitchin' dem bag offa Paulus de cook, an' we got plenny san' right heh!"

Anole kicked up a small mound of sand with his feet, laughing, and Ava laughed with him. Each knew the other as a good person, and knew that their math-and-memory game had come out a fair draw.

Ava reached into her purse and pulled out her wallet. She always kept the low-denomination bills in front, so now she riffled through them surreptitiously to pull out the sum she needed, without displaying the total of her cash.

When she had handed the money to Anole, and he had counted it, Ava said, "Now what?"

"Now yo jus' enjoy yo-se'f. Ah go into trainin'. Yo won' hear nuttin' from me until Ah have yo bag all zipped up nice an' full. Ah plan to climb de mill de night of Coterie. It happen on the Solstice every year, and' *dis* year, Ah like dat. Solstice be de longest night o' de year, gettin' dahk earlier, an' stayin' dahk later, than any other night. Plus, all de Mattisons be busy-busy dat nite, wit' all de socializin'. Ain't nobody gonna be watching a little ol' anole climbin' up a sugah mill.

"Ah ain't gonna call yo de next day, neitha. Ah be tired. An' enjoyin' my Chiva." Anole raised his head high and turned it from side to side, as though catching the taste of fine Scotch in the air.

"Day afta dat," he continued, "dey be parade, and dat mek it too hahd fo' yo an' me to get togeddah. Next day be Christmas Eve. Mebbe yo hear from me den, and mebbe not. I got fambly to be wit'."

Ava's heart sank. She had waited so long to free her son, and hated hearing that there'd be a longer wait before she actually had Charley with her again. Still, what Anole had said seemed reasonable, at least from his point of view. She was surprised, too, at his reference to his family; the idea had never occurred to her. But Ava felt warmed, tender, thinking that Anole had family to be with at Christmas.

"Your plan sounds fine," she said. "And when you hand over the zipper bag, I will make my final payment to you for your labor and your risk. We will both be hoping that the risk is minimal, though that will not affect the fair payment that you will receive."

Anole stood, holding out his hand to Ava's. When they had shaken on their deal, Anole said, "Ah like doin' business wit' yo, Missus Collier. Yo'd be a good woman to go to sea wit'."

Ava understood that she'd received a supreme compliment. Crews on a sea voyage had to trust one another's knowledge, expertise, and honesty.

As she drove back to her hotel, she mused. It would be on the year's longest night that Anole would free her son. And after the Solstice, the days would get brighter.

December 22

Anole stood at the base of the sugar mill, looking up, visualizing his climb. He checked the security of the grappling hook and the rope that he had tied to his waist. These were the essential tools for getting into the mill and getting out of it again. Anole imagined that when he stood in the wide base of the mill's interior, looking up to the top rim, the steep slope of the walls would seem to close in on him, next to impossible to scale. He was not so sticky-fingered as to be able to hang upside down for long; he knew he would need the rope to help him climb out.

Getting in, of course, was the easy part. Anole found a toehold at a chunk of embedded coral head; a finger-hold at a projecting limestone lay just one easy stretch above the coral. And so he began his reptilian climb up the steeply sloped wall.

Chink by crevice by crack, Anole inched himself to the top of the mill. His claw-like fingers found the slight lip provided by the counter-sunk wood ceiling. He grasped it firmly, then stopped to rest, snapping his head sharply in one direction and then another. Somewhere, some eyes might be watching him.

Getting over the top lip of the mill would be a crucial move. Even though Anole had dressed entirely in dark grey, even though he had smudged his face so that sweat would not make it glow, he knew that he could be seen by anyone who happened to look directly at him. A silhouette would make him easier to see. That could be fatal.

Anole crept the rest of the way up the mill, and over the lip, staying close, close to the rock. He sat pressed against the dog-house-like structure that supported the wind blades; he avoided the edges of the trap door. Reaching into a pocket of his coveralls, he pulled out the can of penetrating oil. When his fingertips had identified the base plate of the hasp on the door, he squirted the oil directly on it, and on the hinges at the opposite side.

He sat and waited for the oil to work, wishing that he had a cigarette. He hadn't brought one, because even such a tiny glow as that would be risky. Anole felt proud that he had thought this exercise through, to the smallest detail.

After a few minutes, he pulled out his Phillips screwdriver and applied it to the crosshatched heads. The screws moved without a hitch. After all, they might have been installed just when the gold vase went in the sugar mill—not that long ago, according to Ava Collier.

Anole removed the fasteners one at a time, placing them carefully in a top pocket of his coverall. He slipped the slim standard screwdriver into the trap door's crevice and levered it up. At last he had access to the interior of the sugar mill.

He peered down, but could see nothing. It might as well have been a bottomless pit.

Except that he had seen the urn, on its rock pedestal, when he had looked in through the door.

Anole detached the grapple from his suit and fastened it to one end of his coiled rope with a deft bowline knot. He hooked the grapple securely over the piece of pipe and tested its hold by pulling hard on the line. Then he uncoiled his rope and dropped it into the mouth of the mill. He found the pocket that held his gloves and put them on.

Still creeping in the lowest possible profile, he eased his body through the trap door. He grabbed the rope, wrapped his legs around it to, and then let the rope lead him down the mill's dark throat. Anole dangled far away from the sloped mill walls, and he swayed a bit, like the clapper in a bell. He dropped more slowly to minimize the swing.

Anole stopped just once, a little more than half way down, to flick his light on briefly; he illuminated the heap of rocks beneath the gold vase. He wouldn't want to kick the damn thing when he landed, spilling whatever was in it that Missus Ava Collier wanted so much. One second or two of light was enough to assure Anole that his drop would lead him a little to the side of the urn, as he had planned.

When Anole's toes touched stone floor, he breathed. He set his feet firmly and got his balance. He took off his gloves and stowed them in their pocket. In the dark, he turned his body toward the vase. He squatted, rolled forward onto his knees, and edged toward the rock pile. Skating his hands across the floor and up the rocks, Anole touched the vase lightly. Then he grasped it tight in both hands. He had worried that it might be cemented to the rock, but the vase was free. He lifted it carefully and sat back on his heels.

Instinctively, unaware that he mimicked Ava's movements at the funeral, Anole cradled the urn, one hand at its neck, one at the widest bulge. It was like holding a baby, he thought.

"Treat this like a baby," Missus Collier had said, and now, once more, Anole wondered what the hell might be inside that vase. He set it down, opened yet another coverall pocket, and produced the empty zipper-locking plastic bag.

He removed the cap from the urn and tried to look inside. Of course, in the dark, he couldn't see anything. He sniffed instead. Something powdery assailed his nostrils. Cocaine? The nice lady was smuggling cocaine? No, this was a different smell. Not like cocaine at all. It smelled something like island air after eruptions of the Montserrat volcano. Kinda like that. Burnt.

Anole settled the opening of his plastic bag over the mouth of the urn. He smoothed the bag down over the urn with great care, then squeezed it tight around the neck. Holding the bag tight-tight between his strong hands, he inverted the urn.

As its contents began to pour into the bag, Anole wished again that he had light enough to make out what that stuff was. He sensed the flow of powder and the dropping of a few small chunks of something solid. He shrugged and settled the bag to the floor for stability. As the bag filled, he raised the urn out of it, inch by inch, still pressing the bag tightly against the urn. Then, with only the neck of the urn in the bag, Anole shook the thing sharply, angling it one way and another, making certain that everything once inside the urn was now in the bag.

Anole spanked the broadest curve of the urn, as a delivering obstetrician might spank a newborn's bottom. Then he eased the neck of the urn out of the bag, taking an abundance of care to be sure that the bag did not tip.

With great relief, he zipped the bag closed, burping it to remove all air and to condense the bag's size. Anole checked and rechecked the seal, making sure that it held fast. He lifted the bag, estimating its weight. About six pounds, just as Missus Collier had said. About the weight of most island newborns—not heavy enough to cause Anole any problem.

He set the bag down with precision, unzipped his coveralls, and reached into the bulging inside pocket that held the bag of sand. Testing its weight in comparison to the other bag, he decided that it was close enough. He opened the sand bag then and poured its contents into the urn.

Anole sighed with relief; he was almost done. He deposited both plastic bags—the one emptied of sand, and the one filled with whatever was in the urn—in the inside zipper pocket of his coverall.

Anole sighed again—this time with deep regret, as he capped the gold vase and set it back in its place on the pile of rock. Too bad to leave it there, he thought; he could have got good money for that thing. He found the hand towel in one of his pockets and used it to polish the urn, removing any fingerprints, any smudge or stain.

Anole felt around for possible stray items that he might be leaving behind. He patted all his pockets and made certain that they were securely closed. Now for the last real work.

He got his gloves, smoothed them over his hands, and pulled on his rope. The grapple and pipe felt as tight as before. Anole grasped the rope firmly and gave a little hop that swung him over to the side of the mill. He made his feet walk up the wall, but his arms lifted his weight.

As he neared the top of the mill, he let his feet fall free of the wall; he pulled the last yard or so with just his arms. Then his head was out of the mill and he breathed fresh air.

Anole wriggled out the trap door and pressed his body against the doghouse as before. He pulled his rope up next and then unfastened the grapple from the pipe. He stowed the grapple and pipe, coiled his rope, and pocketed it along with his gloves.

He stopped for a moment, blowing out one great breath to release his tension. He gave himself time to settle down.

Then Anole found the screws for the hasp, eased the trap door shut, and refastened the hasp. He got the towel out again and rubbed the door and its hardware clean. He'd leave no trace—none at all—that anyone had been inside the sugar mill, or even on the top of it.

Anole turned his head one way and then the other, stretching so that he could see almost behind him. And then he turned his body to make sure. No car lights, no house lights, no boat lights, no nothing. He leaned out to see around the doghouse. More nothing. He stopped a minute, cocking his head to one side as he considered every action one more time. Then Anole began his simple climb down.

He tried not to think about the powder-filled zipper bag tight in his inside pocket. He thought about nothing except getting into the boat and returning to his home.

Only when he was there, safe in his own hovel, did Anole think it was safe for him to take a look at what he had risked his life for. He reached into the coverall pocket that held the bag, grasped it tightly and checked its zip lock before pulling it free from the pocket.

He held it to the light, shook it a little. Then Anole shook his head.

Dust! Nothing but damn gray dust. And a few small chunks of something just about that same dull color. Not much to get for all this money and all this effort, Anole thought. He never would understand Continentals, not in a million years.

Anole uncorked the Chivas Regal and started in on some serious drinking.

DECEMBER 23

Ava was awake early, and pacing the floor of her hotel room. Anole had said that he would not call until the day after Christmas, still three days away. How would she fill her time? Arid eons of time, punctuated by humid minutes. And the long nights were the worst part.

So Ava was grateful that, on this day at least, she would have something to occupy her mind. Sandi Leland had called the day before, apologetic that she and Ken had neglected Ava for so long.

"Tomorrow is the big parade," she said. "It's the follow-up to Coterie's major event each year—the coronation of their social set's King and Queen. The wealthy women have chosen to call themselves 'Coterie,' and they make a very big deal of allowing the commoners to view Royalty's elegant costumes. During the parade, the duchesses throw candy down to their underlings." Sandi put a sarcastic inflection to her final word.

"So!" she continued, "Ken and I always have a parade-watching party. Please come, Ava! We're right on the parade route, and there's no better place to view the festivities."

Ava hadn't been enthusiastic when she heard Sandy's invitation; she hadn't promised to attend. But this morning, she found herself warming to the idea. A party might be the best possible thing for her this day, taking her mind away from Anole and the threat that he might have been found out. So she'd need to get moving; Sandi said everyone would arrive in time for breakfast.

Ava drove out of the hotel's parking garage. As Sandi had suggested, she took back streets, avoiding the parade route, which was already blocked off. From the top of a hill, Ava could see all the way across the harbor, to Anole's lagoon. The road that she drove on dropped precipitously toward the fishermen's village and the blue water beyond.

She found Ken and Sandi's townhouse half way down that slope; she maneuvered into a parking spot in front of an iron gate. The gate led to a flagstone patio, and to the entry to the Lelands' home—a refurbished hundred-and-fifty-year-old Danish townhouse. When Ava rang the bell there, Sandi opened the door wide.

"Ava!" she clasped the woman's hand in both of hers. "We are *so* glad that you would come." She stepped back, further opening her home to Ava. "Come in, come *in*!" Sandi lapsed into an imitation of island patois. "On dis day, alla we togeddah be islan' folk an' pah-*tee*."

Ava looked around a large room that seemed to provide living, dining and kitchen areas combined. Heavy beams overhead echoed dark, aged slabs of wood flooring, but light poured in through tall windows and French doors that opened onto a gallery.

She saw familiar faces—Rick Rowland and Brooke Randolph, Mark Dotson. It seemed hard to believe that this group had been unknown to her less than a month ago. It astonished her that seeing them would bring her so much comfort. But where was Craig Buchanan?

She turned to ask Sandi, but the young woman was chattering away as she draped strands of carnival beads around Ava's neck. She offered a silly hat and gestured toward huge baskets brimming with noisemakers, feather boas, masks, and toys. "Help yourself," Sandi said. "Find what suits you, then fight your way through the throng to the kitchen. I've set up a food buffet on the counters there. So load up a plate and then just sit wherever."

Before Ava could move, Ken came to greet her. "I've got a little holiday gift for you," he said. He laughed at Ava's puzzled look, then said, "I found the VIN number of Charley's Escalade."

"That's a wonderful gift, Ken, Thank you!" Ava said, her voice solemn and sincere.

"Let's go in the den," Ken suggested. "It's quieter there, so I can tell you what I've learned."

When they were seated, Ken pulled his billfold from a pocket and fished out a small piece of paper snugged into a credit card slit. He unfolded the paper and spread it out on the table for Ava to see.

"VIN number 1S4FF68S7XL553952," Ken said without preamble. "VIDOT—our islands' transportation department—recorded transfer of the Escalade from Charley to a Mister Emile Longet of St. Martin's."

"St. Martin's?" Ava asked. "Isn't that an island north of here? Not one of the Virgins?"

"Correct," Ken said. "It's outside our territory, and past the British Virgins as well. I think that's significant. The buyer of Charley's Escalade, Longet, confirmed that he had purchased the vehicle, but—" Ken paused, obviously for effect. "He does not have it! He told me that although Mattison had promised to ship the Escalade to him, it never arrived. Longet was impressed that Mr. Mattison refunded his money in full, with a little extra thrown in for his trouble."

Ava frowned. "So where is the Escalade now?"

"At the bottom of the sea." Ken threw his hands up and shook his head as though he still had a hard time believing it. "Story is, the Escalade somehow slid off the barge en route to St. Martin, and sank. Believe that, and I've got a bridge to sell you."

Ava nodded distractedly, caught up by a chill, remembering the tail light sea glass, and the words in her dream, *Red light breaks at the bottom of the sea.* Ava felt that somehow she had known all along the story that she was hearing now.

Ken saw her distress and said, "I'm really sorry, Ava. I feel that I've failed you."

"Oh, I wasn't thinking anything like that!" Ava answered. "Certainly you haven't let me down at all. In fact, Ken, I think this is huge. You've done a great piece of work. How can I thank you?"

"Thank me for a dead end?" Ken shook his head. "You gotta be kidding."

Ava smiled gently. "It's true that losing the Escalade ends any hope that we'll ever answer some of our key questions. We'll have no fingerprints, no powder residue, no—" Ava gulped, then continued. "No blood splatter pattern. It might have helped us to have that information. But you and I both know that the Escalade didn't slide off that barge accidentally! And that's a confirmation of a sort—the kind that I need at least as much as I need crime lab facts."

"I see your point," Ken nodded. "Still, I'm sorry I couldn't have brought even better news."

"Thanks again, my friend," Ava said, and shook Ken's hand.

Together, they headed back to the main room, where Ava found Craig standing with a good-looking woman.

"I'm sure glad you're here," Ava said, walking close to him.

"Me too, Ava," Craig answered. "And look what Santa Claus brought me." He took the hand of the woman who stood beside him. "Ava Collier, meet my wife Janice."

Janice gave Ava a hug. "I've heard so much about you!"

"Janice has given me the best Christmas present ever," Craig said. "She and the kids are moving down here. To stay. Janice has bought a top-rate ladies' clothing store here, and she's going to run it."

Before Ava could think what to say, Craig shoved something into her hands. "Hold on to this."

Ava looked at it, a fancy booklet printed on heavy paper and held together with gold twine. She shrugged, and looked up at Craig with a silent question.

"That's the program Janice got at the Coronation last night," Craig explained. "Think of it as a play list for today's parade. You'll see that most of the debutantes and their escorts are solid scions of families represented, by hook or by crook, in the boardrooms of Mattison enterprises."

Ava studied the Coronation program carefully. Ronald Huffington was King Taíno, she read. Certainly he would be appropriately regal—but hardly indigenous, despite his title. Ava made a wry smile, thinking of Hatuey. She wondered if the true Taíno would ever come to such a parade, and decided that he would not.

She read other familiar surnames—Hendley, Hamilton. "This may be a more interesting parade than I ever could have imagined," she told Craig.

Then Ava turned to Janice: "Tell me more about this extravaganza."

The young woman grinned. "Oooo, it's juicy!"

"Over the years," Janice told Ava, "it has proved generally true that the debutante crowned queen is the one whose father is willing to provide the largest supporting sum. Slightly less affluent families provide daughters to complement the queen's court. Debutantes came from the other islands as well. Of course, Maura Mattison was queen in her day—before she met and married Charley.

"Every queen requires a king. He is most often some years older than the debutante—a rising businessman of the Coterie class. This man is married, with a young family of his own. I'm certain that Charley would have been crowned King Taíno within a few years, if he had lived. His grooming for the position had already begun.

"I must tell you," Janice continued, "that some of us—those who enjoy visiting Hatuey in the rainforest—find a certain irony in the king's name. But I suspect that those of the Coterie class would be baffled by our opinion." She winked.

Just as Ava responded to the wink with an understanding smile, the Hibernia Academy's marching band appeared, leading off the parade. High-schoolers strutted down King Street in emerald green uniforms, complete with ostrich-plumed shakos. Behind them followed four Mercedes convertibles, carrying the Doyennes. Ava recognized Clio among them. Properly hatted and gloved, the Doyennes directed subtle 'Queen Elizabeth' waves toward the on-lookers.

The first float following the Doyennes carried the most recent former queens. Maura must have been there, some time in the past. Arabian stallions followed that float, prancing as though unaware of the weight of riders clad in pompous regalia.

Charles should have been there, with those Cavaliers, Ava thought. And perhaps by the next year, he would have been in the carriage immediately behind them, the one bearing King Taíno. When Ava put a hand over her mouth, Janice came to stand beside her. Craig took her hand and squeezed it.

The Queen's float appeared. "That's Clio Mattison's niece," Janice said. "Her Majesty Eileen, of the House of Clary. All the information is the program Craig gave you."

Ava nodded; she had read that. Now she focused on Eileen Clary, who "carried silver scales of kindly justice in her right hand," according to the program.

"That's ironic." Ava pointed at the words, and Janice chuckled.

"Oh, but it's sooo *Doyenne*," she said. "Those ladies are sooo proud of what they have done for the good of the simple people on their island."

"I'll bet."

"Well, really they have, in a way. Over the years, the need for debutante finery established a small cottage industry on Dos Marias. Skilled needle crafters work all year long to create the richly beaded dresses and their complementary long trains. Bestowing that labor on uneducated, but carefully coached, islanders convinced the matrons of Dos Marias that they were doing their part for the local economy—and not even under the aegis of an Economic Development contract. In fact, the training of local women to make debutante dresses had preceded the rise of the EDC concept by several generations."

Ava frowned. "And how did you learn all this?"

"Even though I haven't been on island full time, I *have* been interested. And as Craig has undoubtedly told you, my passion is clothing. So I found out about these dresses. Now look! Here comes the princess!

"Rumor has it that the Doyennes had planned to name this position 'Shining Horizons,' complementary to the theme. But they had to make a last minute change! The Coterie could hardly appear to be endorsing Horizon Radio, after B.B. Bennack had that 'scandalous' interview with you! One can only imagine the pain that cost the Mattison family!" Again, sarcasm coated Janice's words. Ava made a small smile.

"So instead of 'Shining Horizons'," Janice continued, "the Number Two girl's title is now 'Princess of the Shimmering Periphery'. And would you believe . . . it's Cassie Hendley, Byron's younger sister!"

Ava looked at the girl closely. Her face, softer than Byron's, still held something of his vulpine, acquisitive intensity. Cassie's ice blue gown gleamed with clear glass beads. Clouds of faintly bluish gauze formed a train that billowed marvelously over tiny hidden air jets. Ava only sighed at the foolishness of that float, and the next, and the next.

The Island of St. Thomas float carried Becca, of the House of Wittman, as Duchess of Microbial Splendor. Janice informed

Ava that Becca's father, one of Will Mattison's closest associates, was the CFO of a pharmaceutical firm on St. Thomas.

From St. Croix came Marianne of the House of Lemtorp, Duchess of Danish Memory, and granddaughter of the Territorial Governor. Her train flowed down the back of the float—a sugar mill, worked in gold thread and sparkling with jewels. Ava closed her eyes against welling tears. The unexpected always tugged hardest on her emotions.

Puerto Rico came next, followed by a number of other Caribbean islands—St. Martin's, Antigua, St. Lucia, on and on.

"Rumor has it," Janice told Ava, "that the Doyennes fought very hard to exclude the island of Dominica, because the dark girl who would ride on the float had chosen the title, Duchess of 1491. Well, the Doyennes thought that was ridiculous, because nothing significant could *possibly* have happened on these islands, so long before their European ancestors arrived." Again Janice winked, and Ava chuckled.

"Some of the Doyennes' husbands argued against them," Janice continued. "The men had business concerns on Dominica, and wanted to avoid an offense that might affect their Bottom Line. Of course the men won the argument. The best that the Doyennes could do was to position that float dead last."

The dark Duchess of 1491 stood in front of a papier-mâché mountain, steadying herself on a wooden staff. Ava thought that her exquisitely worked gown of woven feathers was a marvel of indigenous handicraft. The long feather cape, trailing behind her gown, depicted forests, streams, shorelines, and strange, mythic beasts.

Just as the float drew even with the Reviewing Booth for Parade Officials, Dominica's duchess put both hands to her shoulders and delicately released two small bows. The entire feather dress dropped to her feet.

Only the tiniest triangular sprays of feather then concealed the three most private parts of the girl's supremely luscious anatomy. And she rode like that, for the rest of the parade, with one fist raised above her head.

The men at the Lelands' party whistled and yelled. The young women echoed Miss Dominica by raising their own victorious fists.

"Good thing the Doyennes were riding in front and couldn't see what she did," Janice laughed. "There'd be half a dozen cases of apoplexy for sure."

It was not until the parade had ended that Eileen and her Court heard of the horror produced by almost-nude Dominica. And the heartbreak of it was, of course, that almost all the parade on-lookers had cheered Dominica as they would never cheer a Coterie queen.

Those who *pah-TEED* at Ken and Sandi's townhouse loved the whole thing. They rehashed every over-the-top moment of the parade. Liquor flowed.

Soon, the conviviality was simply too much for Ava. As Sandi began to uncover platters of sandwiches and salads, Ava grasped the opportunity to say her thank-yous and good-byes.

December 24

Anole glared at the heap of grey coverall, still rumpled on the piece of plywood that he called a floor. And that coverall still held the plastic Ziploc bag. And it was Christmas Eve.

Shit! Three days he couldn't make himself go near the damn thing. Three days he couldn't touch it, or get rid of it. Three days he just kept wondering what was that damn bag of grey dust that he'd risked so much for.

Only one thing sure, he didn't like it, and he wouldn't have it around another night. Damn sure wouldn't have it in his place on Christmas Day! Anole stumbled from his shelter and up the path to the domino shack.

"Anybody hear from Regional?" he asked.

"He be busy dis day," one of his buddies answered. "Yo know people runnin' 'roun' shoppin' like crazy."

"Well, can Ah use de phone an' call him?"

"Go ahead on."

He dialed the number and waited for the cabbie to answer. "Regional! Dis Anole. Ah need yo to come out heh quick-quick an' pick up sump'in' at my place. Ah won' be deh. Yo can jus' grab it and go. It won't take yo long."

Convincing Regional to make the trip took some time, however, and Anole had to promise to pay for the mileage. That led to telling Regional where and how to deliver the package, and then Anole had to go through the whole persuasion routine again.

Taxi driver Regional Delaney only agreed to carry out Anole's request because he remembered Ava Collier. He recalled the woman's sad, solemn face, and he hoped that whatever he was to deliver would bring her some joy. He felt that she needed that; she seemed such a nice lady, to be so unhappy at this joyful time of year.

Regional prided himself on doing things right. He didn't like being in Anole's camp, he didn't like this current situation, and he didn't want to know any more about it than he could already imagine.

Just as Anole had described, Regional found the zipper pocket in the sneak thief's grey coverall. He pulled out the plastic bag it held, and carried the strange-looking thing to the trunk of his car. He didn't stop at the domino shack to say goodbye to Anole; he just drove away.

Regional left the bag in his car when he parked in an alleyway behind the Mattison mini-mall. His wife Babylorne worked as a seasonal wrapper in one of the shops there. He described to her the size box he'd need, and how he wanted it wrapped, in a bright holiday paper. Regional stressed that the top of the box should be wrapped separately. And he said that he wanted a big red bow in the center of that top. Festive.

When Babylorne was done prettifying the empty box, Regional asked for a roll of tape to take along. He carried the box and the tape to his taxi, opened the trunk, and settled Anole's plastic bag carefully inside the gift box. He taped the lid on.

Fares kept him busy for the rest of that day and well into the night. He had to go out to Mattisons, to pick up a package. Funny thing was, that package was for Ava Collier too, but it was a little thing. Regional put it in the trunk of his cab, right next to the big box holding that bag that he got at Anole's camp.

Tourists hurried everywhere, hoping for island bargains or looking for some kind of fun. Nobody went to the airport, so

Regional did not have to open his trunk. The two Christmas packages for Ava Collier remained undisturbed there.

But the thought of the mysterious plastic bag, stuffed into a festive Christmas box, disturbed Regional's sleep that night.

DECEMBER 25

First thing Christmas morning—Babylorne was still sleeping off her exhaustion from the Eve's frantic package wrapping—Regional drove his taxi to Ava Collier's hotel and parked. He got the packages out of the trunk and carried them to the hotel entrance.

The doorman told him what room to go to, and he went directly there, carrying the large, bright holiday present, with the smaller one in his pocket. No one gave him a second glance, but he still felt uneasy. And he had to wait at the room door a long time before Mrs. Collier came.

"Yo frien' Anole aksed me to deliver dis," Regional said to her. "He tol' me to tell yo Merry Christmas."

Mrs. Collier took the box without a smile and weighed it in her hands.

Regional stood there, waiting. Anole had told him that Mrs. Collier was going to pay for the delivery.

Mrs. Collier loosened the tape holding the top onto the box. She took one quick peek inside and then firmly closed the box once more.

She looked grim, and Regional expected she'd send him packing. He wouldn't be surprised if she did, because nobody would be pleased to get something like that on Christmas Day. He wouldn't have any trouble understanding why she wouldn't give him any tip, but if she didn't pay, like Anole said, that was another matter. Regional couldn't imagine how he would work that out with Anole.

But Mrs. Collier didn't get mad. She even smiled, just a little bit, cradling that box like it held the crown jewels.

"I have another package for you too," Regional said.

He handed her a small, brown, plastic bag. The Mattisons hadn't even wrapped whatever they were giving this nice lady, and that embarrassed Regional.

Mrs. Collier peeked in that bag too. And then she smiled again, a real smile that brightened up her whole face. That surprised Regional more than anything.

"Wait a minute," Mrs. Collier said. "Let me get some money."

She turned to get her purse and pulled out two fifty-dollar bills. She held up the hundred, saying, "Take this to Anole with my thanks." Regional took it.

Then Ava held up another fifty. "And keep this for your trouble," she said.

Regional pocketed Anole's hundred and his fifty as he hurried back to his cab. If this was Christmas, Continental style, he'd had all of it that he'd ever want.

Ava sighed a deep, contented sigh and patted the box that Regional had delivered. She had her son home for Christmas. That was all that she could ask for, all that she could possibly want, on this Christmas Day.

And yet, she had something more. Clio Mattison had sent her a small voice recorder with a sticky note attached. "Listen to this when you get back to Texas," was all that it said.

Surely this must be the tape we've been looking for! Ava thought. It seemed odd that Clio suggested she wait till she was in Texas to hear it, but Ava knew that she did not want to listen to the tape this day.

She simply sat with her son. She remembered. She cried.

After a while, she picked up her phone and made a flight reservation back to Texas.

DECEMBER 26

Gotta get airborne, Mom! Ava heard Charley's voice, as clear as day. It woke her at sunrise, prodding.

Ava looked at the package on her dresser and sighed. Incredible, she thought, that the brightly wrapped box held all her son's earthly remains, silent and grey.

She thought of his words in the dream, *Gotta get airborne.* It had nothing to do with her plane reservation; the phrase had been one of Charley's favorites, always a prelude to the suggestion that they go sailing. Ava sighed: The time had come.

She called Winston Watley, at Spanish Cove Marina. She reminded him that they'd met, when she went sailing with Craig.

"Yas Mom," Winston agreed. "I do remember yo."

"You have some small sailboats for rent, don't you, Winston? I'd like to take one out today."

"Yas Mom, we can do dat fo' yo."

"And would Alma be able to fix a snack for me?"

"Dat too. An' she put in a small bottle of rum. Late Christmas gift, yo might say."

At the gift shop in the hotel lobby, Ava bought a small, covered basket. Back in her room, she lifted the bag of Charley's ashes out of the garish Christmas box and set it carefully in the basket. She did it without looking—sensing, but not able to bear seeing, this last remnant of her son.

She carried the basket out to her car. With Charley in the front seat beside her, Ava headed for Spanish Cove Marina.

Winston hurried to meet her as she parked the car. "Yo boat be shiny and ready," he said. "She waitin' fo' yo at de end o' the right han' dock deh. She a nice little day sailor, fit for single-handin'. Yo won' have no trouble wit' dat sweet boat."

Alma came with Ava's food hamper and stowed it on the boat for her. She was hardly back on the dock before Ava loosed the boat's bowline. She was eager to be on the sea with her son, one last time.

Ava passed by Restaurant Niçoise and skirted the tip of Dos Marias. She saw Out of the Blue, and Falling Down. She sailed by the boardwalk, where the bum had befriended her. She spotted Pirates' Den and the Keg Wharf. Bright paint gave her a glimpse of the District Attorney's office building. Each landmark also represented a gift freely given, a friendship, or a blessing that she had received on Dos Marias. She would hold them in a grateful heart; they would strengthen her in the days to come.

When Ava sailed past the Mattison compound, she fastened her eyes on the sugar mill. She saw it now as a symbol of endurance, and of one's ability to set things right. She did not notice Clio, standing on her gallery, looking at the day.

Ava turned toward open sea, putting the island behind her. At a deep spot that seemed right, she turned her little boat into the wind and dropped the sail. She ducked into the cabin to pick up her MP3 player, a cup of dark rum, and the basket that held Charley's remains.

Ava walked to the boat's stern and sat there to sip her rum, made from the same molasses that held old mills together. She had learned that the mid-range of distilled rum yielded the best flavor, "the heart of the spirit," so she sipped it in reverence.

Staring into the sea, Ava turned on her music: first Enya's "Caribbean Blue," and then the aching reverie of Leona Boyd's "Adagio for Guitar and Strings." She pulled a piece of paper from the pocket of her shorts and read aloud a few lines from Tennyson that she loved, and that Charley had loved, ending:

For tho' from out our bourne of Time and Place
The flood may bear me far,
I hope to see my Pilot face to face
When I have crost the bar.

Ava opened the basket and lifted out the plastic bag. For the first time, she had the courage to study the bag's contents. And she knew: *This is not Charley.*

This grey ash, that she had schemed to obtain, was only earthly remains, and not her son. Charley was already free, had been free from the moment that bullet smashed into his body. In all Ava's time of grieving, the essence of Charley, pure spirit, had lived wherever Ava's thoughts carried her.

She slipped her hand into the bag of ash and cupped a bit of it into her palm. As she raised her hand, a whiff of breeze lifted some of the ash, spiraling it into the air.

Gotta get airborne, Mom.

Ava heard her son's happy voice and let him go. She moved her hand gently, parallel to the sea, letting ash sift slowly from her fingers to settle into the blue depths. She scooped ash from the bag again and again, knowing that it was not Charley, but knowing as well that she wanted and needed this closure.

Ava's fingers stumbled over coarser bits of bone as she committed them all to the deep. At the end, she held the bag upside down and shook it, ensuring that she had released Charley's earthly remains entirely. Her son was now, in every sense, free.

A faint ripple stirred on the surface of the water. More ripples joined it, growing into wavelets. For a brief moment, the water seemed to boil. A large eagle ray rose to float for a second or two atop the tumult that it had made. In that ephemeral moment, Ava recognized that some of Charley's gray cremains lay upon the eagle's back.

My boy is loving this, Ava thought. She smiled. She laughed. *Charley is really loving this.*

The ray shook its wings emphatically; bone and ash went airborne. Silently the eagle flew beneath the surface, the cremains followed, and the ocean covered everything.

The image of the eagle ray that stayed with Ava was not of Charley's ashes being shrugged off. The ashes had soared with the eagle. Strong wings carried her son, then sheltered him beneath a wide mantle. Charley's ashes were safe at last. And Charley, the heart of the spirit, was free.

"Go in peace, my son," Ava said aloud. "Go always in joy."

She swirled the MP3's dial to Yanni's *In the Morning Light*. The delicacy of that composition fit this quiet moment, afloat on the sea, and the tune's central passages lifted Ava, as the ray had lifted her son's earthly remains.

Ava raised the boat's sail once more and headed toward El Niño Cay. She circled it to get her bearings, then chose a spot to set her anchor fairly close to shore.

She found lunch in the hamper that Alma had packed, and something else too. A crumpled white paper napkin nestled in the bottom of the basket. Ava smiled.

She carried the napkin onto the deck before spreading it open. There she revealed the thing that she had expected: a smooth chunk of sea glass. It told her, as the others had, that she was on the right track.

Ava cradled the sea glass in cupped hands, lifting it skyward as an offering, a confession, the elements of a prayer:

> *I may never learn all the details of the night my son died.*
> *I may never have proof positive that Charley was murdered.*
> *But I know.*

Ava took another sip of the rum, knowing that it was Communion indeed.

DECEMBER 27

Charley's friends surprised Ava by coming to the airport. "We needed a last goodbye," they said.

"You can always come visit me in Texas," Ava responded.

"Oh, we will, we will!"

When Ava's plane was airborne, they stood watching it. "Has the time come for us, too? Should we be heading home?"

"Not yet. Not quite yet. Let's have one more ride on the merry-go-round."

Airborne over the Caribbean, Ava fished in her purse for the voice recorder that Clio had given her, equipped with an ear bud attachment. She thought that she was ready to hear it now. She believed that, in this public space, she might hear in an objective way. She could not—would not—cry, surrounded by these strangers on the plane. Ava pushed the ear bud into place and turned on the recorder.

But it was not the recording of Charley's final night. It was Clio's voice that she heard.

CLIO'S STORY

Sweet is revenge—especially to women.

—Don Juan, Lord Byron

DECEMBER 1

Clio Clary Mattison stood on her east gallery, watching the sun stretch sleepy gold arms to awaken the still-dark Caribbean Sea. Clio imagined that the sea balked, as she herself had resisted, when her husband roused her from another night that had provided no restful sleep.

And now December had come upon them. Christmas month. Coterie month. The peak social season for the Original Settlers on Dos Marias. Clio sighed.

She was always busy—too busy—in December. At least, Charles' funeral was behind them now, and she expected that Ava would leave the island soon. That sad chapter had ended; another would begin. History moved inexorably onward.

Clio turned her eyes to see an emerald hummingbird, already task-oriented, hungrily sipping nectar from the yellow blossoms of a Ginger Thomas tree. Ground doves cooed like gentle foghorns; males displayed puffy breasts mottled with the colors of ripe mangoes. Wild roosters, croaky as old schoolteachers with laryngitis, rivaled for dominance in their morning announcements. One solitary frigate bird caught a high current of air and soared out of Clio's sight.

Dos Marias, she sighed, *how I love you*! She cherished her island, as had eight generations of her family, living and dying on two green mountains washed by azure sea. Sugar mills, the island's enduring sentinels, reminded every modern inhabitant that another sort of life had once pulsed upon the place.

Clio was proud of her heritage; she freely admitted that. But she had never allowed herself to be haughty. Clio considered *grateful* to be the appropriate word. She felt grateful to be descended from a noble line (her maiden name, Clary, being the first true surname recorded anywhere in Europe), then grateful to pioneering forebears who chanced a journey from Waterford, Ireland, to a new world. Clio felt thankful indeed that those ancestors had found Dos Marias lovely, and that they had added to the island's beauty, in their own way, over ensuing centuries.

She was proud that her family heritage continued through her daughter Maura, the only child that she and Will had produced. When Maura married Charles Collier, Clio and Will had given the young couple a fine home on a choice piece of beachfront property.

Clio had insisted that Will put the property in both the children's names—Maura Mattison Collier and Charles Alden Collier. The boy's mother had always called him Charley, and that's how Maura had introduced him to her parents. But after their marriage, Will had insisted that everyone on island should call the young man "Charles."

And, in truth, Clio had to admit that she liked the ring of the name "Charles Alden Collier." She doubted that those Texan Aldens had any affiliation to the historic ones of Plymouth, Massachusetts. Still, it pleased her to think that her grandchildren would be assumed to carry a doubly impressive heritage of early settlers in the Americas.

Charles Collier had proved himself an astute businessman on Dos Marias—although Will carped that he was a hardheaded one at times. And Maura and Charles had seemed happy. Even Will conceded that. Who could have imagined that things would all turn out so sadly?

If only, if only . . ., Clio thought. *If Maura had married Byron, not Charles.* Maura had never known life without Byron Hendley. He had been a part of her idyllic island childhood. They had built sand castles together and shared secrets. They had showed each other their nude, budding bodies. They had touched, explored, giggled. But Maura had never wanted to marry Byron. She had always wanted more than Byron, someone better than Byron.

She wanted to go somewhere better than the local college, too, and that was no problem. Her parents expected that of her. Maura enrolled at Sweet Briar because it was in the South, and she thought it would be warm. She loved the freedom of being at Sweet Briar, loved learning who she was, and who she could be, beyond an island Mattison. But the state of Virginia, in winter, proved much too cold for Maura; she dropped out of school after only one year. She came home to Dos Marias.

Economic Development Centers were discovering the promise of the island then. Young MBA graduates flocked there, exciting the Coterie. The senior ladies who ran that island social group organized a series of Tea Dances for the young people—as if such antiquated events would interest sophisticated college grads from big cities.

Be that as it may, Maura attended the tea dances as a post-debutante should. It had been clear to Clio that none of the men Maura danced with held her interest for more than one spin around the floor—until she met Charley.

He told her that he came from a small Texas town, but that its population was larger than all of Dos Marias. Charley said that it was warm in South Texas, almost always. He told Maura about stylish Dallas, and bustling Houston, and historic San Antonio. He promised to take her to those big cities. Charley's drawl and gentle wit made Maura laugh, and so she loved him.

"At last, Mama!" Maura had told Clio happily, "I'll have it all—my life-long best friend Byron, my wonderful exciting Texan Charley, and always, my Daddy's enduring support." After a pause, Maura added: "Oh! And your support too, of course, Mama."

Gradually, though, Maura began to change. She lost the sense of independence she had learned at college, as the three men in her life formed a competitive triangle. Maura found herself trapped between the conniver, the newcomer, and the archconservative. She became more like Clio, compromising and kowtowing to Will. And Clio regretted that deeply.

Maura had confided in her, worried about the conflicting concerns of her three men. Maura worried, too, that she was beginning to see Charley differently. She realized too late that the Dos Marias he envisioned was not the one that she knew and loved.

Maura began to share her mother's opinion that Charley and others like him threatened the traditional Dos Marias way of life. Her voice grew shrill as her moods became frantic. And then she was not the girl that Charley had fallen in love with. She was a Mattison, and she called her husband "Charles."

So Clio worried for her daughter. And now she was sorry that Charles was dead. But on top of that, she fretted: Why did such a tragedy have to happen right now?

The telephone rang, interrupting Clio's muse. When she heard Ava's voice on the line, Clio made her voice gentle and compassionate. They went through the customary "how-are-you" routine.

Then Ava asked about Maura's baby. Clio could not think fast enough to phrase her response gently. And Ava cried, distraught to learn of Maura' miscarriage. Clio cried with her. Neither one of them would ever be a grandmother now.

Clio and Ava also shared a deep resentment toward Will Mattison—but Ava would never know of Clio's feelings. Ava *should* know, however, the how and the why of Maura's miscarriage. That had been a hard decision for Clio to make, but she knew that it was the proper one.

Once more, Clio thought through the events leading up to the miscarriage, as Maura had described them to her.

Maura had agreed to go to the Keg Wharf with Charles, though she never felt entirely comfortable with his friends. She said that Charles was quiet all evening—mopey, as though he had something on his mind. So Maura had been glad to see Byron walk toward their table.

He had made a toast to her. And another to the baby. Maura had stood and curtsied and smiled. Byron had patted her belly. Charley had scowled, cursed, pulled Maura back down, beside him. But then Byron tried to take her hand, and Charley tried to push him away, and somehow the table went over.

After that, Maura said later, everything became a blur. Somehow, she took a terrible blow to her stomach, and that frightened her. She told Charley that it was time to go home. She tried to get into their car, but Byron was there too, and somehow Charley fell. Then Byron kicked him.

Parker came. He helped Maura get Charley into the car, and she drove home. It was hard to drive, while her stomach hurt so badly.

Maura did not call Clio until after she had Charley home, and in bed. "Mama, I'm bleeding! I'm afraid I'm losing the baby," she said. But by the time Clio arrived, the spotting had stopped, along with pains that Maura had feared were contractions. Clio and Maura could do nothing, then, but hope for the best.

The weekend after the fight, Byron invited himself to dinner at Maura's. "We have to talk," he said. "We have to work something out." Maura had expected Byron to make some sort of apology for knocking her down, making her almost miscarry. He did not, and that hurt her. Byron only wanted to ask Charles for money to pay some debt that he owed the Consortium. And Charles refused to do that. Rancor festered.

On Thanksgiving night, Maura insisted that Charles follow tradition and "go out with the boys." She believed that the two of them must keep up appearances. So they went out, their separate ways, and when Charles returned home, Maura was already in bed. That was when the nightmare began.

Afterward, Maura called, and Will was out the door like a shot. By the time Clio had dressed and followed him to Maura's home, Will had already done what he believed he had to do.

Now, remembering that awful night, Clio grimaced, pressed three fingers firmly against her forehead, and geared herself for the days ahead. Ava Collier, like any Continental, just could not imagine the delicate balance demanded by life on island. No one, reared as Ava was, could possibly understand the compromises that island women—women like Clio—had to make every day. Such compromises were mandatory, if one were to continue a dignified life, in the face of ever-increasing precariousness. But surely some women, even in Texas, had husbands like Will. Those women would understand, even if Ava could not.

Clio walked out onto her gallery. The little sugar bird was there, her dear pet bird that did not require a cage. Clio opened a small plastic container and shook a fourth-teaspoonful of sugar into her hand. The sugarbird perched on her thumb and began to eat.

Clio Mattison reviewed her plan for revealing the truth to Ava Collier.

DECEMBER 24

The Coronation, and the Parade were behind her at last! The events had seemed *unbearably* trivial, Clio thought, though of course necessary. *Noblesse oblige.*

What she had to do this day was so much more important. She unwrapped a new voice recorder and began to speak into it.

"Dear Ava, I hope that you will not find this recording a disappointment. It is not the one you have been seeking. My husband's henchman—that's as good a name for him as any, I suppose—has destroyed the recording of the argument that preceded Charley's death. I had hoped to obtain it myself, but Will was a step ahead of me, I'm afraid. I'm desperately sorry about that. Nonetheless, my purpose here is to reveal to you exactly what really happened on the night that your dear son died.

"The first part is just as you have been told: Charley and Maura went out separately that evening. Charley returned home first, and found Maura already in bed. She had been spotting for days, and by this hour she realized that she was losing the baby. Charley believed that Byron had caused the slow-motion miscarriage on the night that they fought on the boardwalk.

"Now, seeing his dreams of a child washing away, Charley was understandably furious with Byron. Maura told me that he said, 'I'll kill the bastard!' Then Charley stomped off into the den and began pulling out some of his guns.

"Maura knew that he was only angry, only ranting the way men rant. Still, she has always hated guns, so she got out of bed and went to reason with him. 'Put the guns away,' she said. 'There's enough dying here tonight already.'

"Charley muttered something. Maura reached for his hand, trying to pry his fingers from a small .22 revolver. 'Don't do this, Charley,' she begged as she grasped the gun.

"Charley tried to jerk his hand away. Somehow the gun went off. And Charley fell to the floor.

"Maura screamed, and the baby inside her just let go. Blood gushed out of her. She believes that she must have fainted then. When she came to, she found herself in a pool of blood—her own, and her husband's.

"Charley was not breathing. She tried to revive him, but she could not. And that is when she called our home. I answered the call. I heard Maura, screaming, 'I've killed him, Mamma! I've killed my Charley!'

"The moment I told Will, he was out the door. He didn't wait for me to dress and join him. By the time I arrived as Maura's home, just a few minutes after Will, he had already moved Charley's body to the car and concocted the suicide story.

"So now you know everything. And since I learned it directly from my daughter, you and I both know that it is the truth. Anything else that you have heard is of Will's devising.

"He took control from the moment he arrived at Maura's home. After that, neither she nor I could do anything to stop him. And, I must regretfully admit, I had my own reasons for wanting to save face in our small community.

"But at the same time, I was so furious with my husband! And heartbroken. We have not agreed on many issues for a very long time. I often strive to set things right, in the wake of his actions. When that is not possible, I devise a subtle sort of revenge.

"Do you remember Doulsie, our house servant? Surely you know that her name is an island version of the Spanish word *dulce*, meaning sweet. I think of my Doulsie as a sugar mill of sorts. She converts my concerns into remedial actions.

"Doulsie and I have had a long-standing agreement. When I say 'a spoonful of sugar,' and mention a person, she knows what to do. Of course, I give her some guidance along the way.

"Doulsie communicated regularly with the man whom you know as the Boardwalk Bum. She instructed him on when and how to give you the pieces of sea glass—intended as little bits of sweet thoughtfulness to bring you comfort.

"Doulsie coached that homeless man, and gave him some money, so that he would get you into the right taxi to take you to Hatuey. Hatuey followed Doulsie's instructions to lead you to Anole. After Will had the radio transmitter blown up, Doulsie arranged new and more profitable opportunities for B.B. Bennack.

"All I ever did, really, was make sure to keep Will busy at Jump-up, until I was certain that Anole had completed his work in the sugar mill.

"I always believed that you had the right to handle Charley's remains in the way you thought best. I expect that, in time, Maura will change, will remarry. And the mill should not be a somber blot on our landscape.

"Do not misunderstand! I loved Charley. But the mill's purpose is to be a symbol of this island's history and heritage. And the disposal of Charley's remains should be your choice, not ours.

"Will is never going to know any of this. I believe him to be incapable of understanding the symbolic meaning of a sugar mill, which is this: It blends disparate elements under pressure, to produce a small, sweet miracle. That meaning defines my life, and the life of this island.

"Over the course of a great many years, Doulsie and I have carried out subterfuges against my husband, when that is clearly the right thing to do. Because these little bits of sugar make the Mattison go down."

◊

Acknowledgements

Anyone who knows beautiful St. Croix, largest of the U.S. Virgin Islands, will quickly recognize it as the inspiration for my portrayal of Dos Marias. I created this imaginary fourth major island in the U.S. Virgins to provide me some latitude in describing locales, politics, and social events. More importantly, it emphasizes that the story I tell is a work of fiction; I have no knowledge of a real set of events such as I depict here. The people who inhabit Dos Marias are likewise creatures of my invention. None of them actually lives on St. Croix, or on the Continent, or anywhere other than in my own mind . . . and now, perhaps, in yours.

Writer Jeff Abbott launched my editing campaign. Readers Andi Overton, Ric Griffin, and Ellen Goldin King offered valuable assistance. I give special thanks to Sally Jordan, who clarified the problems in an early draft, and Ellie McCoin, who read with an artist's eye. My understanding husband, Bob Davis, encouraged me through many re-writes. Finally, and perhaps most importantly, I must recognize Amy Glenney and Leah Johnson, an elementary teacher and a librarian in San Antonio, Texas, who encouraged a young girl to believe that she could write.

Many people and sources provided inspiration for various passages in my story.

Rockport, Texas, in Aransas County, is indeed named for the Virgin of Aranzasu, as is documented in *ARANSAS: The Life of a Texas Coastal County*, with I wrote with the assistance of William Allen. It was published by Eakin Press in 1997.

During the three years I lived on St. Croix, I saw vagrants on the island very like the ones I describe in this story.

Information on Virgin Islands EDC corporations can be found at http://www.usvieda.org.

The quote about Latitude has been *attributed* to Mark Twain.

The St. Croix Landmarks Society published *Divers Information on the Romantic History of St. Croix, from the Time of Columbus until Today,* by Florence Lewisohn. I adapted some of its information on sugar mills for use here.

Leo Robin, Richard A. Whiting and W. Franke Harling wrote the words and music for *Beyond the Blue Horizon.*

Country song-writer/singer Kenny Chesney composed *Don't Blink.* His home on St. John overlooks a lovely bay where my husband and I often anchored..

The acoustical instrument known as Steel Pan originated on the island of Trinidad in the 1940s. Bill Bass of St. Croix, considered one of the premier steel drummers in the Virgin Islands, inspired my "Steel Pan Sam" and provided information about the construction of steel pans, via an article published in *St. Croix This Week.*

Wikipedia (http://en.wikipedia.org/wiki/Centipede) provided information regarding centipedes.

Carol M. Bareuther's article in *This Week* magazine for St. Thomas/St. John, May/June 20007, cleared up some of my confusion about local lizards, as did my conversation with Elizabeth Armstrong, of The Buccaneer Hotel, St. Croix.

John Ciardi's eloquent lines appeared in *Saturday Review* on June 2, 1962, and October 6, 1966.

Rob Armstrong's musings on dogs, signs, and coffee shops at St. Croix contributed to my fictional WHDM call-in program.

Marty Schladen's interview [*St. Croix Avis,* December 28-29, 2003] with Ernest Isaac John (Tooqurouck), a full-blooded

Carib who lives on the island of Dominica, inspired my Hatuey.

Much about the early Carib and Taino people is speculation. Eric Lawaetz' exhaustive history, *St. Croix/500 years/Pre-Columbus to 1990*, outlines some theories concerning them. Bartolomeo de Las Casas' *Brief Account of the Devastation of the Indies* (1542) is indispensable for any research on this period. I also gleaned valuable information from "The Taino Survival" at the lasCulturas.com website, and from *Smithsonian* magazine October, 2011.

I am not aware of an Arawak myth such as the one I have Hatuey telling. Its inspiration came from the late Elsom Eldridge, of The Educational Center in St. Louis. I paraphrased ee cummings for Hatuey's expression, "in the magical time before *if* became *is*."

Angela Spenceley included delightful island aphorisms in her *A Taste of the Caribbean Cookbook*. I learned others at a Quelbe symposium at the Caribbean Center for the Arts. I have used them throughout this story.

"Road Kill" is the name of a hot dog stand operating on the island of St. Croix. I assume that its proprietors, Rose and Joal Andrews (polad812@yahoo.com) will appreciate my plug for their great food.

Special thanks to Brent Sullivan, my son, who enlightened me on the proper techniques for scaling, entering, and exiting a sugar mill.

The lines of poetry included when Ava took her son's ashes to sea are from "Crossing the Bar," by Alfred, Lord Tennyson.

A long-lost friend shared his experience with a manta ray while depositing the ashes of a loved one. I hope that he would approve of my reshaping it for use here.

This final illustration is of a baobab tree. Africans honored it in the center of their villages, for the baobab gives many gifts.

They brought seeds of the tree to the Americas, and this one stood on the grounds of The Buccaneer Resort, on St. Croix, where I worked at one time. To me, now, this baobab represents the many I have listed above, who helped bring this story to fruition.

Printed in the United States
By Bookmasters